MEET ME IN THE MIDDLE

MEET ME IN THE MIDDLE

YVONNE HEIDT

SAPPHIRE BOOKS

SALINAS, CALIFORNIA

Editor - Heather Flournoy
Book Design - LJ Reynolds
Cover Design - Michelle Brouder

Sapphire Books Publishing, LLC
P.O. Box 8142
Salinas, CA 93912
www.sapphirebooks.com

Printed in the United States of America
First Edition – April 2017

This and other Sapphire Books titles can be found at
www.sapphirebooks.com

Dedication

For our dear spirit sister, Monica.
We Love you.
Please stop turning off the lights.

Acknowledgment

For my readers, thank you for your patience. It's been a long couple of years. Your notes, letters, and posts, make everything worth it, and keep me writing. Thanks for killing the insecurity demons!

There isn't enough room to thank Sandy enough for her patience, love, and understanding. Putting up with me isn't an easy job, it requires knowing how to have three conversations at a time, knowing when to encourage, and when to push. She is a Saint. Really.

Thank you Chris for bringing me on board with Sapphire Books Publishing. I look forward to a wonderful journey and I promise to keep better deadlines! The welcome I received from my new Sapphire sisters was awesome.

Shelia Powell – always a friend and inspiration. Thanks for kicking me out of the nest this time.

Special thanks to Layce Gardner and Saxon Bennett for their early encouragement. Without them, Aislin wouldn't have come out to play.

I'd like to also thank Heather Flournoy, L.J Reynolds, and Michelle Brodeur. You all made it all easy and fun!

Maralee Lackman, I love you. Thank you saving my bacon – always!

Cheryl Matthews, it's been a year of loss. Big hugs and love to you.

JD Glass, thank you for picking up the bloody pieces and helping me put them back together. Love.

And last, but never least, another big curtsey and hugs to Suzie Baldwin, my big sister who is still my underpaid (read: as-in-none), publicist, and cheerleader. I love and appreciate you.

If I've forgotten anyone, please forgive me. I'm late for a deadline. Again!

Chapter One

*M*ore tea, dear?"
"Yes, please."

Two women sat at a small bistro table, lovely fragrant flowers in a crystal vase between them.

Although seemingly close in age, their appearances were vastly different. The woman on the left wore a white, flowing dress in a beautiful red rose pattern, her upswept golden hair revealed a long graceful neck, and many diamond rings flashed fire in the sunlight. Two impeccably groomed Afghan Hounds flanked her chair as she poured the tea, bringing to mind the picture of high society.

Fine china tinkled musically as the other woman, dressed in comfortably worn jeans and a fisherman's cabled sweater the color of Irish cream, held up her cup for a refill. Her locks were hidden under a large black cowboy hat, which also shaded her face. She sat her cup back in the saucer with a graceful hand that wore only a plain gold band, resembling a photo of down-home country.

The women sat in companionable silence as they drank their tea and nibbled on chocolate biscotti.

When their cups were again empty, the scenery changed.

The trees were replaced with yellow walls and they sat on an island of brown granite. The dogs sat silently at their feet, the air heavy with anticipation and *importance.*

The woman in the cowboy hat looked around the small cozy kitchen they'd just appeared in, wiped a tear from the corner of her eye, and straightened her back. "Okay, I'm ready."

"Are you sure?" the blonde asked as she jumped off the counter.

She nodded just as a ball of black and white fur streaked into the room and barked furiously at the intruders. He was clearly confused at why the other dogs wouldn't react, and in fact, ran right through them into the opposite wall.

"Well then, let's get started, shall we?" She walked over to the kitchen garbage can and with a perfectly manicured hand, shoved it over on its side, and trash scattered across the floor. The mutt immediately turned his attention toward the contents with a manic energy.

Their eyes met and they smiled at each other before the Afghans, and they themselves, faded away.

෨෴෨෴

Aislin O'Shea stared at the large stain spreading on the crisp white shirt she'd only been wearing for twenty minutes. She looked at her watch, and then spilled the remaining hot coffee in her lap.

"Holy crap! That burned." The absurdity of what she'd done made her laugh. "Who else *does* that?"

There wasn't time to change; she'd already pulled onto the long driveway to the estate, and by her estimate, nearly forty-five minutes late at that. She never should have taken that nap after a full day in her veterinary clinic when she knew she was going to help her sister tonight.

Darcy was going to be livid. It was nothing new for her oldest sister to be upset with her. No matter how good Aislin's intentions were, the harder she tried, the more she screwed up.

She blew her bangs out of her eyes and added another task to her mental to-do list. The long messy layers needed to be trimmed eight months ago. She hardly ever noticed because she wore her hair up in a knot; it was safer for her that way. She shuddered when she remembered some of the substances she'd discovered in her hair in the past.

Aislin happened to glance into the rearview mirror and was horrified to find she'd only applied eyeliner, shadow, and mascara to the right lid.

She darted a quick glance to the passenger side of the old bench seat and remembered her purse was on the counter.

At home.

A napkin on the dash was her only option at the moment. She scrubbed at the makeup while she parked her truck, fondly named The Beast.

Darcy was standing at the service entrance of the estate's rear door with her hands fisted on her hips. Her bright red hair was pulled back in a severe bun, which only made the anger on her face more apparent. Aislin took a deep breath, and felt grateful her sister didn't have a spatula in her hand this time.

Oh sure, they looked all innocent, until you got smacked with one.

She finger-combed her hair and pulled it into a quick ponytail. It wasn't until she jumped out of the truck and hit the ground that she noticed she'd forgotten to put her tennies on.

Quickly rewinding the afternoon, she remembered

sitting on the bed with the white shoes on the floor in front of her when she'd heard a huge crash in the kitchen.

Mikey had dumped the trash again, his favorite thing to do for attention. Aislin had run down the stairs still wearing her slippers, and found him joyfully spreading the garbage through the entire first floor. She could have sworn she heard him laughing.

It was only after she was done cleaning the mess she'd noticed how late she was, and then ran out the back door—in her pink fuzzy slippers, now covered in various yogurt colors, wet coffee grounds, and a couple of stray SpaghettiOs. Aislin kept her eyes on the path, and didn't dare look up until she reached her sister.

"Seriously?" Darcy's voice nearly screeched. "Are you kidding me?"

"Um." Aislin peeked out from under her bangs.

"You look like you just rolled out of bed. Really? Did you wet your pants?"

"Of course not! Don't insult me." Aislin wished she could disappear. She'd already put in a full day in the clinic, and really was just here to help. She hadn't meant to fall asleep after work. "Of course not."

"Ace, you know how important this job is to me. How could you?"

"I—"

Darcy interrupted and Aislin tried to tune her out. Not out of meanness or inconsideration, but she'd heard it all before. When Darcy began making wide arcs with her arms as she lectured, Aislin expertly ducked out of her way.

Finally, as Darcy didn't seem to be letting up, Aislin tried another tack. "It's not as if I did it on purpose. And really, now that I think about it, it's your fault."

Darcy opened and closed her mouth, apparently struck speechless by the accusation for a moment before jabbing a finger at Aislin's appearance. "What? How could this possibly be *my* fault?"

Aislin bit the side of her cheek to keep from grinning at Darcy's expression. To her way of thinking, it was perfectly clear. "I was doing just fine on time management until Mikey dumped the trash can. You see, it had been full, and I couldn't just leave him in the mess."

"Mikey is *your* dog!"

Aislin nodded. "Yes, yes he is. But don't you think for one minute I don't know that you, Mom, Brianna, Kathleen, and Heather didn't drop him off on my porch. I'm not stupid."

Darcy sighed and her demeanor instantly gentled. "No, darling, you're not stupid. Spontaneous, a little impulsive, and easily distracted, but never dumb."

She pulled her in for a quick hug, and Aislin was surrounded by the scent of warm vanilla. When she pulled back, she noticed the tears on Darcy's lashes. She hadn't meant to make her cry by reminding her why they'd left the dog on her porch. Her loss had affected everyone in her family.

"Do you have anything at all in your truck you can wear?" Darcy asked.

The door behind them opened and her youngest sister, Heather, appeared wearing a perfect blond party ponytail. "Darcy," she hissed. "We need you right now. There's a problem." Heather stared at Aislin and then gasped dramatically. "Really, Ace?"

"Go on, both of you. I got this." Aislin rolled her eyes at Heather and then shooed Darcy toward the door. "I'll find something."

When the door closed, Aislin turned back toward her truck, an old Chevy that had seen better days. A little bit white, a lot of rust, and a faded blue primer color, it stood out like a sore thumb in the back where the Whitmans' maids, gardeners, and just about anyone else in their service parked their nicer cars.

Aislin squared her shoulders and chided herself for comparing it at all. She would never bear to part with The Beast—not ever.

She ran her fingers lightly over the large dent in the front fender and thanked it once again for taking the kick from a vicious, pissed-off bull that was aiming for her head at the time.

Aislin stopped the memory before it continued by quickly opening the passenger door. She involuntarily winced at the screeching sound of metal on metal and ignored the various trash scattered on the floorboards. She'd get to it.

Eventually.

After she pulled the bench seat forward, she spotted a large black gym bag tucked behind it.

Aislin opened it. Along with a pocket of grief, a clean white lab coat was folded neatly inside. She shook it out, put it on, and traced the name embroidered on the breast pocket before buttoning it over her stained catering shirt.

The bag was full of veterinarian supplies, tools, medications, tubes, and emergency supplies. Though she hadn't remembered it was in the truck, she remembered when she'd packed it.

Before.

It was how she measured her life now.

Before. After.

Aislin ordered herself to breathe past the lump in her throat, and forced herself to keep looking.

In a roomy side pocket she found a pair of white Keds. Shannon always kept a clean pair in case she needed them.

The memory started a constrictive fluttering in her chest and her throat tightened. Telltale precursors of a panic attack. Aislin tried to calm herself, slow her heartbeat. She'd had some small victories doing that in the past.

She sat on the wide running board and took several deep breaths.

When her ears stopped ringing, she opened her eyes to focus on something else, anything to distract from the symptoms. One of her tricks was to spy something nearby she considered pretty, then explain to herself why she loved that object.

There was so much to choose from here. The grounds of the estate were stunningly gorgeous: the grass, flowers, and statuary—even around the parking lot, the area was immaculate and magazine perfect. She concentrated on the blue and beige violets, the white and pink blossoms in the trees lining the driveway, and the riotous colors of blooms spilling from stone planters.

The distinctive sound of...*No, don't think about wasps!*

Aislin took another deep breath. The distinctive buzzing of...harmless honey bees nearby.

Better.

Several moments later, the pressure in her temples abated and Aislin traded her slippers for the tennis shoes.

They were two sizes too big, but still looked

infinitely better than the sticky, fuzzy pink pair she threw back in the truck.

Too bad they also came with ten thousand pounds of grief. She would have to deal with it and be careful she didn't trip at the event. Though Darcy never let her serve the guests anyway; that job fell to her younger sisters. The graceful, slender siblings.

Everyone loved Kathleen, Aislin's other younger sister, and Heather, who were known collectively as the O'Shea blond bookends. Aislin was stuck in the middle, the only brunette, and her innate clumsiness made her a back-of-the-house type helper. She didn't feel bad about that—she preferred being in the background. It's why she became a veterinarian. Animals were forgiving, and they didn't care she had social anxiety.

Aislin was content to be a part of the whole. Besides, not everyone could be as charming as her younger sisters, or as polished as her older ones. The O'Sheas helped each other, whether it was in her own small clinic, her parents' bar, or her sister's catering business. They all wore many hats for one another. It was the way they were raised.

She'd just balanced herself to force the door past the warped hinge when a man in a tuxedo ran up to her and grabbed her arm.

"Oh, fabulous. You're here!" He took the bag, slammed the stuck door in a smooth motion, and grabbed Aislin's arm. He dragged her down a path and around the side of the house before she came out of her shock.

"Hey!" she yelled.

When he stopped to look at her, she kicked the offender in the forearm that gripped her.

He screamed, dropped the bag, and cradled his

injured arm to his chest. "What did you do that for?"

Aislin retrieved her stuff, and turned to run back to the kitchen entrance.

"Where are you going?" the man asked. "The horse is down this way." He pointed down to a curve in the path.

"What horse?" Aislin was confused, and took a second to reassess her attacker. He was over a foot taller, but she was used to that, being the shortest of five siblings, and standing five foot nothing. His bad for underestimating her—she kicked ass in her self-defense classes.

He tossed his multicolored blond hair out of his eyes and glared at her. "You kicked me!"

"Obvious answer, you were dragging me."

"My name is Louis," he said slowly. "I live here, and I don't have time for this. Hurry, I need you." He ran down the path and around the corner.

His urgency was contagious, so Aislin followed him. When she rounded the bend, she saw the huge building.

Horse. Stables.

White coat, black bag.

Crap.

"Wait, I'm not..." Aislin now ran in an attempt to catch up with him, but he'd already disappeared past the giant doors.

Out of breath, she reached the entrance and waited until her eyes adjusted. Louis didn't appear to be having any of it. He ran back to her, took Aislin's hand, then dropped it before he jumped back again.

"You're not going to kick me again, are you?"

Aislin laughed. "You should have seen the look on your face." *Wait, this is serious.* "Listen to me carefully, Louis," Aislin said. "I'm not a—"

"Last one on the left," he said, then got behind her to push.

It was all she could do to keep her balance until she reached the large open stall where a gorgeous mare stood in the corner, covered in sweat, breathing heavily, and, to her, obviously in labor. "Oh, she's beautiful," Aislin said. "Arabian?"

Louis nodded frantically. "Please help her. She looks horrible."

Aislin checked the brass nameplate on the door: Crystal Blue Persuasion. "What do you call her for short?"

"Blue."

Just as Aislin tried to tell him again, Blue folded her legs and lay on her side.

"Go to the caterers in the kitchen and ask for Brianna."

"Why on earth would I do that?"

"Just do it. I'll stay with her."

Louis wore an expression that conveyed he clearly thought she was crazy, but took off toward the house. Aislin slowly approached the mare, wanting to assure her that she was her friend. "Hey, Blue. I'm going to check you out now, okay?"

She took her time with the mare, giving her opportunity to learn her scent, and hopefully perceive her helpful intentions.

After Blue snuffled her hands with warm breath, she laid her head down and relaxed a bit. Aislin preferred to be slow and steady. In her opinion, there was nothing worse than a doctor you've just met shoving their hands in private places without even taking the time to get to know you a little.

So, since she couldn't take the horse to dinner—
ha-ha—before they got seriously acquainted, she'd at
least make sure not to be intrusively rude.

≈≈≈≈

Zane Whitman was standing near the kitchen's
swinging door when she heard her brother's raised
voice. She looked around it to see him gesturing wildly
at a couple of the women in white shirts.

She hadn't known there was a problem with the
catering. At least, she hadn't had one yet. The food
was delicious, the alcohol flowed, and the timing of
the trays was perfect so far. Even her picky stepmother
hadn't complained.

Zane hadn't been very involved in the details and
she'd warned Imelda, her father's fourth wife, to keep
out of it. The professional event planners she'd hired
did a superb job to make sure her father's retirement
gala was going perfectly. She'd better go and rescue the
staff before any of the guests sensed blood and moved
in for the kill. They were a mean, gossipy bunch.

Before she reached them, one of the red-haired
cooks ran out the side door with Louis. What the hell
was going on?

He'd better not be bonking another maid or her
ex—make that plural—and making promises he had
no intentions of ever keeping. He could be a major
slut, and Zane had lost more good help and friends
by his actions than she'd like to count. And sadly, she
admitted, she almost always missed the help more.

She put her champagne flute on the bar, and then
slipped out the back door to try to cut them off and see
where they were going.

The stables. And he was still running, pulling the cook behind him.

Blue.

Zane took off after them.

The instant she reached the doors, she saw the commotion. Instantly worried, she raced down to the end. Blue was not only a retired champion, but a cherished companion as well. She pushed by her brother. "I'll deal with you later."

Inside the stall, a teenager with a white coat was at Blue's rear doing God knows what, and the cook was whispering into her horse's ear, stroking her neck to soothe her.

"Does someone want to tell me, *right this instant*, why the caterers are delivering Blue's foal?"

The girl laughed and looked up at Zane. The light of the stables illuminated her face, and Zane nearly stepped back. She was definitely an adult, and a striking woman at that.

The brunette snapped her glove. "I'm Dr. Aislin O'Shea. The foal isn't breach, Blue's contractions are steady, and her heartbeat isn't irregular, so let's just see how she does naturally."

As if waiting for the doctor's diagnosis, Blue gained her feet again and walked to the far side of the stall.

Zane's tension eased and looked back to the caterer. "So, who are you?" she asked.

"Brianna."

"Oh, that explains everything." *Not.*

The vet's phone pager went off. "Oh," she said, then laughed. "Apparently, there's an emergency at the Whitman Estate."

"I'm confused," Louis said. "I called half an hour

ago."

"I think you called the old service. It must have taken them a while to reroute the emergency call to Aislin," Brianna said.

Zane pinched the bridge of her nose. "Dad's making his big announcement in ten minutes. We have to be there. He's officially turning the firm over."

Her brother looked so clueless in the chaos she almost felt guilty for calling him a slut, until two seconds later, when one of Zane's friends walked out of the office across the hall.

The woman shot Louis a venomous look, adjusted her dress, and strutted out of the stables in her sky-high heels.

"Really?" she asked him. "Have you any shame at all?"

Louis shrugged and grinned good-naturedly. "If I hadn't been here, we wouldn't have known Crystal Blue was in labor."

"Where is our manager?"

Before he could answer her, Zane heard loud snoring. She looked over the wood wall to the next stall. Barney was lying in the straw with two empty bottles of expensive champagne, apparently snagged from the party, curled against his chest.

"When he wakes up, he is so fired."

"I agree," Louis said. He gasped, then ducked down again.

"What is *wrong* with you?" Zane wondered if he was trying to hide from a jealous husband or one of his previous conquests of the evening.

"Imelda!" he whispered from behind the wall.

Zane smoothed her expression before she turned to face her stepmother.

"Your father is waiting for you both. I don't know why you're hiding in there, Louis. He's worked so hard. How could you do this to him?" She wiped delicately at the corner of her eye.

"Please," Zane said. "Spare the drama, your mascara is waterproof, and Dad's not here to witness it. Go on, we'll be right in."

"Oh, snap," Aislin said when Imelda disappeared. "That was a good one."

"Excuse me?" Zane looked at her.

"It means you scored. You know, an insult?"

"Ha!" Louis said.

"I know what it means." Zane let the sarcasm drip from her tone while she took another look at Aislin. Her makeup was smeared but even so, her blue eyes contrasted vividly against the mass of her dark, messy topknot. It caused a little tug in Zane's imagination, wondering what her hair would look like against all that creamy skin. She hadn't had her wits about her since she walked into the barn. Maybe she was on her third glass of champagne instead of her second.

That would explain the little attraction, as Aislin didn't resemble Zane's type at all.

"You should probably clean the doody off your shoes before you go," Aislin said.

Zane looked down. Her preciously expensive red-soled shoes were covered with manure. *Doody indeed.*

"We need to get you upstairs to change them before Dad's speech," Louis said.

"Don't worry about us. Blue's doing great. You can check back in after the party," Aislin said, and then looked down at her coat, now sporting an assorted array of red and brown stains. "I shouldn't go back into the kitchen anyway."

"You never actually made it *into* the kitchen," Brianna pointed out.

Zane was torn. She had a duty to her father, but she also wanted to stay with Blue. It had absolutely nothing to do with Dr. O'Shea. She stretched her neck until it cracked and released the tension trapped in it. *Much better.* "I'll be back. If you need me before then, please come up to the house."

"I assure you," Brianna said, "Blue is in good hands."

Louis grabbed her arm and began pulling at her. "Hurry, before Imelda comes back."

Zane looked at Blue, Aislin, and Brianna in turn, shook her head, and followed him out.

❧❧❧❧

"What is that look you're giving me?"

"Ace, it's my face. It always has an expression on it." Brianna smiled.

Aislin laughed. "Please just tell me what's on your mind."

"Sure, and if you didn't see or feel it, little sister, you ought to be ashamed of your Irish. Or, lack thereof."

Aislin smiled. "You sounded just like Granny with your brogue all turned up."

"Aye. And what fun would it be if she didn't pop through once in a while?"

"Right?" Aislin laughed. "Now spill."

"Okay, if you're going to play stupid. I saw how Zane Whitman was looking at you. I also saw you take more than a second look at her with an expression of your own."

"I did not." Aislin's cheeks warmed. "She is so not my type, she's in another stratosphere."

Brianna looked genuinely puzzled. "Tall, platinum-haired, green-eyed, and beautiful is not your type?"

"You know what I mean."

"Honestly, Ace? I'm sure I don't."

"People like her go out with models and socialites named Buffy and Prudence, blue-blooded, pretentious ice princesses dressed so sharp they cut you just looking at them, all while looking down their noses at you."

"You are pretty much shorter than everyone, Ace."

"Okay, I'll give you that one." The pull she'd felt in her belly when she initially saw Zane returned with a buzz, but she would never confess it to her sister. She didn't want to admit it to herself.

"Honey," Brianna began.

Aislin held up an imaginary microphone and mimicked a five o'clock news reporter. "Zane and Louis Whitman, the impossibly good looking twin heirs of the Whitman fortune empire were named after their grandfather's favorite western authors. The siblings both joined their father's law firm straight after graduation from a prestigious Ivy league law school and acing the bar." Aislin pointed to the wooden slats. "Here they are at whatever social event, every hair in place, in the company of jet-setters and tall, impossibly thin models. Oh, and the family also breeds champion horses as a quaint little hobby."

Brianna laughed. "You're so dramatic, Ace. It's not like that."

"It most certainly is. I know. I have a lot of alone

time to actually watch and read that society crap."

"You know what's funny?" Brianna asked.

"Mmm?" Aislin worked to pull herself out of her little fantasy.

"That you can remember that, but never an appointment time that you've checked three times."

"What?" Aislin had to laugh. It was true. "For the life of me, I have no idea how details stick in my mind with no rhyme or reason. If I could change it, I would."

She remembered she hadn't recognized Louis. "Oh crap. I kicked him."

"What?"

"Really hard, too."

Before she could explain, Brianna's phone beeped, and she answered it.

Aislin could hear the gist of the conversation. It involved a particularly fragile Shih Tzu and an impending litter of puppies. From what she could gather, the frantic owners were standing in front of the closed clinic, paralyzed with fear for their precious Queenie the fifth—or maybe it was the eighth. Aislin wasn't sure, as they were Brianna's clients.

"I'll be right there." Brianna slipped her phone into her jacket and started what was surely an apology, but Aislin waved her off.

"I don't mind staying, really. It looks to be hours yet, right? We'll be fine. Darcy will just have to handle the party without us."

"Okay, I'll go and tell her. She's already miffed with you. Call me if you need anything," Brianna said. "I'll be back."

Aislin nodded. Her heart ached a little. The warm, earthy smell of the horses and the well-kept barn tugged at her memories. It had been a long time since she'd spent any time in one.

Another before.

The evening was young and she'd already waylaid a panic attack and managed to shove down memories that hurt. Good thing she'd had a lot of practice in sidestepping them. After her sister left, Aislin murmured to the horse. Blue was sweet of spirit and leaned toward her as if for comfort.

It was fine with her; they could help each other through. She'd always had an incredible bond with animals, a way to soothe. Sometimes, Aislin was sure she heard their thoughts.

She took a deep breath and looked into Blue's pain-filled eyes.

"I know you're scared. I promise, I won't leave you, and when it's all said and done, you're going to be a mother. Isn't that wonderful?"

Blue's beautiful long neck bowed to Aislin's chest and bumped her.

"We'll be fine," Aislin said. "Just fine."

Eventually.

Above in the rafters, the women sat and watched. The blonde turned to the other. "And so it begins."

"Didn't seem all that smooth to me." She tugged the hat lower over her face.

"Ah, all we can do is nudge, be subtle. There's always free will."

"Yes, there is that." She sighed. "And now we wait."

Chapter Two

Two hours after her father's announcement, Zane saw trouble coming and braced herself for the possibility of an ugly scene. Her ex-girlfriend, Giselle, more than a little drunk by her appearance, weaved toward her in a crooked line through the party guests, her champagne sloshing carelessly over the rim of her glass. Zane steadied her when she would have stumbled, and guided her to the chair next to her. "Careful," she said. "I think you've had enough."

Giselle tightened her lips, narrowed her eyes, and when she opened her mouth, Zane cut her off before she started shrieking and spoke in a quiet but sharp tone. "You will absolutely not make a scene here in this house."

Zane knew the rebellious side of Giselle's personality was simmering. With a firm hand under her elbow, she ushered Giselle to the side hall where she leaned her against the wall and was relieved to see her driver approach. "I need you to take her home," she said. "I prefer it to be quiet and discreet."

Bill rolled his eyes, but Zane knew it was just for show. He'd been with the Whitmans forever and would do anything for her—just as she knew he'd already arranged transport, and escorted Barney, the drunken stable manager, off her property, because she'd asked him to.

He'd also had been present at enough functions

where Giselle had been, let's say, less than proper.

"As you wish," he said in a perfect British accent, which never ceased to amuse her since she knew he was from Atlanta. "Would you like me to also take her *friend*?" Bill shuddered visibly when he continued. "The one in the micro-mini red paper dress?"

"Anise." Zane nodded and nearly shivered herself. Giselle had brought her and crashed the party uninvited. She'd completely ignored the reality that, being Zane's ex, she hadn't been on the guest list herself. When she'd shown up earlier, Zane had, against her better judgement, let her in rather than cause a scene at the door. She should have known better.

Neither had shown any class by showing up at all, let alone being dressed appropriately for a trashy nightclub and not a posh soirée. They'd stuck out like sore thumbs amidst the formal attire, and made themselves very welcome to the expensive free alcohol.

Giselle slid down the wall and landed in a pile with barely a sound. "It might be easier than we thought." Bill's eyebrow twitched.

"Excellent."

Zane took a last look, then turned and went back to the main party. Oh, there'd be some whispers and gossip tomorrow, there always was. But at least she'd avoided the spitting catfight with the inebriated ex-girlfriend scene and hadn't given much ammunition otherwise.

Christ, I'm too old for this.

She scanned the room. The party was finally thinning out, and she deemed it safe to go check on Blue. Unbidden, a little voice in her mind chimed in. *And maybe the little vet. Or caterer, or whatever she is.*

Zane shook her head. She was aware of her good

looks and the effect she had on people, both male and female. She'd never had a problem finding company. The problem was she'd never wanted any to last for long. She formed no deep attachments to the women that came in and out of her life. She was more than surprised by her attraction to the little doctor—she wasn't her type at all.

Ludicrous.

She took the back stairs, changed her shoes again, and wrote a generous check for the caterer's tip. It had been an excellent party and everyone loved the food, so in her opinion, it was well worth it.

Zane made her way to the side door in the kitchen where they were in the process of packing up their supplies.

"Great job, thank you."

"We aim to please." Darcy smiled politely and finished zipping her black coat.

"Really?" Zane asked. "You're going to act as if we didn't go to school together?"

"I didn't think you'd remember. Me, that is. You were only there for a few weeks junior year."

"Of course I remember." Zane didn't want to be rude but she was anxious about Blue and in a hurry. "We'll catch up later, okay? And again, the food was excellent."

Darcy's grin looked genuine this time. "Thank you."

Zane discreetly passed her the sealed envelope. "I, uh, have to go. I have a horse in labor."

"I look forward to catching up with you," Darcy said. "Thank you and have a wonderful evening."

"You too." Zane sidestepped another person bringing out trays, and walked along the side path.

When she reached the last stall in the barn, she leaned against the doorframe and looked inside. Dr. O'Shea was on her feet rubbing gentle hands along Blue's swollen belly, whispering what Zane assumed were reassurances in a soft voice. The sight tugged at an unfamiliar yet nostalgic place she couldn't readily define. She slipped into the stall quietly, sat on the clean hay in the corner, and was soon able to make out her conversation with the horse.

"Oh," Aislin said. "Sure, you're a gorgeous one, aren't you?" She turned and made eye contact with Zane but continued in the same soothing voice. "She's doing great and going to push that baby out soon now." Aislin looked back at Blue. "Aren't we, darling?"

Zane felt some of her own tension leave as she herself felt the impact of Aislin's calm voice. Her shoulders relaxed a bit.

"She's foaled before."

"Hmm? How did you...never mind. Vet, sorry. Yes, but her babe was stillborn." And it still hurt. Zane had been heartbroken for her beautiful horse. "Is she—?"

"Relax. Her heartbeat is a little elevated because it's almost time."

Relieved, Zane nodded then scooted over when Louis entered and sat next to her.

"Now what?" he whispered.

"We wait," Aislin said.

※ ※ ※ ※

The stalls' upper doors were open along the outside walls, allowing the breeze in. Aislin saw the gold rolling hills of Marin County against the purple evening twilight on the horizon, and the air smelled of a hundred different flowers finding new life in the warm spring.

The atmosphere was quiet and hushed.

Aislin sat apart from the twins and closed her eyes for a moment. She heard them whispering but didn't pay much attention. Right now, this second, with the warm air teasing her hair, the smell of hay and horses, she could have been in another stall and another time with Shannon.

Before she had time to fall further into her memories, she sensed Blue's internal anguish seconds before the horse made her distress audible and folded herself to lie heavily in the straw.

Aislin moved into position and in a short time was able to help guide the foal. Her assistance hadn't actually been necessary; the birth was a smooth one.

Blue heaved to her feet, and nosed her foal to do the same while she cleaned her. Aislin made sure everything else went competently with the afterbirth and with the new mother's maternal bonding, then quietly backed out of the stall, leaving Zane and Louis talking to Blue and her beautiful young filly.

Whew. Thank the baby Jesus there were no complications. She was terrified to think of the consequences if there had been. As lawyers, the Whitmans were certainly the type to sue the marrow from her bones.

Aislin had nearly made it to the door when she heard Zane call out behind her.

"Dr. O'Shea?"

Damn it. Her pulse rate increased as she turned around. "Yes, is something the matter?"

Zane walked toward her, and Aislin tried not to

notice how her long legs covered the distance quickly in a confident stride. She could stand here all day and say Zane wasn't her type, but the physical desire circling low in her stomach told her something quite different.

And that just pissed her off.

"No," Zane said. "Nothing's wrong. I was going to invite you in and give you something to eat. You've been sitting out here for a long time with Blue."

"Oh, no that's okay. My sister brought me something." At Zane's questioning look, she added, "Darcy?"

"The caterer? I wasn't aware you were sisters."

"Yes, everyone in that kitchen was related to me." Something about the way Zane muttered "caterer" raised Aislin's hackles. In her experience, wealthy people didn't even notice the hardworking service class they hired every day. She was fiercely loyal, and she didn't want to stand here and explain how they each helped out in all the family businesses. It was a given in her world. More importantly, none of her damn business anyway.

She wanted to escape. "Goodnight, Ms. Whitman." She hoped she'd managed to put enough ice into her voice to sound cold and dismissive. She didn't have much practice being rude.

Aislin tried to spin and make an awesome exit, but she realized too late she'd stepped on the toe of the ill-fitting shoes, and squealed when she began falling.

She was completely unprepared for the strong arms that caught her before she hit the ground. Under the heat of mortification, she experienced a jolt of pure lust.

Humiliation won, and she batted Zane's hands

away from her body. "I've got it," Aislin hissed at her.

"Are you sure?"

"I'm fine." Still mortified, Aislin stared at the ground. Ten times awkward didn't even begin to describe what she was feeling, and she didn't want to look at Zane as she knew her face would be bright red. She also recognized how filthy she was. "I just need to clean up."

Before she could escape, Zane took her arm again. "Absolutely not, that's the employees' restroom. I'm taking you to the house. Did you twist your ankle?"

"No, I don't think so."

Zane led her on a garden path that wound around an elaborate pool grotto and through a set of French doors. The enormous room they entered could have fit Aislin's entire house inside it.

Her skin heated under Zane's grip on her arm. She already felt out of her comfort zone and Aislin's nervous system was threatening to overload.

"Here you go," Zane said, and then gently pushed Aislin into the bathroom before closing the door, leaving her alone.

She could feel a handprint tingling at the small of her back.

Enough. You are not attracted to that snotty amazon. Employee restroom indeed.

Her mouth dropped open as she looked around the stunning bathroom. Large, lush plants stood on pedestals, the rich slate floor revealed hints of copper, and a four-foot bronze fairy graced the quartz counter, contrasting the chips of blue glass within.

Aislin approached the sink and her reflection in the mirror.

Holy crap.

She quickly stripped off her filthy coat, rolled it into a messy ball, and shoved it into her bag. The evidence of Blue's birth didn't bother her as it was natural, but it seemed a thousand years ago she'd spilled the coffee that stained the front of her shirt.

Her hair was sticking out and snarled, and if that wasn't enough—and it was—her mascara was smeared worse, actually worse, than it was hours ago.

She considered how her day went, and knowing it was impossible to make another first impression, Aislin simply did what she could and washed her face and hands.

Her appearance and the luxury of the bathroom underscored that she was out of her comfort zone and, at the very least, out of her league. No one knew that better than Aislin herself.

That lesson was learned the hard way after living through the pain and humiliation of the separation of social class during her school years. All of the O'Shea daughters attended an exclusive Catholic school, but her parents worked extreme hours and brutally budgeted their pockets to accomplish that. Most of the student body was substantially better off financially than her family.

Her high school boyfriend—*whose name will never be mentioned again, Amen*—his family wasn't just rich, they were old-money wealthy, and lived just a few miles down the road from this estate. They'd been embarrassed of their son's association with a girl who was obviously from the other side of the tracks. Adding insult to perceived injury in this upscale county, her family owned and operated a pub. No fancy letters after their surnames, no ma'am.

She'd been innocent and gullible at fourteen, and

Aislin had been stupid in love. She'd lost her virginity to him at sixteen while he whispered false promises and declared his love to her.

She'd been dismissed so easily. *C'mon, Ace. You knew this couldn't last, and you're certainly not worth my trust fund.* He'd laughed at her confusion, went off to Harvard without a backward glance, and left Aislin's heart crushed at her feet. Her sensitive soul absorbed his cruel words about her worth and status. They cut her to the bone.

Good enough to sleep with, but certainly not good enough to marry. *What a freaking cliché.*

Since then, she'd been extremely leery of anyone she viewed as above her. She'd always been an average student, but after the trauma, the situation turned out to be the fire that lit Aislin's desire to succeed, the impetus that propelled her into college successfully.

Aislin threw herself into her studies, earning scholarships and working part-time at O'Shea's to put herself through grad school.

She finally forgot him when she met her college sweetheart—who wasn't rich, definitely not male, and so not who her family expected. Despite that, they took Aislin's coming out with grace and love.

Her mother told her she already had five daughters, so what was one more after all?

Stop!

When she'd successfully used her imaginary scissors and cut the memory train again, she left the bathroom. She wouldn't give the asshat—*whose name will never be spoken again, Amen*—the power to make her feel small today. It must have been the opulent estate bringing her old insecurities to the surface.

So, what was Zane's game?

God, what's wrong with me today? It wasn't as if she weren't a doctor. No one else had her permission or the right to dictate her value or worth. Not ever again.

She knew that logically, but some of the voices in her past were harder to forget than others. They often came back to taunt her into arguing with them again.

She made her way back to the great room where she saw a coffee service set up on the end table. Low flames lit the massive stone fireplace, and though she couldn't name the artists of the oils decorating the walls off the top of her head, she'd bet her practice they were famous. It was definitely a masculine room, but not, in her opinion, over the top, as she'd expected. She stood and tried to decide whether or not she should sit on the furniture as her pants were covered in doody.

"Cream or sugar?"

Aislin flinched and turned. She hadn't heard Zane walk up behind her. She wanted to say no thank you, but had to clear her throat instead. Zane had changed into hip-hugging yoga pants and a white shirt that showed a generous expanse of tanned skin and taut muscles as she moved. Her hair was loose and fell past her shoulders to the middle of her back.

The stiff, intimidating executive Ms. Whitman was nowhere to be seen. That woman wasn't her type, but this casual, less severe Zane could be.

As soon as she acknowledged the thought, it scared the bejeezus out of her, and she could only shake her head.

What is wrong with this picture? Oh yeah, I'm in it.

Zane sat on the loveseat, fluidity in motion. Aislin chided herself for being so fickle. She knew she was bordering on the edge of foolishness, and wanted to exit before she made an ass of herself.

Louis, still dressed in his tux, glided into the room, as graceful as his sister. They seemed to float in the air rather than through it. God had sure been generous the day he created the Whitman twins. Watching them only reminded Aislin she was as nimble as a bull in a china shop, and that was on a good day. No, she didn't belong here. Attraction couldn't overcome incompatibility. She didn't have anything in common with these people.

"Good, you're still here," Louis said. "I wanted to thank you again for coming so quickly today."

Aislin hesitated. "Um, I was already—"

He held up a small card. "I'm confused. This reads 'Shannon Riley.'"

"It's an old one." Aislin swallowed around the lump in her throat. "Where did you get it?"

"The old Rolodex in the stable's office. Is Dr. Riley no longer with your practice?"

"Something like that," Aislin said softly.

"In any case." Louis enthusiastically shook her hand. "Blue and babe are doing excellent. I'm happy you made it."

Aislin smiled politely and tried to take her hand back, then became uncomfortable when he continued to grip it. Was that a gleam in his eye? His interest was the last thing she needed. She had to get out of here, and quickly. "It's late, and it's been a long day. I'm going now."

"So soon?" Zane stood and walked to where Aislin was standing. She still hadn't gotten over how different she looked. Softer, approachable.

Aislin picked up her bag, and when Zane touched her shoulder, the snap of an electrical shock stung her from continuing her quiet admiration.

"Ouch, sorry," Zane said. "Here, I'll walk you to the door."

Aislin followed her down the long hall, mumbled good-bye, and breathed a huge sigh of relief when the night air seemed to clear her head a bit.

The whole day had felt surreal.

It wasn't until she had jumped into her truck, driven down the driveway, and turned onto the main road that she realized there hadn't been any mention of payment. She freely admitted there was no shame in her game in this situation. Her clinic did well, but was always in need of something.

Still, she ran.

Aislin didn't want to be attracted to Zane.

She'd have Sabrina send her a bill in the morning.

There would be no reason to see Ms. Whitman's, um, face again.

※ ※ ※ ※

Zane watched Dr. O'Shea run around the side of the house and wondered why she'd felt the need to leave so quickly. She could hear the loud engine traveling down the driveway.

They hadn't discussed her fee, but she would get the office's address from the business card. She returned to the family room, found Louis had substituted whiskey for his coffee, and then shook her head when he offered her some. "I've had enough to drink today," she said. "And it's late."

Louis toasted his highball anyway. "Well, since I'm wide awake, between lawsuits and marriages, I'm quite bored." He leaned back in the club chair. "That doctor was very, let's say, cute."

Zane felt a stab of annoyance. "Don't you ever give it a rest? You're such a dick."

Louis sputtered and put a hand to his chest in mock defense. "I'm so insulted." He grinned at her. "She's adorable, like an Irish pixie."

She glared at him. "She's not your type, Louis."

"She's not yours either, sister dear. But that didn't stop your tongue from hanging out."

"Don't be absurd. It most certainly did not." *Did it?*

"Good," Louis said. "Then you won't mind if…"

His deliberately incomplete sentence dripped with innuendo, and Zane knew he was fishing for a reaction, something he could pounce on. If he'd actually seen her spark, or had even an inkling of her desire, he would have gone for her jugular. They were extremely competitive and had vied for more women in the past than she wanted to remember.

Not all of them, she justified to herself. Most of them were calculating social climbers that were after money and the golden prestige dating a Whitman could bring.

Dr. O'Shea didn't remotely fit into that category.

Which led her to another thought. With their mutual broken relationship history, maybe she and her brother ought to expand their dating pool to include women who didn't bleed blue and cry ice crystals.

Now there was an idea. At least she didn't keep marrying the damn gold diggers.

Zane was tired, too tired to banter with him, and she really didn't want to scrutinize the hint of jealousy his comments had prompted. Instead, she headed to the back stairs, then called out to him over her shoulder.

"Give it your best shot, Master Whitman. She'll turn you down flat."

When she reached the top, she heard him yell back at her in a snarky tone. "Or you. She'll shut you down as well."

Nothing wrong with her gaydar. Zane flipped him off, though he couldn't see her. Childish, she knew, but it still made feel better.

We'll see.

❧❧❧❧

Aislin pulled into her driveway and tried to ignore the screech of the truck's shocks, which were shot. That and the way her engine continued to knock and run a full ten seconds after she'd turned the key off. She patted the dash before she got out, and promised herself she'd check the oil in the morning.

Or, eventually.

Her house and attached clinic weren't far from the Whitmans' ranch in miles, but it might as well be on the other side of the moon. Here, the norm was ranch style with the odd two-story here and there, houses that had normal-sized yards with flowerbeds and flagstone paths. Large trees dotted each block and arched over the small avenues. It was a pleasant neighborhood, full of colorful characters. She stared up with pride at her small piece of the world.

She'd worked hard for it, and it was all hers.

Now.

Since she was in her own front yard, and because it had been building all day, Aislin finally let the memory loose.

Shannon.

Once, she would have met her at the door with kisses and laughter.

That time ended three years, six months, and twelve days ago.

An internal video battered her and memories of Shannon flew across her mind's eye: her green eyes and long red hair, each and every beloved freckle of her Irish ancestry stamped across her nose, her shy smile and welcoming laugh when Aislin met her at Texas Aggie. Long nights of cramming for exams sprinkled with a thousand more at home in the evenings, simply loving each other.

And always, the memories ended abruptly with a hurricane of grief that tore Aislin's soul in half the night Shannon was killed.

In the beginning, she didn't think she could bear the pain and not die from it. Her mother and sisters had made all the arrangements and took turns taking care of her.

It took six months before she quit looking out the windows, willing Shannon to come home. More than a year before she stopped seeing her in the grocery store, just outside her range of vision. It was just recently that Aislin didn't feel as if she were slapped in the face when she spotted any woman with long red hair. She was numb for a long time.

She still had panic attacks, and some days her skin felt as if it were on inside out, but they were getting to be fewer and farther between.

Unfortunately, she still had days like this one, and it had held several slippery points. As she replayed them, Zane's image intruded, and Aislin shook her head. She needed to give it all a rest and stop overanalyzing every detail of her life, present and past.

It was exhausting, and in Zane's case, a waste of time. There was nothing there to be had anyway.

Mikey began frantically barking before she turned the key in the lock. When she opened the door, he bounded out at Aislin, jumping like a pogo stick. Weighing in at a whopping fifteen pounds, he was an indeterminable breed left on her doorstep several months ago. Aislin strongly suspected her mother and her sisters, but not one of them would cop to it. When she'd confronted Darcy earlier this evening, the look on her face pretty well confirmed it. But she'd let them keep their subterfuge. She knew they did it out of love.

She bent over to pet him and welcomed sloppy kisses. Aislin looked nervously down the hall but she couldn't yet see any destruction, and that was always a good thing. Mikey barked, whined, and growled in turn, as if telling Aislin all about his night. It was adorable and she laughed.

Mikey followed her through the clinic while Aislin checked on a couple of boarders she currently had in-house. A springer spaniel whose owners were on a cruise, a young mixed breed puppy who was in for observation after she'd removed a tumor from his leg, and a stray cat recovering from starvation brought in by a local rescue several days ago all seemed to be doing just fine.

Aislin knew Mikey wasn't panting and dancing beside her for any other reason than to stick his tongue out at his caged counterparts. She'd determined it was his doggie version of neener-neener. Aislin handed out treats and cuddles before she returned to her house.

Before she turned the corner to the breezeway, she felt a chill that caused the hair on her neck to rise.

Aislin turned back around and saw a tall woman

run down the same corridor she'd just been through.

The quick glance of long, red hair stung her eyes. She knew that figure.

"Shannon?" Aislin called out and ran to catch up with her.

Logically, she knew it couldn't be, but she'd just seen her, dammit.

She could smell her favorite Escada perfume, the scent that had haunted her for years now.

When she stopped running, she was in front of the swinging doors, and one of them was still moving.

Her heart ached and fresh goosebumps ran up her arms and legs.

Aislin didn't hesitate. She pushed past the doors, desperate to get another glimpse. She heard the click of her office lock and ran toward that.

"Shannon?" Her whisper carried through the dark room.

The soft thud of something hitting the carpet nearly had her tinkling her pants. She bit her cheek sharply to keep from screaming and turned on the light.

A picture frame lay upside down three feet away from the shelves.

Aislin crossed to it and picked it up before sinking to her knees and holding it to her chest.

It was of their graduation. So young, so in love, so joyful in each other's company.

The chill of the room left, leaving only a small trace of the scent behind. She curled on the floor and let the tears she'd been holding back all day fall freely.

Aislin was hurt, confused, and felt as if she'd been stabbed.

Again.

From her perch high on the bookshelves, the blond woman shook her head. "Why did you do that?"

"I didn't mean to," Shannon said. "It's the first time she's seen me in three years, six months, and twelve days."

"Time means nothing to you or me," the woman said. "Aislin's unrelenting sorrow has kept you invisible."

Shannon floated down and sat beside Aislin. "I just want her to be happy. That little rendezvous we set up didn't go as planned. I thought you said—"

"Remember, we can only arrange possibilities. We can't help how they react."

Shannon stroked her hand above Aislin's hair. "Then we try again."

The ringing of a bell sounded in the room.

"Round two."

≈≈≈≈

She registered Mikey's tongue licking her ear an instant before she heard his whining. She must have fallen asleep.

Aislin looked down at her empty hands then gasped when she turned and saw the frame back on her shelves.

Had she imagined the entire thing? She could have sworn it was real.

Maybe she'd finally snapped and gone crazy.

Granny's voice intruded in her thoughts. *Crazy people don't sit around and wonder if they're crazy. They just have a good time.*

"Aye, Granny. And I wish you were here, too."

Her back felt stiff and hurt. Aislin stretched out

the kinks and went back to the other side, to her house.

Reality sucked right now, but she had to face it. She still had to take a shower before bed. As she stood in the hot water, she let the tears fall again.

What did all of this really mean? Exhaustion won and Aislin let the only explanation that made sense fall into place. The two near-panic attacks, the memory onslaught of finding their shared black bag, and taking care of Blue must have taken her stress level over the cliff.

Zane's face intruded on her rationalization. She blinked hard as she turned off the shower, and convinced her tired mind and soul it had nothing to do with being attracted to someone who wasn't her type at all.

Aislin raced to the warmth of her bed, fought Mikey for ownership of the fluffy pink comforter, and turned out the light while he turned in circles round and round at her feet.

She was nearly asleep when she heard irregular thumping noises on the stairs, then a loud motoring purr two seconds before a heavy weight dropped next to her on the bed. "Late night, Merlin?"

The cat meowed and ran his cheek against hers several times while kneading the covers with one foot. Aislin had removed his other leg in surgery.

Another waif, someone had abandoned the mangled gigantic cat in a cardboard box during the night by the clinic's back door. When she'd found him, there had been so much blood she was certain he was dead until she'd touched him. He'd opened one beautiful amber eye and started purring nearly as loud as a drink blender.

Aislin and Brianna cleaned him as best they

could, and assessed the damage of what looked to be a vicious attack by either dogs or raccoons. In the end, the tom cat had lost an eye, a leg, half his tail, and one ear. Though the remaining one was pretty torn up as well, she'd been able to save it.

What else could she name him but Merlin? The cat certainly must have magical powers to survive. She knew he had to be in pain, but he never showed it. As he got better, large patches of skin remained scarred and bare when his fur refused to grow back.

When some people first laid eyes on him, their natural reaction was to take a step back in apprehension, and it broke Aislin's heart each time they did. She'd heard whispers he'd been nicknamed Frankenkitty, though no one would dare say it to her face.

Even so, Merlin had a seemingly bottomless reserve of love for everyone he met, and all other animals. Aislin was ferociously protective of him.

Her mind quieted little by little, Aislin felt herself relax again. She was used to Mikey's nightly loud snoring, and Merlin's motoring purr led her straight into a deep sleep.

The damn sirens were going off. Her phone was ringing.

Behind the bedroom curtains, red and blue lights spun and it made her dizzy.

A sense of dread passed through her, and the sound of her racing heart smothered the sirens and the telephone.

She turned to Shannon but her side of the bed was empty. Drowsy, it took her a moment to remember she'd been called out of bed for an emergency.

Aislin had offered to go with her, but Shannon

had only smiled and told her to go back to sleep. She remembered snuggling back into the comforter, grateful not to leave the warm bed.

She checked the clock—that was two hours ago. She got out of bed to look out the window. As soon as she parted the curtains, she saw the state patrol car in her driveway.

Nerves cramped low in her belly. Two uniformed officers got out and headed to the front door. The knocks only sent more fear down her spine and her legs shook as she descended the stairs. The treads multiplied and stretched out the distance to the hall entry. Time slowed to a crawl.

A dog began to bark incessantly.

Aislin woke. Mikey was staring into her eyes and then licked the tears from her face. She hadn't had the dream in a while, but should have expected it. Shannon had been on her mind all day.

Maybe that's why she'd seen her ghost, too.

She curled into a ball and desperately wished she had kissed her good bye that night.

Chapter Three

Zane finished her morning appointment with time to spare. Her next and last one of the day, was a working lunch at noon. Now was as good a time as any to settle up with the doctor.

She found herself anticipating seeing her again. And honestly, she couldn't remember the last time she looked this forward to the challenge of getting to know a woman. It was a feeling usually reserved for the intellectual battles she fought in the boardrooms.

She imagined Aislin falling into her arms with gratitude after she graciously announced she was going to hire her exclusively to care for the Whitman stable of horses. After which she would tilt her head back and stare into Zane's eyes with wanton appreciation and a veiled invitation to take more. Her full lips that most women pay thousands in collagen injections for, but never quite pull off, would open slightly and her pink tongue…

Whoa.

What was really going on here?

Her so-called relationship with Giselle lasted approximately nine months, and they'd been broken up for three as of today. It wasn't as if she were starved by abstinence.

Zane would be the first to admit that being linked to the model was flattering as well as shallow on her part. They went to the right parties, saw and were seen by the right people, had their picture in the right columns. There didn't seem to be any end to Giselle's energy. It was inexhaustible, and the girl could party.

There had been occasions when Giselle had been on assignment in some tropical locale or other that Zane would fly out to for a few days to join her. After the initial lust wore off, Zane found herself bored and a little surprised that she couldn't hold an entire conversation with her. She had the knack of turning everything said back on herself, what *she* wanted and needed. Giselle was a completely self-centered narcissist.

How come it hadn't bothered her sooner? The relationship's final demise was a conversation that dripped with manipulation, and suggested that maybe Zane could procure Giselle her own little black American Express card.

Not paying your bills, sweetheart.

Giselle was great eye and arm candy, but Zane couldn't picture a lifetime of catering to the girl's ego, and chose the exit instead. It hadn't been pretty and Giselle had badmouthed Zane from San Francisco to the French Riviera. Zane was only relieved that the charade was over.

In the aftermath of the breakup, several of Zane's acquaintances, some with great enthusiasm and relish, shared stories of Giselle's infidelity. She herself hadn't been unfaithful, but she figured that was mainly because she was exhausted and couldn't keep up with Giselle, let alone an additional woman. Zane chalked up the experience to a pre-midlife crisis and believed she learned a good lesson not to date women born in a different decade.

The breakup hadn't stopped Giselle from showing

up at the same social functions, and Zane hadn't been driven to the point yet where she'd felt the need to permanently banish her entirely from the exclusive social circle.

After her stunt last night, she was reconsidering her generosity toward Giselle.

Zane turned at the corner as per the snobby English accent on her GPS, checked the address on the sign, and pulled into the tiny, crowded parking lot of the clinic, which was hidden behind trees and large rhododendrons in the mostly residential neighborhood.

O'Shea's Small Animal Veterinary Clinic.

Zane read the sign, paused, then read it again. Anger started bubbling somewhere in the vicinity of her lower stomach, and moved up to the top of her head.

Small animal vet?

As in, Not Equine.

This imposter had been at Zane's house, taking care of her coveted champion purebred Arabian, and she was a small animal vet? Well, she'd just see about that. She slammed the driver's door of her Mercedes shut, then stormed up to the entrance.

She stepped into a small waiting room and into complete pandemonium.

A young boy held a leash connected to the collar of a very rambunctious black Lab who was currently running circles around him, causing another dog resembling a huge rat in an elderly woman's lap to bark hysterically in a nerve-pinching tone.

Another woman shakily held onto a cage that held some sort of colorful, screeching colossal bird that flapped its wings and ordered every living thing in the room to "Shut up, ath-hole!"

The boy's face turned red before he began to laugh hysterically. He also repeated the phrase in an altered high-pitched, ear-shattering voice. "Shut up, ath-hole!"

Zane noticed a man snoring in the corner who must be the boy's father, because no one here reprimanded him.

Dear, God. This is insane.

"Can I help you?" asked the receptionist. The plaque on the desk read "Sabrina" in pretty cursive letters. She resembled a younger version of Aislin, but appeared much more polished.

How can she stand it? Zane pulled herself out of her nervy shock and squared her shoulders. "You can. I need to speak with *Doctor* O'Shea. Immediately."

"Which one, and do you have an appointment?" she asked.

Zane detected the sweet, sugary tone as sarcastic. "Aislin. And no, not on purpose," she snapped back at her before she dared a quick glance to the bedlam still in progress.

"Then it's going to be a long wait. As you can see…" Sabrina swept a hand toward the crowd. "There are a few people ahead of you."

Zane's eyes narrowed. She had excellent observation skills and the girl was patronizing her, she was sure of it. Sabrina appeared the type to consider herself guardian to dragon's gate. She pushed her annoyance down along with her still simmering anger, and instead turned on her charm, the jury's million-dollar-killer-smile, to try another tactic. "I just need one moment of her time." She paused for effect. "Sabrina. Please."

"Shut up, ath-hole!"

"Stop it, Billy," Sabrina said, then giggled when Zane's expression faltered. "Sugar won't help you either. Still not happening."

"Ath-hole, ath-hole!"

From behind the reception desk, the swinging door opened and Zane saw Aislin appear with a gargantuan orange tabby in her arms. The second she noticed Zane, her face flushed and before she could say a word, the cat leapt from her arms in a blur, which brought the black Lab puppy exuberantly running over to investigate while dragging the boy on his leash.

It happened in slow motion. The leash wrapped around Zane's ankles and swept her clean off her feet to crash to the floor. Zane started to scream, but it was cut off by the puppy's tongue when he smothered her face with kisses.

She tried to fend off the dog and bury her mortification at the same time, but she was still easily capable of seeing that when Aislin and Sabrina leapt to help her, each were obviously holding back their laughter at her predicament.

Billy Boy had no such tact. Great big belly laughs filled the waiting room to join in with the enraged yowls from the cat, the explicit profanity pealing from the bird, and maniacal barks from the other dogs. Even the little old lady hid her smile behind her hand.

From the position on her back, she watched Sabrina quickly and efficiently quiet the animals, then grab a piece of candy off her desk to shove in little Billy's face.

Aislin helped Zane off of the floor and directed her down the hall to her office. She coughed several times but it wasn't effective enough to cover her amusement. Zane was embarrassed beyond belief, but chose to hold on to her original icy wrath.

"I'm so sorry," Aislin said while helping Zane into the chair opposite her desk while obviously trying to compose herself. "Are you okay?"

"No, I'm not *okay,* Dr. O'Shea." Zane stared down at her suit pants now stained with who-knows-better-not-ask-what. Indignant, she shoved back a long lock of blond hair that escaped her tight bun. "Damn it, these are *Armani.*"

"I said I was sorry." Aislin's features tightened in what Zane defined as a prim. Aislin clasped her hands together in front of her. "It was an accident. I'll be happy to have them cleaned for you."

"Yes, you will," Zane said, but was already sorry the laughter faded from Aislin's demeanor until she remembered why she came in the first place. "You're not a veterinarian."

Those expressive eyes changed yet again. "I am *too.* My diplomas are on the wall behind me."

"Not a real one. Not a horse vet." She leaned forward to emphasize her next words. "You're a *dog* doctor. What the hell were you doing taking care of Blue?"

"And cats! Oh, and birds, snakes, guinea pigs, and the occasional ferret." Aislin checked them off with her fingers. "Besides that, I tried to tell your brother when he was dragging me down the walkway, but he wouldn't listen."

"Do you have any idea of the complications that could have come up?" Zane was on a roll, comfortable in her argument and convinced she was in the right. "Blue is a champion, a *racehorse,* not a damn dog."

Aislin's mouth dropped open and Zane saw the flush begin on her neck and spread up to her cheeks.

Aha, got her. Now, go in for the kill.

"Delivering a foal is nothing like delivering puppies." Zane stood up then closed the distance between them. She looked down and pinned Aislin with a steely glare.

Aislin's eyes narrowed, but she didn't back off. "I'm well aware of that, *Ms. Whitman.* Again, I tried to inform both you and your brother yesterday, but you steamrolled over me. As your type usually does."

"My type? What the hell does that mean?"

"Nothing. Whatever."

Zane's glance caught Aislin's chest as it moved under her white lab coat. It was hard not to, as she was radiating electricity and temper. As attractive as that was, she'd liked her much better when she wasn't angry. Zane wanted to disarm her further, so she gave her the same smile she'd shared with Sabrina a few minutes ago, with just about the same results. Aislin stepped away from her as if she were a snake. Oh, no. That's not right. She *treated* snakes, which brought her back around to her argument. Zane stalked back to her briefcase, opened it, and pulled out her checkbook. "What do you charge?" she asked through clenched teeth.

She couldn't find her balance with Aislin. She was right, damn it, and she refused to have Aislin manipulate her way out of impersonating an equine veterinarian.

Aislin folded her arms across her chest and glared at her.

"Well?" Zane tapped her pen on the desk. "I assume that because Blue is a horse, the price increased. I imagine your cost also went up when my brother and I steamrolled over you and assumed you were a real vet."

The silence stretched, and Zane began to feel awkward. Aislin continued to stare, and she almost resembled what Zane thought a pissed-off fairy might look like. "Never mind," Zane finally said, then scribbled out an amount before tossing the check onto Aislin's desk. "I'm sure this will cover it. And then some."

"Thanks." Aislin picked it up and then her eyes widened. "This is too much."

Zane smiled, amused. "Don't be ridiculous. You may not be a real—"

"Get out!" Aislin shouted. "Leave my office right now." She grabbed Zane by her elbow, steered her out of the room, and dragged her down the hall "I don't need your freaking money or your fancy pants attitude."

"You're mad because I'm trying to pay you?" Zane slid dangerously on her heels but managed to keep her balance. She was stunned. Aislin was a lot stronger than her size suggested.

Aislin shoved her back out into the waiting room.

Zane stood and stared at the door after it swung back in her face. What just happened? She'd not only lost an argument, but her entire place.

"I'm not as nice as my auntie. I'll take that." Sabrina plucked the check from Zane's hand while escorting her out the clinic's entrance. "Have a nice day."

Before the door shut completely, Zane heard Sabrina mutter under her breath.

"Ath-hole."

⚘⚘⚘⚘

How dare she? Aislin was livid, and the surge of adrenaline she'd received after throwing Zane out showed little to no sign of abating. She'd been so surprised to see her she'd lost her grip, and the cat had no trouble jumping out of her arms. Actually, that was funny, and she didn't care one whit it might be small-minded of her to think so.

Aislin cringed to think of how she'd answered the accusation of not being a real vet. *Really, Ace? "Here are my diplomas"?*

God.

Where were her zingy comebacks? She'd been distracted by the green fire in Zane's eyes, and the way the morning sun had played across her cheekbones.

What was truly disturbing was how quickly her ire turned to lust when Zane had towered over her. In the space of two heartbeats, anger had turned to desire. Aislin wanted to say something clever, she wanted to kiss Zane, and she wanted to run away as quickly as possible.

Then, she thought, *then,* as Zane all but vibrated with electricity and Aislin's temper had reached a boil, she'd had the nerve to try and disarm her with a thousand-watt smile. Oh no, false charm would not work on her—the Irish cut their baby teeth on it.

Aislin wanted to smack that look off her face, so instead just glared at her.

Then before she could say anything, Zane had whipped that checkbook out like a sword. The woman turned on and off her wiles like a faucet, and actually went on to imply she'd fleece her.

Aislin's attention went to the photo on the shelves. She traced a finger along the frame and her temper drained.

She supposed she could have told Zane she'd had experience with delivering foals and calves with Shannon, who was the livestock veterinarian at their clinic. But at that point, Aislin had been deeply insulted, the warmth had drained from the room, and she'd have rather hell freeze over before she'd tell Zane anything personal.

With the infuriating ease of the *über*wealthy, she'd thrown money at her.

Zane Whitman, so confident in that role, graciously giving her enough to run the clinic for a month.

No matter that she'd hurt and insulted Aislin.

What else could she have done but kick her out?

The phone on her desk buzzed and Aislin hit the intercom.

"Auntie, your next patient is waiting."

"Thank you." *Please don't let it be Billy.*

"It's Billy and his new puppy."

Aislin pushed the button to disconnect.

Just. Freaking. Awesome.

ᘐᘐᘑᘑ

"I'm going to lunch with Mom now. Your mother just called my cell and said she wasn't coming back in until around three."

"Okay." Sabrina handed her a bank slip. "Could you drop off the deposit and please say hi to Gran for me?"

"Sure." Aislin smiled, then hitched again when she saw the amount. Even though she'd told Zane to take it back, she couldn't help but be grateful. Their clinic did good business but many of their clients were on a sliding scale payment program that she, Shannon, and Brianna had implemented when they opened.

They'd all agreed they would rather treat the sick animals when their owners were going through hard times, even if it meant operating at a loss. They also volunteered their medications, supplies, and services to a local rescue shelter. It had been a tight month, and Zane's check would go a long way to offset it.

A very long way.

When she looked up, Sabrina's eyebrows were raised.

"What?" Aislin asked.

"You should have seen the look on her face when she left."

Aislin's feelings were still stinging, but she wasn't spitting mad anymore. She never could hold on to a grudge or be mad for more than a little while. "She accused me of impersonating a real vet."

"What?" Sabrina slammed her pen down on the desk, and Aislin knew she would have leapt to her defense and ripped into Zane had she heard her earlier. "Well, then. We hate her."

"A strong word," Aislin said. "I'm looking at it from her point of view, and I could have handled it better. I should have told her that Shannon and I often went on barn calls together after I knew they had one of her old cards."

"Oh, Auntie Ace, I'm sorry."

Aislin waited for the sharp pain that usually followed the mention of Shannon's name, but it didn't appear over the dull ache she carried most days. "It's okay, Sabrina. Really. It's not like we have to see her again, right?"

"Well, I hate her, but she is hot." She paused for a moment. "Aha! I knew it. Is that a twinkle in your eye, Auntie? Maybe she's okay. If she doesn't talk."

Aislin snickered. "She's a lawyer."

The phone rang and Sabrina visibly held back her laughter as she answered it. Aislin waved and took the opportunity to slip out the door.

Chapter Four

A islin's mouth watered as she watched Darcy slicing corned beef for the Rueben special being served that day at O'Shea's. "Come on, just a little taste? Do you want me to beg?"

"Absolutely not." Darcy laughed. "I hate it when you're pitiful." She dropped a small morsel on a napkin and slid it over to where Aislin sat at the counter. "I don't know why you and Mom don't just eat here."

"Because." Aislin paused while she chewed. "God, that's good." She waved her napkin. "If we do, there are always a thousand interruptions."

As if on cue, Heather burst into the kitchen through the swinging door. "Hey, Ace. You helping in the kitchen today?"

"Thanks, but no. Did my time. I never got paid for it after Dad started deducting the broken dishes out of my paycheck. Nobody runs it better than you, babe."

When Heather smiled, the room lit with joy. She'd always been the bubbly one. She was the baby, so she could afford to be. She'd had plenty of examples set by her sisters before her. Aislin let her bask in the compliment while she prayed her mother would hurry up before Heather started jabbering about wedding plans. "How are you, sweetie?"

"Oh, you know, busy. We're going to look at dresses at six, don't be late." *Walked into that one.* Aislin grimaced behind Heather's back then turned it into a grin after Darcy shot her a dirty look. She kind of hoped the surgery scheduled after lunch would run over. She reached for every little excuse, anything to get her out of seeing her sisters and mother clucking in one room crying over wedding gowns.

As soon as Heather went out one door, Kathleen walked in the other.

"Oh good, Ace, I caught you."

"See?" Aislin asked. Darcy raised an eyebrow then turned back to the stove.

Aislin gave up and smiled at Kathleen. "Caught me for what, sweetie?" She accepted her hug. "How's the baby?"

Kathleen rubbed the small bump. "Completely different from the boys. It had better be a girl."

"I don't know," Darcy said. "With my four and your two, Dad's curse still seems to be in effect."

"May you all have boys just like you," the three of them said in unison, then laughed.

"I still have hope," Kathleen said a bit desperately. "Brianna had Sabrina."

"When she was in high school," Aislin agreed. "That was before we drove Dad crazy."

"True," Darcy said. "But I'm not taking any more chances." She used her fingers in a snipping motion. "Took care of that, didn't we, John? she shouted into the back of the kitchen.

"What?"

"Never mind," Darcy called out sweetly. "Go ahead, Kathleen."

"What? Oh yeah. Ace, this morning your horoscope said that you're to have an interesting stranger come into your life, or you're going to fall for someone. Something like that."

"Kathleen!" Heather popped her head in the door. "A little help here please?"

"Oops, I'll tell you the rest later. Gotta go." Kathleen kissed Aislin on the cheek and disappeared into the restaurant.

Darcy snapped her fingers. "Zane Whitman."

"Shut up," Aislin said. "There is nothing, absolutely nothing there."

Aislin was getting a headache, and well on the way to convincing herself it was a migraine, she was almost sure of it. She took her chance and backed away from the kitchen while Darcy's back was turned, then hit something solid.

"Where are you going?" Darcy asked.

Damn, she's sneaky.

Aislin spotted the dreaded spatula in her left hand and sidestepped around her. "Home. I think I'm coming down with something." She held a hand to her forehead.

"You are not getting sick. If I have to go tonight, so do you. It's mandatory we all show up. Besides, if we skip this? Heather will be so mad she'll pick out the ugliest bridesmaid dresses she can find."

Heather was normally sweet, but Aislin imagined being bitten by the invisible pretty little fangs she'd grown when she'd gotten engaged. Aislin sighed dramatically and gave in. "Ug. Okay, I'll go."

Aislin's mom bustled in the back door and kissed her cheek. "Sorry I'm late." Her blue eyes sparkled, her dimples flashed. Her mother was often mistaken as one of the O'Shea sisters herself. She was a small woman with boundless energy, even after raising five grown daughters. She still carried her authority like a five-star general.

She tilted her head and looked Aislin over with a practical eye. "Okay, you're not losing weight, and your color is good."

"Mom, I'm not twelve." Aislin knew her mother still worried about her. Her entire family had spent the last couple of years cocooning her in bubble wrap, afraid she might break again. She let her fuss with her hair a little and then stepped back from her.

"Are you ready?"

"You're the one who was late." They had a standing twice monthly lunch date. Her mother made time for each of her daughters, and when the family extended to in-laws and grandchildren, she made time for them as well at the regular busy Sunday dinner table.

The O'Sheas loved their chaos. And Aislin wouldn't have it any other way. She checked her watch. "I have to get back to the clinic in just a little over an hour. We have afternoon surgeries."

"Then what are waiting for? Move it." Her mother nudged her toward the back door.

They walked the two blocks to Vinnie's. The two families had been in friendly competition for years and took the time to patronize each other's establishments. After being seated by the young waitress, her mother placed their order.

She wondered if she should mention seeing Shannon's ghost the night before, then decided she didn't want to bring the pain into the light. Her mother grieved nearly as hard as she had.

Aislin had just lifted her water glass to her mouth when she spotted Zane walking in the front door. Her hand shook and water sloshed over the side of the glass. She hissed and startled her mother whose back was to the door. "Aislin, what's the matter with you?"

"It's her." And of course, she was with a blonde. Her mother started to turn around.

"No!" Aislin said. "Don't look."

"I give up." Her mother sounded exasperated. "What or who are we not looking at?"

"Never mind." Aislin picked at the tablecloth.

"Oh, for God's sake." Her mother turned anyway. "Who is that?"

Aislin sniffed. "Zane Whitman."

"Oh?" Her mother wore an innocent expression. "Is that the family Darcy catered for this last weekend?"

"Don't play dumb with me. I know that Sabrina called you the second Zane left the office this morning." She tried to keep her gaze from the back of the room. Zane had proved herself to be the elitist snob Aislin originally thought she was, and she wouldn't spare her another thought.

She had nerve, all but accusing Aislin of malpractice and then throwing her money around as if it were confetti.

Her mother wisely, in Aislin's opinion, chose not to say anything more on the subject and they talked of Heather's upcoming wedding instead.

"If she puts me in chartreuse, I'm not going."

"Darling, if she picks out purple polka dots on hot pink satin, you will not miss your baby sister's wedding. You will wear it and love it, for her sake."

Aislin grinned and took another bite of her chicken fettuccine. "I know, but a girl could hope, right?"

❧❧❧❧

Yvonne Heidt

Zane had a perfect view of the women sitting by the window. She had no problem recognizing the two as mother and daughter. They had the same mannerisms, both gesturing and talking animatedly with their hands, both dark heads close as if conspiring with each other.

When Zane heard Aislin's bawdy laugh, her system zinged. It almost made her regret that she'd been the one to make her angry earlier.

She halfway listened to the client sitting across from her at the small table, and made the appropriate uh-huhs, and mmm sounds when there was a pause.

"You're not listening to me."

Zane nodded with her eyes still pinned on Aislin. Marion slapped the table and Zane flinched. "What?"

"I said you're not paying attention."

Zane mumbled an apology and tried harder to pull her attention away from the window. It irritated her Aislin The Imposter hadn't left her thoughts and had gotten under her skin.

Like a tick.

She stared back at Marion while she went on and on about her latest divorce until she felt two holes burning holes in the back of her head. Zane felt the pull, looked at Aislin, and stared right back at her.

For one moment, everything else disappeared. The conversation lulled, and all motion stopped in the restaurant. The magic broke when she determined Aislin was smirking, actually smirking, at her. Conversation around her picked up, and time slipped back into place.

Zane took a deep breath when she watched Aislin stand and then head to the ladies' room. She gave her a few minutes, patted her lips with a napkin, and excused herself from the table.

She strode to the back, and a yelp of pain greeted her as she swung through the door.

"Ouch! You ran into me."

Zane was embarrassed and quickly chose offense for her defense. "Well, what were you doing skulking behind the door?"

Two bright red spots appeared on Aislin's cheeks before she turned away to check her face in the mirror. "I was not skulking, I was leaving."

Now she felt bad. "Here, let me look at it." Zane tilted Aislin's chin up and checked. Her nose was pink, but she couldn't tear her eyes off Aislin's lips.

Zane blinked when Aislin smiled cheekily at her.

"Are you impersonating a doctor?"

The lightening-quick change in mood startled Zane. "No, just protecting myself from a personal injury lawsuit." Zane gave in to impulse and kissed the tip of Aislin's nose. "There, all better."

When Aislin stepped forward and melted against her side, Zane was disarmed once again. She was enveloped in the herbal scents in Aislin's hair, and reminded of the smell of spring flowers in the morning air. She dropped another kiss on the top of her head, before Aislin stiffened and pulled away.

Zane felt she must be coming down with something. She rarely gave in to impulse but Aislin had jump-started her nervous system, and sped up her pulse in ten seconds flat.

"I think your *friend* is waiting for you."

High from the adrenaline, she wasn't sure how to react. Should she explain the woman was a client and receiving legal advice? Temper danced in the small space between them. Zane didn't owe her any explanations, but continued to be intrigued by her own behavior. Since she seldom, if ever, denied herself anything she wanted, Zane bit back her retort. Instead, she blurted, "Have dinner with me."

The look of genuine surprise on Aislin's face was beguiling. When was the last time Zane had done anything spontaneous? Her entire life was brutally planned out and calculated to the last minute.

Aislin's mood appeared to have shifted once again. "I'm sure your date wouldn't appreciate it. I have to go." When she caught her reflection, Zane quickly shut her mouth, and left.

Zane walked back to her table. She was right the first time: Aislin wasn't her type. She assessed Marion with a critical eye. Now, *she* was. The tall, willowy, blond, sophisticated type. *Fake boobs, hair dye, starved, collagen, and shot up with snake venom. And Lord, what did that just reveal about me?*

Then there was Aislin. Petite but curvy, and from the unexpected hug, Zane now knew her breasts were wonderfully natural. Her moods shifted so fast, it made her dizzy. She caught sight of Aislin at the counter, paying the hostess. Now that she wasn't so close to her, she took in her outfit—black leggings and a white oversized man's dress shirt. She had on high-top Converse tennis shoes for crissake.

She deliberately turned to Marion who could have modeled for a magazine cover that day: hair ironed perfectly straight, flawless complexion, and a ten-thousand-dollar smile.

When she heard the bell on the door, Aislin's sprinkles of freckles and crooked eye tooth superimposed over Marion's face.

I may just be in trouble here.

ᘐᘐᘐᘐ

Outside, Aislin picked up her pace, forcing her mother to walk faster.

"What happened in the bathroom?"

"Nothing," Aislin mumbled. "At all."

What had she been thinking? Hugging that woman?

"I saw Ms. Whitman follow you in there. Do I see all the little hearts flying in your eyes?"

Aislin gasped. "You do not. She's not my type." Her mother didn't answer and adjusted her stride to keep up with her. "Besides, did you see the woman she was with?"

"Mmm."

"She was all Karolina Kurkova and Brooklyn Decker sitting there in her slinky silk suit. That's her style."

"And who exactly are they?" her mother asked.

"Really, Mom? Just the current gorgeous supermodels." Aislin hated that she felt an inkling of jealousy when she thought of Zane wrapped around that woman. She tried to suffocate it and remember the kind of woman she *was* attracted to.

Shannon.

Now she'd done it, and the band of grief tightened around her heart. She felt both guilty and sad. Damn Irish emotions anyway, they flew all over the place. At least hers did.

All. The. Time.

Aislin exhausted herself.

She stopped at the back door and held it open for her mother.

"Aislin," she said and swept a lock of her hair away from her face. "Maybe she's not good enough for my little girl."

She appreciated her mother's effort to make her feel better, and hugged her tightly. When she saw the time on her watch, she squealed. "Omigod. I'm late, I have to run."

"Go," her mother nudged her. "And you better show up tonight, or I'll make damn certain Heather picks the chartreuse."

Aislin waved over her shoulder and couldn't stop the laugh that bubbled out. She knew her mother well enough to know she'd do exactly that.

❦❦❦❦

Zane continued trying to make sense of her time with Aislin in the restaurant while she dropped Marion off at her car, and then parked at the office. Maybe she was bipolar, and good Lord, don't they have medications for that?

There continued to be nothing wrong with the way her body felt against hers. Two days ago she'd never heard of Aislin O'Shea, and now, within twenty-four hours, she could think of little else. After putting on her lawyer hat, the one that left emotion out of her equations, she replayed every encounter. Zane had a gift, one that enabled her to recall complete conversations and details.

When she pulled into her driveway, she felt the stupid grin on her face and slammed her hands against the steering wheel.

She left her car in the circular lot in front of the big house, and detoured on her way to the front door.

Zane kicked off her heels, rolled up the cuffs on her slacks, and walked barefoot down a path and through the grass down to the lake.

She loved springtime, the breezes that brought the scent of flowers. Aislin smelled like spring.

Shut up.

Zane's grandfather, the one who'd named her, had built the mansion for his beloved wife. It was her grandmother's favorite place and she loved to read by the peaceful water. She felt her shoulders relax, and chided herself for not coming here more often, not taking the time to enjoy what was right in front of her. Antique wrought iron tables interspersed chaises covered in colorful cushions along the water's edge. How long had it been since anyone in the family had spent time here?

It was on this spot she'd come out to her mother, Bella, when she was fourteen. It was also here that she cried when her mother died less than a year later from cancer. Her father had been stricken with grief, and the insecurity of raising two teenagers had him remarrying within months and sending them both to boarding schools shortly after.

At thirty-three, it remained unbearable to think of her mother. Zane pushed the feelings down coolly. She was good at it. She'd been doing it most of her life.

Zane continued to pick out memories around the beach. It was next to that tree she'd kissed a girl for the first time. It hadn't gone any further, but the sweetness of that moment came back to her, and she let it ease a trace of her grief.

She lay back on a chaise, turned her face to the sun, and tried to relax, imagining the worry moving from her shoulders, down her arms and fingers to drop

into the sand. It was a childhood ritual her grandmother
had taught her, but it worked.

Right up until Aislin intruded.

In her mind's eye, Aislin danced along the sand
in a gauzy white gypsy dress, turning in circles while
her hair fanned out in the wind. She smiled shyly at
Zane, showing her dimples, and started toward her.

Zane opened her eyes and sat up. She blinked
twice and the vision disappeared but the muscles in
her lower abdomen remained tightly coiled. What
the hell was that? She ruthlessly attempted to focus
on something else, anything would do, but could not
shake the feeling she had to see Aislin again.

She was never out control, ever. Emotions led
people to do things that weren't logical. And when you
depended on someone, really depended on them, they
either died or sent you away.

Her hands curled into fists, her serenity ruined.
Zane angrily wiped her palms against her slacks, and
sat straight up. As far as she was concerned, she was
the original ice princess, and anyone unlucky or stupid
enough to cross her in any way learned in no uncertain
terms who they were messing with.

Zane felt something hit her chest and looked
down to find water—no, tears—dropping from her
face. She wiped them away but they continued to fall.
It was a mistake coming here. The loneliness she hid
behind her designer corporate suits felt bigger here in
this place she loved, and she should have known better.

It was preferable to remain unattached from
others in general. She had business associates, family
in the area, and her pick of available socialites.

People easily controlled.

Or bought.

Predictable people.

Oh God. Is that what she'd become? Boring and predictable?

No, that she wouldn't allow. In her mind she sorted out the emotional turmoil, placed them back into their proper boxes, and stood up. She was a successful and strong woman; she would not let childhood grief dictate how she lived as an adult.

Zane stalked back to the house and up the stairs where she ran smack into Louis.

"Whoa, where you going, Zany?" He grabbed her arms to steady her.

Zane batted his hands away. "I didn't even see you, I'm sorry."

"Have you been crying?" Louis studied her face.

"No," Zane said. "Why would you say that?" She didn't want to think that her feelings were being broadcast so openly.

"Because, little sister, I have made plenty of maidens weep. I know what it looks like."

Zane chuckled. "You're only seven minutes older, and so full of yourself."

"Seriously, what's wrong?"

Nope, not getting into it, Zane thought. *Distract, evade at all cost.* "What are you doing home?" She didn't wait for him to answer, turning down the hall toward her room.

"No so fast." Louis caught up to her at the door. "This isn't about me."

Sometimes Zane hated having a twin that knew her as well as himself. "Do you think I'm predictable?"

"Like the sunrise," Louis said without hesitation.

"Nooo." Zane threw herself back on the bed and pulled a pillow over her face.

Louis pulled it away. "Wasn't that the right answer? I was proud of myself for a second."

"Would you want to be boring? Is that what you look for in a relationship?"

Louis snorted. "With three failed marriages and my paying enough alimony to support a third-world country, hardly."

"See?" Zane pushed the hair back that fell in her eyes.

Louis looked confused. "What are we really talking about here?" He drummed his fingers against his leg for a few seconds then snapped his finger. "I get it. It's the O'Shea woman, and she has you in knots."

"Is not."

"Uh-huh."

Zane glared at him until he looked away. She always won the staring contests.

"What do you want, Zany?"

"I don't know."

Louis sighed. "Me, either."

"Hence the three failed marriages." She laughed. "You're such a bad actor. That wasn't dramatic enough."

"At least I tried." Louis sounded defensive.

Zane softened. "I'm sorry. I don't know where all this is coming from. I was sitting at the lake, thinking of Mom and Nana, how full of life they both were. Always laughing and loving, and how they made a room better just by being in the vicinity, you know?"

Louis nodded. "And?"

She looked down at her lap. "And, I couldn't remember the last time I laughed, really laughed, deep in the belly, tears in the corners of my eyes, laughed."

He nodded again. "You're the serious twin, and I did everything opposite just to spite everyone. You're the one they count on, Zany." Louis crossed to the door, and Zane wondered if he would have left if he'd seen her reaction to his remark.

He'd turned too late, after she'd wiped the emotion from her face. "Gotta go," he said. "Are you going to be okay?"

Zane waved him off and lay down, curling herself into a ball around her pillow. She closed her eyes when she heard the click of the handle as it shut behind her brother.

She used to take great pride in just that. How different would her life be if she'd been the carefree, impulsive sibling?

Would she be happy?

She considered that Louis was thrice divorced, and decided probably not.

Love hadn't done him any favors either.

༄ ༄ ༄ ༄

Aislin looked at the time. She'd stalled long enough. The small surgery room was spotless, the old Labrador was resting comfortably in the kennel, and she tried not to regret that everything went off without a hitch. Of course she was glad Rex came through the procedure with flying colors. She'd just hoped it would take longer.

Now there were no more excuses between her and the scheduled fitting for the bridesmaid dress that was probably hideous.

She imagined imaginary blocks of cement covering her feet, and they slowed her walk toward the reception area of the clinic where Brianna waited for her.

"It's not that bad, Ace."

"Says you," Aislin said. "You weren't the one that answered yes when Heather asked if her red pants made her ass look big."

Brianna laughed. "Dumbass."

ᴥᴥᴥᴥ

Zane paid for her purchase and then strolled down the strip of the exclusive mall. When she stopped to adjust her Neiman Marcus and Bed Bath & Beyond bags, she heard catcalls and loud laughter coming from the store next to her. Curious, she looked at the window display, and saw a plethora of wedding paraphernalia. She'd not much to do with these female rituals before. Zane had never been that girl, the one who planned her wedding from a young age. She'd considered it pointless and frivolous.

She felt a quick tug of recognition when she glanced at the brunette and stepped inside to check her out. There was a large alcove to the right and from there she could see an entire clan of women toasting with champagne glasses and giggling.

When she recognized Brianna and Darcy, she ducked behind a potted palm that separated the area from the dress platform against the wall. She split the fronds and peeked again. Was that Aislin in the horrid pink dress? She looked flushed, and Zane wondered if it was because of the champagne she was drinking or that her family appeared to be teasing her mercilessly.

All in all, though, they looked to be having a great time together, and for a rare moment she felt a longing for something she'd never had.

Sure, she was close with her brother, but other

than an elder sister who was sent to boarding school when Zane was young and a cousin, she had no consistent female relatives to bond with while growing up.

She felt bad for Aislin in her current predicament and wanted to hear better, so she edged closer.

I like big butts.

I like big...

Zane was horrified and slapped at her blazer pocket. She was going to kill Louis, dismember him limb from limb.

Butts and I cannot...

She edged backward into a circular rack of wedding dresses, and tried to silence the phone and hide at the same time.

Butts...

Zane couldn't be caught spying on Aislin; it wouldn't be dignified. Especially after the argument they'd had. She crouched in the center and listened, but all she heard was her own heart pounding. The O'Sheas were silent.

They can't hear me, can they? The dresses rolled back on the rack with a snap. "Stalking me, Counselor?"

Zane started at the tips of the pointed pink pumps and looked up slowly, past the ugly dress, until she saw Aislin surrounded by her sisters. The women were all holding their sides, and as a unit covered their mouths, but it did little to hide their explosive laughter.

Zane felt a hot flash starting on her neck that spread to her face. God, she was humiliated. "No. I dropped my phone." She swept her hands across the floor blindly to make it appear as if she had.

I like big butts and I cannot lie.

"It's coming from your pocket." Aislin pointed.

Peals of laughter from all of the women surrounded Zane, genuine hilarity that was contagious, but she refused to join because really, it was at her expense.

She stood tall, patted the hair that escaped from her bun, and tried to find her pride somewhere in the middle of disgrace.

"So," Darcy asked between giggles. "How are you?"

Zane picked up her bags. "Fine, thank you. I was just leaving." She ran out of the store, flustered she could still hear their laughter two stores down.

She seethed on the entire ride home. She was going to kill him.

Zane dropped her shopping bags on the marble floor in the foyer, kicked her heels off, and with murderous intent charged up the stairs, calling for her brother.

Each empty room she came upon only increased her anger. "Louis, I'm going to kill you. Where the hell are you?"

He appeared at the bottom of the grand staircase holding a sandwich. His cheeks were puffed with a large bite he was still chewing. His eyes widened and his jaw dropped. A mouthful of ham, cheese, and mustard hit the spotless floor. "What on earth happened to you?"

"What?" Zane glanced toward the large mirror on the landing. "Oh." Her normally perfectly groomed reflection did not meet her. Instead, a wild version stared back. It was yet another and more than a good enough reason to kick his ass.

"It's your fault." Zane descended on him while he appeared frozen where he stood. She pulled out her phone and shook it at him.

Louis choked, apparently on what was left in his mouth. He bent over, coughed several times, and gasped for air.

Zane's concern overrode her revenge, and she rushed over to pound him on the back. After several seconds of trying to help him, she realized he was laughing and shoved him.

"Please," Louis said. "Please tell me you were in the middle of a serious meeting when it went off."

Zane had several insults ready to hurl at him, but remained speechless. Louis continued laughing, tried to be serious, then his exuberance erupted again.

"There is something seriously wrong with you," she said.

And while she said it, she had to ask herself what was going on inside her own head, which recently included crying in the middle of the afternoon, spying on a gaggle of women...not obsessing on Aislin.

"She's not my type," Zane muttered under her breath. She left Louis to his mirth in the foyer and went upstairs to her room.

Zane crossed to the bathroom. She wanted a cold washcloth to put over her eyes. She had better put herself back together. Control was the name of the game, and she had it in spades.

Damn skippy.

But directly following her little pick-me-up speech, a swath of dark hair interrupted her next thought. Well, that and a pair of brilliant blue eyes. Oh, and the big smile showing a little, crooked eyetooth.

Zane punched her pillow. She thought of going downstairs to do something, but found herself unable to move. She stared at the ceiling and watched an endless parade of women she'd gone out with, a bizarre runway show in her mind, the models beautiful, but interchangeable.

Disgusted with herself, she turned out the light.

She was aware of dozing off and on. At one point, she thought she'd heard the sound of her mother's beloved dogs, their claws clicking on the hardwood.

But there hadn't been pets in this house in a very long time, not since her mother died and she was sent away.

Zane strained to catch the noise again, but convinced herself it had only been a whisper of a memory because she'd been thinking of her.

She lay back down and saw her hand in the glow of the alarm clock. Aislin had cute little hands and she wondered what it would feel like to have them slide against her bare skin and stroke her in interesting places.

And while she was dreaming anyway, why not have a slender thigh between her own that pinned her to the bed?

Zane wanted to think about something else, but the fantasy was good, and it pulled her into sleep.

⁂

Aislin pulled the truck into her driveway. Thankfully the dress ordeal was over. She wished she felt relief but was still mortified about the pink dress Heather had picked out for her. How come she had to wear the Pepto-pink one?

Heather's explanation that she was the middle sister and should stand out in the wedding party wasn't consolation, and didn't hold any water as far as she was concerned. Aislin was convinced Heather was holding a grudge. The hideous color washed out her complexion, the frills and ruffles made her feel silly. Besides, she hadn't worn a dress since...

Well, since.

Before.

She walked to the clinic through the breezeway and unlocked the door. Current boarders barked, screeched, and meowed. The cacophony set up a general racket. In spite of the distraction, she searched for Shannon's image in the hallway, and when it was not forthcoming, Aislin hurried back to comfort them and see they were bedded down for the night.

Treats and love for everyone and everything that had a tail.

Or not, she thought as she pet the Doberman.

It was a routine she loved each night, and one that had kept her sane.

After.

Aislin cleaned the final kennel, fluffed the last blanket, and then turned off the main lights, waiting in the darkness to see if she would spot her again.

She could still see her way to get back to her own door on the other side of the connecting breezeway. After she unlocked it, Mikey performed his spastic I'm-so-happy-you're-home dance around her legs, nearly tripping her several times on the way to her kitchen.

Mikey's eyes bugged out as he frantically jumped up and down. Aislin gave up and sank to the floor to hug him. He slobbered on her while making little whining sounds in the back of his throat. How could she not adore him? It didn't matter if she was gone five minutes or five hours, the welcome was always the same.

So what if he got into the garbage once in a

while? She glanced to the corner where the trash can usually sat and was proud of herself. She'd actually remembered to put it on the counter before she left.

Mikey sighed happily and curled into her lap as she sat on the cold tile. Aislin leaned against the lower cabinet, stroked his fur, and because she was comfortable, began talking to him.

"I ran into that Zane Whitman again," she said. "She was hiding in the bridal shop."

His soft brown eyes looked up at her from under his bangs and he tapped her calf with his paw. The gesture tickled her, as if he understood she was talking about the same Zane who put her in such a tizzy earlier. Mikey had gotten an earful then as well, about her high-and-mighty attitude and the way she'd implied Aislin was a fraud. Then she had the audacity to ask her out in the bathroom of the restaurant while she was on a date.

"I know, I know. Three times in one day. The nerve of her showing up again surprised me as well. You should have seen the look on her face when she got caught spying on us."

Mikey barked.

Aislin laughed. "Okay, now you're freaking me out a little." She gently picked him off her lap so she could get up and cross to the canister that held his treats. She watched him do his happy dance all over again. "Here you go, baby."

She checked the clock and groaned when she saw it was only nine o'clock. She hated that hour; it felt too early to go to bed, too late to do anything else. It was a non-hour as far as she was concerned. She could read for a while, or watch something she'd recorded, but neither one sparked any real desire for her. She didn't feel like turning on the computer or talking with anyone.

She was still in limbo, and wondered how long she would stay there.

Visible in the window above her sink, the full moon's glow called to her. Aislin took a bottle of water from the fridge and stepped out onto her deck. The breeze brought wonderful smells from her blooming garden, as well as the scent of cedar coming from her new fence, built to keep Mikey from finding new escape routes.

Mikey scrambled off the porch to do his business. Aislin loved watching his pure joy of motion, but was grateful the new addition kept her from having to chase him down the street. Again.

Merlin leapt from the deck railing and landed next to her before curling at her feet and purring up at her. Aislin sipped her water and thought of Zane hiding in the circular clothes rack. She sprayed the liquid out of her mouth and sputtered when she began to laugh all over again. The giggles continued even as she coughed and then stood to raise her arms up as her mother always did when something went down the wrong way. She caught her breath and began to dance with Mikey jumping at her feet.

And since it felt so good, Aislin swayed and swirled to the music of the night in her moonlit garden.

Alone.

"No, not alone, Ace. I'm here, and I'll dance with you into your future." The love Shannon felt for Aislin poured forward in a flash of blue energy as she flowed unnoticed beside her.

Chapter Five

Zane sat in the clinic's parking lot and waited for the last car to leave. She'd spent the day obsessing on her acute humiliation at the bridal shop, but somehow ended up here anyway.

She didn't know if she wanted to apologize to, or jump Aislin. The pros and cons list she'd written hadn't given her a clear direction as she'd hoped it would.

She'd driven here with the idea that kissing her would finally loosen the fascination Aislin inspired.

Zane hadn't felt normal since she'd met her.

Nerves sang along her skin and the second she'd knocked on the door, she wished she hadn't, but there was no time to run—she'd already heard the click of the deadbolt. Zane had a second to register the pleasure of seeing her before Aislin's expression turned from surprise to closed.

"You."

"Is that how you greet your patients, Doctor?"

"No, Counselor, and you're not my patient, unless of course you sit up and beg while you bark prettily for me," Aislin said with a hint of a grin, then let her inside.

Through the closed blinds, a shaft of late afternoon sun pierced the dim room, dust motes floating lazily in the beam. The clock on the wall seemed to grow louder in the silence, and to Zane, each second sounded sharper, clearer.

Aislin licked her lips and Zane felt an electrifying kick of hunger.

She more than wanted short, sassy, curvy Aislin.

She's not my type, she's not my type.

Zane tried repeating her mantra but her body disagreed. She was on fire.

She advanced toward her until Aislin was stopped abruptly by the side counter which held flea and tick medicines. Zane placed a hand on either side of Aislin's body, boxing her in.

Just one kiss.

She leaned to close the tiny distance, and relished how Aislin's pupils dilated, her lips parting in anticipation.

Intoxicated, Zane anticipated softness, another inch and she…

And she sneezed violently in her face.

"Ewww, gross!" Aislin's voice raised several octaves.

Zane tried to apologize but another sneeze erupted instead, followed by three more. The force of them had her backing up toward the door.

Aislin glanced down at Sabrina's desk and grabbed a box of tissues. She plucked a couple out and approached Zane slowly, arms fully extended to hand them to her. "Are you okay?"

Zane was mortified, which is why her voice was snappy when she discerned Aislin's amusement. "I'm fine, damn it."

"You don't sound fine. Maybe you should sit down." Aislin tried to steer her to a chair but Zane wrenched her arm away.

"Stay away from me."

"Pardon?" Aislin said. "You came to see me."

Zane drew herself straight and looked down her nose. "A mistake obviously." She could see the front door from the corner of her eye and, dreaming of a dignified exit, she spun toward it.

"Watch out!"

The warning was too late.

Zane saw stars when she crashed into the metal magazine and book rack. When her heel slipped on a glossy cover of *Gone To The Dogs*, her legs went out from underneath her, and she crashed to the floor on her back.

For the second time, she found herself staring at the clinic's ceiling, and while she noticed there were no dust bunnies under the desk, she couldn't help but hear Aislin from somewhere behind her. It was obvious she was trying not to laugh, and ended up sounding like a strangled goose.

A few seconds went by until Aislin dropped to sit on the floor and began to rock back and forth. "I'm so sorry. You should have seen the look on your face!" She rocked more vigorously. "Oh God, I have to pee."

Against her will, Zane felt herself grin. "Ah well, you seem to have this effect on me."

The air shifted again, and Zane felt her blood turn hot silver. She didn't feel the effects of the fall yet, but her skin tingled in interesting places.

"No arguments from me, Counselor." Aislin helped Zane to her feet and into a waiting room chair. "Anything broken?"

"You're the doctor," Zane said. "Want to check?" *God, I must have bumped my head. That was asinine.* Just as Aislin leaned closer, Zane sneezed again.

"Again, gross. Are you sick?" Aislin asked. "I

really hope not. I hate to get the flu."

"I'm *not* sick. I never get sick." And if she was, she'd never admit it. "I must be allergic to you."

"To me?" Aislin asked. "That's just stupid."

"Is that a professional diagnosis, Doctor? Take two aspirin and call me?"

"Shut up!"

As soon as she heard the words come out of her mouth, Zane knew she'd lost control again. She needed to leave before she made it worse.

Aislin giggled.

"Now what?" Zane asked. "Is there something on my ass?"

"No, I was thinking of my sister Kathleen's prediction that someone was coming into my life. Or maybe she said someone was going to fall for me. Something like that."

Zane joined her in the laughter. "Well, since this is the second time in about the same place, I'm going to assume the falling for, as in literal."

"Looks like," Aislin said.

A large animal appeared from around the corner behind Aislin, hobbled in on three legs, and beelined toward Zane, growling and showing his fangs.

Zane backed up again and screeched. "What the hell is that?"

If looks could kill, Aislin's eyes shot daggers. "That's Merlin, and he was here to welcome you." She picked up the cat and held him close. "You hurt his feelings, he's sensitive."

"Are you fucking kidding me?"

"Get out!" Aislin shouted. "We don't want you here."

"Fine. I'm leaving, I'm sure it's nothing more

than a silly crush anyway," Zane said and walked out.

"Good!" Aislin yelled before she slammed the door.

Zane got into her car and wondered where she lost control. She was so hot and bothered when she got here, now she felt sick and hot. When was the last time she was this stirred up? Twelve? She must be coming down with something. It was the only logical explanation for how she'd completely lost her mind.

By the time Zane got home she realized Aislin was right, she *was* sick and getting worse by the moment. When she'd walked into that clinic she was a perfectly happy, healthy, and sane woman.

And she left sicker than a *ha-ha* dog. She smirked at her own sarcasm then grimaced when the headache gave her a sharp jab in the temple.

Zane made it into the house and then upstairs to her bathroom to take her temperature. All the while remembering the vow she'd made when she was thirteen.

When her mother was sick, the Whitman wealth ensured that doctors would make house calls, and provided the nurses who came in shifts twenty-four hours a day.

But all the best-money-could-buy care and all the medicine in the world hadn't made her mother any better or saved her.

Zane had developed extreme hatred for anything medically related, and though she knew it wasn't logical as an adult, she continued with the belief she'd never be sick, and kept the promise that she would never put her faith in doctors or hospitals.

She stared at the electronic reading on the thermometer. One hundred and two, that couldn't be right. She took it again with the same result. Zane groaned and headed for her bed, grieving her mother who had once nursed her through childhood.

From their perch in the corner, Shannon shook her head. "This is going to be much harder than we thought"

"We don't always get what we want, as fast as we want." The other woman crossed her legs. "That being said, we'll have to try again. We have nothing but time. You yourself know that."

"That we do. Only now it's going to be harder. Zane insulted her baby."

"Not the smartest move, no."

"Dumbass," Shannon said, then laughed. The boxer bell rang in the opposite corner. "What are we on now, round three?"

The other woman smiled. "Something like that."

⚬⚬⚬⚬

Aislin glared at the closed door and listened until Zane's car drove away. Merlin cuddled against her chest and clearly conveyed how upset he was over the confrontation. She adjusted his heavy weight and scratched his cheek, whispering to him until his motor ran and he drooled while his eyes closed in ecstasy and he kneaded her arm with gentle claws.

She'd been so proud of herself today. She hadn't thought of Zane at all.

Well, hardly. Any thought less than fifteen seconds didn't count in her book.

In the morning, when she started thinking of Zane's long, elegant fingers and wondered what it might feel like to have them slip through her hair and tangle at her neck to pull her in for a long, lose-yourself kiss.

Hadn't she shut it down immediately?

It had to have been at least three hours before she found herself fantasizing about Zane's lips sliding from a passionate kiss to nip at her neck.

And yet two more before imaginary Zane pinned her to the wall and she felt pure heat when her thigh slipped between Aislin's...

"Stop it!" Aislin yelled into the empty room and startled Merlin who was becoming really heavy. She didn't want to put him down, but her arm fell asleep.

Zane had ruined it by showing up. Aislin was better off leaving the fantasy where it belonged.

In her head.

Oh, the visual was perfect. Zane in her casual faded jeans, her hair down around her shoulders, and she smelled amazingly of Cool Water.

As Zane had moved closer the scent surrounded her, moved through her, a shot of tequila to her senses. Aislin felt magnetized to her gorgeous, heavy-lidded eyes. Bedroom eyes. Seduction was clearly on Zane's mind.

Until she opened her mouth.

When she turned toward the hall, she noticed a yellow piece of folded paper on the floor. Zane had to have dropped it.

"After she fell on her ass," Aislin said gleefully to Merlin. She checked herself and her attitude, but when she unfolded the paper, she let her emotions fly again. Her eyes widened, and she stared at the words in shock. She read them out loud to Merlin.

Aislin O'Shea

Fact: She's adorable.
Counter: She's not my type.
She stimulates insidious thoughts.
Circumstantial crush?
1ˢᵗ Defense: Kiss her and get her out of my system.

"Aw, look Merlin, she thinks I'm cute. She's not my type either, but it stings a little to know she thinks the same. Insidious thoughts, she said. Did you know there's a horror movie out by that name? I think I'm insulted."

Wow, really? Zane must have hit her head too many times. Things were easier when Aislin was in high school. Do you like me? Check yes or no. She ordered herself to ignore the little thrill that Zane thought she had a crush on her because really, the last line felt like a slap in the face.

"And, she lost her chance, sweetheart." Aislin nodded to Merlin who had jumped onto Sabrina's desk. She grabbed a Kleenex to wipe the drool from his chin.

Aislin shook the note at the cat. "Who does this? I think I might be offended, what say you?"

As if on cue, Merlin's tail shot straight in the air and twitched.

"I agree," Aislin said, then went about her evening chores. It remained difficult to put the encounter out of her mind, but she redirected her attention to the animals.

Sadie, the dachshund who'd had earlier complications with her spay procedure, was up and showing she felt much better. It had been touch and go, and Aislin was happy it turned out positive.

She spent a little extra time with each animal,

and basked in their unconditional love, another thing she loved about her job. Animals were much easier to deal with than humans.

The only exception that night was an English bulldog named Petunia, who stared at her with sad, sad eyes before she turned her back to her.

"I get it sweetie," Aislin said and left the bone where she could reach it.

She also checked Brianna's patients after reading their charts to make sure they had what they needed.

With everyone fed, watered, and drugged if they needed it, they were bedded down for the night.

Even after Zane's confrontation, everything was well in O'Sheaville.

No, Aislin corrected, not a family problem, but personal. All was well in Aislinville.

Just think, she'd almost been disappointed she hadn't kissed her, right up until she insulted Merlin and later found the note.

Sweet baby Jesus, Zane wrote a memo. The humor hit her. Zane really was a smarty pants. Good thing they knew where each other stood now.

Smack dab on opposite sides of the railroad tracks.

Chapter Six

"Oh, for Christ's sake, Brianna, I am *not* going to call him back."

"Sabrina told me he's called three times today."

Aislin slammed the chart she'd finished writing in on the desk. "So, what, we're back in high school now? And she's having her brother call to say, 'Ooh, Zane likes you'?"

She had a revelation. "Are you in on this?" She narrowed her eyes at Brianna. "You are! I can see it. Your eye does that twitchy thing when you're lying."

"Am not!"

"Are."

Sabrina walked into Aislin's office. "I'm sorry to bother you. Mom, Auntie, can I interrupt your intellectual doctor debate?"

"No," Aislin said.

"Yes." Brianna crossed the room to stand at Sabrina's side.

Aislin refrained from sticking her tongue out. The best things about working with your family could also be the worst. This was one of those times and she felt about twelve years old. "Grow up," she hissed at Brianna on her way out. She'd just heard the bell announcing her last appointment with Spot and his owner who had brought him in for his yearly checkup.

Unfortunately, she finished with them before Sabrina left for the day, and the second she was done, the reception line in her office rang.

"Yes, Sabrina."

"Would you please talk to Louis? I'm asking pretty please. He's not going to stop until you talk to him."

It was the frustration in her niece's voice that affected Aislin. At the very least, she could give him crap for the number of calls he'd made that day. As far as she was concerned, he had no right and no reason. She wasn't going to see Zane again.

She could have called herself.

"Okay, fine. Put him through, babe." Aislin sat at her desk and rolled her eyes when she pushed the extension button. "What do you want, Louis?"

"You need to come over here and see my sister."

"I certainly do not," Aislin said.

"No really, you have to." Louis voice trailed off into a whine while he rattled several symptoms that Zane was exhibiting.

"Well, Zane seems to think I'm not a real doctor," Aislin said. "Have her call her regular physician."

"She doesn't have one."

Aislin nearly smiled. "Because she never gets sick."

"Something like that. Please tell me you'll come, she's driving me absolutely crazy."

"You and me both," Aislin muttered.

"Pardon me?"

"Nothing. I suppose I could take a quick look at her." Aislin took pity at the desperation in his voice and searched her memory for her grandmother's natural remedies. They could work, if she could get Zane to take them.

"You'll do it?" Louis sounded relieved.

"I will, but at the first sign of trouble, I'm out of there."

"Come soon," Louis said. Aislin heard the phone disconnect.

She waited a moment, then she heard Sabrina snicker. Of course she listened in on the conversation, and Aislin would bet big money that both she and Brianna knew exactly what was going on. Before she could bust her, Sabrina hung up on her as well.

Aislin took her time cleaning, changing her clothes, touching up her makeup. Not because of Zane or anything. She just wanted to look professional, that's all. As she gathered herbs and such for Granny's poultice, she didn't hold much hope that Zane would be receptive to the medicine as it wasn't actually a prescription and made in a lab. Of course, according to Zane, Aislin was an imposter anyway.

She gave Mikey a bone before stopping into the clinic again to check the medicine locker. Aislin perused the array and answered the phone automatically when it rang.

"Ace," Darcy said.

"I'll tell you tomorrow, promise. Bye." She hung up the receiver and absently dropped the medicine bottle she'd been holding into the bag, and went out the front door.

When she started her truck, she caught a glimpse of her fresh face in the mirror and grinned wickedly. *I'll show you silly crush.*

Aislin pictured Zane flat on her back and at her mercy. That could be fun. The internal flush it caused had her reaching forward to turn up the AC and ordering herself to behave.

But the heat between them for those few moments

was etched into her memory. Zane probably hadn't thought it a big deal as she'd written in that stupid note that their chemistry was a crush that needed to be dismissed. It wasn't as if they'd gone on a date or anything. Time and again Zane proved that their kinds didn't mix well.

Still, the closer she came to the ranch, the faster her heart raced. Her nerves sang as loud as the radio playing classic rock while she sped down the private road.

Aislin took her time parking The Beast and getting her things together before she walked slowly to the door. She absolutely didn't want to appear anxious or anything. She was still pissed at her for both the note and insulting Merlin.

"Oh, thank God, you're here." Louis's grip was hard as he grabbed Aislin's arm and began to pull her to the staircase. Given his height, Aislin had to run to keep up with him or lose her balance and fall. *Déjà vu*. He dragged her through the massive foyer, up the curved stairs, and down the long hallway.

When she tried to slow him down, he took her black bag full of supplies from her other hand and pulled her faster. "Hurry."

His tone alarmed her. "Why? Is she worse? Maybe we should take her to the emergency room or something."

"No. Esther just quit, and I'm going to kill Zane."

Aislin stood at the closed bedroom door and by the time she blinked, Louis was gone. How could he disappear so quickly? *Chicken*. They probably had secret passageways built into the walls.

She straightened her spine and pulled her shoulders back before knocking sharply on the door.

"Go away, I'm dying."

Aislin grinned. She had four sisters—these words held no power. They actually meant "come in and mess with me because it will be great fun to rile me up while I'm helpless." She rattled the knob and was rewarded with a muffled scream, a loud thump, and some rather creative swear words. Aislin was impressed.

Her hand was in the air to knock again when the door opened with a rush. Aislin startled and took a step back.

Zane held her foot, hopped up and down, and snarled at her.

The cool, perfectly groomed attorney wasn't anywhere in sight. This version had snarls in her hair, smeared mascara, and wore a pajama top buttoned crookedly.

Aislin tried, she really did.

"Stop laughing at me. It hurts." Zane turned and hobbled back to the bed. Aislin waited until she faced her again.

"Your brother called me." Aislin held a hand out in a stop motion that brooked no argument. "If you say anything at all that I deem insulting, I'll turn around, walk out, and leave you to die the miserable and long death you deserve for being so mean."

The flash of temper faded from Zane's eyes. The comment seemed to have hurt her. "I'm not mean," she said.

Aislin held her sarcasm. "Okay then, you're sick...Oops, not feeling well."

Zane nodded and then blew her nose. "That's right. You're not here to gloat are you?"

"The thought occurred...I'm kidding, stop looking at me like that. I'm actually here because you're—"

"Indisposed?" Zane's voice sounded childlike, almost hopeful.

Aislin put her bag down next to the bed. "Sure, we'll go with that." She tried not to gape at the luxurious suite, but it was hard not to. A large fireplace dominated one wall, an arched entrance to the left indicated a sitting room, and to the right, because the door was open, she saw a walk-in closet that appeared to be as large as her living room at home.

Zane sneezed and Aislin's attention was drawn back to her. She walked over to the gigantic antique four poster bed that looked as if she would need a step ladder to get into. "Did you move your office in here?"

Zane's response was a grunt. Aislin began stacking papers, folders, magazines, and notepads, piling them on the nightstand before crossing back to Zane's side of the bed.

"What's in your black bag, Doctor?"

Because she heard the suspicion in her voice, Aislin curled her hands into claws and cackled. "Poison apples and sharp instruments, my pretty."

Her comment startled a laugh out of Zane, which turned into a severe coughing fit that had her nearly hanging off the side of the bed.

Aislin patiently waited it out, alternating between patting and rubbing her back until Zane moved and threw herself back on to her pillows. Aislin put a hand on her forehead. Zane was burning up.

Aislin headed to the bathroom. "Oh. My. God," Aislin whispered and instantly fell in love with the decadent Roman-style room. Marble floors and counters gleamed in the late sun from three skylights, and the cobalt sinks matched the luxurious towels hanging on pewter rods. And oh, the deep pool-sized tub in the center of the room had her reverently wishing for a bath. A white chaise graced the area by the window. Baskets of soaps and hand towels were artfully placed around the room.

If this were her bathroom, she'd never leave. Aislin lovingly swept her finger across the faucet before running the cold water, and grabbing the nearest washcloth, she tried not to feel like the country bumpkin who had never visited the city.

Who lives like this?

She had shared a single bathroom with her sisters. It was probably the reason she had a thing for them. Bathroom envy. It was definitely a thing.

"Did you get lost?" Aislin heard Zane whimpering from the bedroom and grinned. She liked this little girl appeal. It was nicer than the corporate, icy image Zane usually projected.

Sick people Aislin could deal with just fine. Still amused, she returned to the bedroom.

Zane tried to run her fingers through her tangled hair and apparently gave up when her hand got stuck. "Aren't you going to take my temperature?"

"No," Aislin said. "Don't need to, it's one hundred and one. As a medical professional, it's my advice that you go to the doctor."

Zane's eyes narrowed. "Not happening." She pointed to the big bag. "Do you have a lollipop in there?"

Aislin bit her tongue to keep back the giggle. She knew it was the fever making her act this way, but it was still adorable. "Let me see." She pretended to rustle in the bag for minute. "Nope, sorry. I do have some dog treats, though. And two aspirin."

Zane pouted but took the pills. "A real doctor

would have lollipops."

Aislin chuckled. "Shows how long it's been since you've seen one."

"We need to work on your bedside manner, Doctor." Zane patted the bed beside her.

"I don't need one, I'm a vet," Aislin said. "My patients don't complain." She pressed the cold cloth to Zane's neck and heard her sharp intake of breath. The sound jump-started her pulse.

It's the fever, Aislin reminded herself again. *And totally not fair to act on it.*

Zane stretched, exposing a large area of ivory skin. Aislin ordered her mind out of the gutter. She was supposed to act professional here.

"Mmm," Zane said. "You smell so good, like the beautiful doctor in my fantasy yesterday."

"Really?" Aislin whispered. This might get good. She refrained from reminding her it was real. And they were arguing. *I thought you said it was a silly crush.*

"Uh-huh, and it was in a clinic," Zane said. "Can you believe that?"

"Outrageous, isn't it?" Aislin could feel her temper brewing so she grabbed the Thermos full of soup that she had filled with her grandmother's recipe, shook it, then opened it. "Here, smell this." Aislin snickered when Zane's eyes widened.

"What's that stench?" Zane retched.

"It's the soup you're going to drink down. Every drop."

"Oh God, it smells...dead."

"Suck it up, princess, it's good for you. An old Irish recipe. Fish oil, garlic. Oh hell, just drink it."

Zane pinched her nose closed and downed the contents. After she drained it, Aislin saw she was gamely trying to keep the concoction down. She knew from experience how difficult that could be.

Aislin screwed the lid back on. "I'm going to leave the rest here with your brother. You'll need to drink all of it."

Zane looked apprehensive. "What was in that again? Eye of newt and dragon's blood?"

Aislin thought of the large alcohol content. "Something like that."

Zane's smile was loopy. "Do I have to dance naked and widdershins around a fire first?"

"Couldn't hurt." Aislin laughed. Just when she wanted to lose her temper, Zane endeared herself again. It was unnerving. She reached back into her bag and pulled out her stethoscope only to realize she was going to have to climb up on the bed to use it.

Zane raised an eyebrow and with a naughty smile she moved over to make room for Aislin.

Who was this person? This playfulness was out of character for the Zane she'd recently met. She looked at the height of the bed again and knew there would be no graceful way to climb up. She placed her bag on the mattress where she would be able to reach it, and took the offered hand up.

And went flying into the middle, on top of Zane. Damn she was strong.

"Oopsy!"

Aislin stared down at her flushed face. *Oopsy? Did she really just say that?* She couldn't help but giggle. She straddled Zane's waist. "Take your shirt off."

"I thought you'd never ask, Doctor," Zane said in a breathy voice and then sat up so fast, Aislin had to lock her knees to keep from being bucked off. She felt lust rocket with the motion, and it took every ounce of self-restraint she had to keep from riding the friction. The heat between their bodies was blistering. Aislin held her breath and focused on finding the container that held the homemade poultice while Zane stripped off her shirt.

"What are you doing with that?" Zane asked, then flopped backward on the pillows.

Aislin stared at her breasts. She couldn't help it; they were perfect and natural. *So much for assuming they were silicone.* She wanted to reach out, touch, and taste.

Her hand moved forward, cupped Zane's breast in awe, and felt enchanted when Zane arched against her caress. When Aislin moved her other hand, she looked stupidly at the bag it held. For a second, she couldn't remember what she was going to do.

"You're such a cute little pixie," Zane said in a baby voice then stopped. "What's wrong with my voice?" She shrugged then grinned again up at Aislin. "You have to take your shirt off, too."

Aislin slapped at Zane's busy hands, but she was stronger and managed to pin Aislin's arms behind her back. Zane's face fell against Aislin's chest and she began to mumble then struggle in earnest.

When she realized Zane was choking, Aislin cracked up. "Let go of my hands, dumbass."

"Oh, that was a close one! I was suffocating." Zane fell back again, heaving for breath.

Aislin was enjoying herself, fully aware that it was at Zane's expense. She wasn't a bit ashamed of it after she'd found the note yesterday afternoon. She opened the container and began to spread the poultice on Zane's chest.

"I'm on fire, my eyes are burning." Zane writhed

underneath her. The room filled with the smell of mustard. "Aaaa, this is hell and you're the devil." Zane laughed. "Want to sin with me?" Then she burst into tears for thirty seconds before giggling uncontrollably.

Aislin instinctively knew this was beyond fever induced. Something chewed at the edge of her consciousness until she caught it.

Oh no, no, no, please no. She scrambled madly for her bag, pulled out the pill container, and looked at the label.

Aislin was frantic. She looked back at Zane. Her mouth was open, and saliva was dripping slowly from the corner of her lip. *Omigod.*

The air ripped with a loud snore, and Aislin realized Zane had passed out cold. She ordered herself to calm down. The dose was only for a large dog, not a tall human woman.

How was she going to explain this? Better to just go, like right now.

Wait, shouldn't she make sure Zane didn't have an allergic reaction?

Of course she should, said Doctor Aislin. But Horrified Aislin thought it was a much better idea to get out of Dodge immediately.

Aislin packed her bag and set it by the door. Okay, she would compromise and sit here for the required time to make certain there were no adverse reactions, *then* she would run.

She carefully climbed up on the other side of the bed then pulled up the sheet to cover Zane's naked chest. *Can't be distracted now,* she thought. *Better just say good-bye to the girls now.* She was certain she'd never be bidden to see them again.

Ever.

Oh God, she hoped Zane wouldn't sue her for malpractice. Her mind raced with new and horrible possibilities. The only invitation she was likely to receive in the future would be a court summons.

The tightening in her chest and darkening vision warned her she had a panic attack approaching. When she realized that, her lungs shut down further.

You will not have breakdown. You will not...

Aislin fumbled for her phone and called Brianna. When the line connected, and before she had a chance to say hello, Aislin blurted, "I think I'm in trouble."

There was a pause. "Aislin, what's the matter, honey?"

She began to wheeze, and Brianna talked in a soothing voice. "Breathe, Ace. Tell me what's wrong."

"I accidently..." Aislin looked at the figure under the covers and began to whisper.

"Ace? I can't hear you. You accidently what?"

Aislin repeated it a tiny bit louder.

"I still can't hear you."

Frustrated, Aislin shouted. "I handed her doggie downers!"

Hysterical laughter came through the little speaker. "It's not funny, Bri." When the laughter continued without pause, Aislin hung up on her, closed her eyes, and ignored the vibrating phone when Brianna called her back.

An hour later when Louis came home, she told him what happened. She'd had to, just in case. The sound of his hysterical amusement followed her down the stairs and out the door.

Zane woke slowly, and before she opened her eyes, was conscious of a dull pounding in her temples.

"Wakey, wakey." Her brother jabbed her in the shoulder.

Startled, Zane screamed, then thought her head was going to split open. "My eyes!"

"Painful, huh?" Louis snickered. "You scream like a girl. Maybe I should have left the drapes closed."

"I'm blind. I must be sicker than I thought." Zane struggled to remember going anywhere last night. "I have amnesia too?" What was wrong with her? "Why are you laughing at me, Louis?" She hated the whine she heard in her voice. "This is serious. What if I have Alzheimer's or something?"

"You went from never being sick, to the flu, and now a major disease, all in a day. Somewhere, Zany, pigs are flying."

"I hate you, Louis. Get out." She threw a pillow at his retreating back.

He continued to talk. "I cancelled your appointments for the day, because I figured you'd be recovering." Louis turned at the door, presumably for his parting shot.

"What?"

"You're not just sick. Your girlfriend slipped you a mickey." He smiled cheekily at her and slammed the door.

Zane sat up, then immediately wished she hadn't as it started a percussion band in her head. She noticed the foul-smelling goopy mess on her chest. Vaguely, she remembered Aislin being on the bed with her, but even when she strained, more details were not forthcoming.

Maybe she should start at the beginning. Which

was when? She was almost certain that it was Friday, but she checked her phone anyway. Yes, and she remembered going to the clinic. That was it for the memory train so far. She went into the bathroom to shower and realized she felt better, much better than she had.

Once she'd changed the sheets and climbed back into the bed, the fog lifted a little higher and she recalled her brother's words. What? The imposter drugged her? Before she got mad, she drifted right back into that floating phase before sleep, where a dark-haired angel with pointy ears rolled around with her on the bed.

When she surfaced again, the late afternoon sun was streaming through the windows. Zane took a deep breath, didn't cough, and hallelujah, she was clear headed.

She felt great. Her thoughts turned automatically to Aislin and she shook her head. The woman took up more space in her mind than any other before her. Zane swallowed the automatic negation she'd formed. Maybe they weren't as far apart as Aislin would like to say they were. And what did she have against her money anyway?

She could tell her about the battered woman program she ran, and…

Screw that. The pixie fucking drugged her! Zane's blood ran hot with anger and was she was ready for confrontation. She jumped out of bed to get dressed and then a flash of her own behavior came back to her.

Omigod. Did Aislin dose me to get away?

The thought was absolutely mortifying. Zane climbed right back into bed and pulled the covers over her head.

She was just drifting off before she felt a weight

on the mattress, as if someone sat down next to her.
Before she could open her eyes, sleep took her.

*Bella floated to the side of Zane's bed, then sat
and crossed her legs. "Oh, my poor baby, she never gets
sick."*

*"She'll be fit as a fiddle right soon. After all, my
Aislin used the best medicine, sure and she did."*

*"Aye, Granny," Shannon said and kept her seat on
the window ledge. "And then she ran for the hills."*

"She should," Bella said. "Doggie downers?"

*Granny laughed and slapped her thighs, which of
course, made no sound at all. "It sure loosened your girl
up, Bella. That daughter of yours is entirely too serious.
I thought things might get interesting for a second
there..." She trailed off and glanced over at Shannon.*

*"It's okay, Granny. I want Aislin to be happy, It's
why we're all here isn't it? To make sure?"*

*Bella nodded. "Zane, too. Who knew it would be
so hard to get them together?"*

"We did," Granny and Shannon said in unison.

"Ding, ding," Bella said.

Granny nodded. "Round four."

Chapter Seven

A islin was on pins and needles, exhausted, and full of raw nerves. Every time the bell rang above the door she cringed, waiting for the fallout. The knots had formed and reformed consistently in her stomach for two days now.

When Brianna was unable to draw any more gossip from her, she finally left, and a grateful Aislin crossed the breezeway to her house.

Mikey dropped a slobbered ball at her feet and she tried to leave her apprehension at the clinic. She looked at his hopeful face and felt guilty when he started whining. "Oh, you poor, poor boy. I've neglected you terribly, haven't I?"

Aislin laughed when he crooned back to her, and seemed to assure her that yes, she had been remiss in her duties.

She picked up the ball and headed to the backyard to play with him.

For the space of a half hour, she managed to waylay the horrification. When it crept in, she continued to talk to Mikey. "It's all her fault, anyway. If she hadn't been so cute in her jammies…she was half-naked, you know. No wonder I wasn't paying close attention." She tried to shift the blame further but knew it was no use. She felt awful.

Aislin should call Zane and apologize. But what if she'd taken out a restraining order or something?

What was it about her that infuriated her so much?

She'd never felt insecure with Shannon. Everything was comfortable and easy with her. Aislin had never worried if she were good enough. Everyone loved her and she fit in wherever she went, whether it was a fancy ball or the dog park. Shannon defied social boundaries.

Aislin had never felt that way. Since high school, when she'd been cruelly told her place, she'd never quite gotten over it. She didn't belong.

Zane had put a hole in her defenses.

Come aboard! The guilt train is now leaving the station.

Sad now, she threw the ball one last time. Regardless of her insane attraction, Zane was way out of her league.

"She's not for the likes of us, Mikey." Aislin knew her heart couldn't take it. She'd spent more time stressing about her than fantasizing.

Aislin had fed the boarders, Mikey, and Merlin, but she herself wasn't hungry.

What on earth was she going to say to Zane when she saw her? She couldn't make herself call now two days later. She just couldn't.

The best thing to do would be to fill up her time and not think about it.

She'd managed just that over the next two days by keeping busy at the clinic and getting caught up in Heather's pitched hysteria over her wedding plans. It wasn't her first choice, but it was a good distraction.

After suffering through another sleepless night, Aislin treated herself to an extra cup of coffee before she crossed through the breezeway.

When she turned the corner she stopped, stunned by the sight of an enormous arrangement on the reception desk.

"Three dozen," Sabrina said.

"Wow," Aislin said. "Who died?"

"Stop that." Brianna grinned impishly as she walked up. She pointed at Aislin. "There's a card."

"And I don't suppose either of you read it."

Both Brianna and Sabrina managed Oscar-worthy shocked expressions. "Of course not," they said together.

"No, of course not. Liars," Aislin murmured affectionately. She knew how sneaky they both were, and she would have done the same thing. You never knew when you would need ammunition. There was always another quarrel and it could make the difference in winning the argument. And that was the point, after all. They were never malicious, but what fun was a family gathering if you couldn't fight with your sisters?

Aislin opened the card and couldn't help but smile.

Doctor, thank you for the house call. It worked. Love and kisses.

No signature.

Sabrina managed to look earnest. "Well, what does it say?"

Aislin closed the envelope and put the card in her pocket. "Nothing."

"What about the love and kisses part?" Brianna asked, then slapped her hand over her mouth.

"Aha! Busted. Spill it."

Brianna's face turned as red as her hair. "Well, a very handsome fellow…Louis, wasn't it Sabrina?"

Aislin felt her stomach fall as she heard they were delivered by him earlier. The flowers weren't from Zane after all. "What are you two up to?"

The question went unanswered when the door

to the clinic opened. A gigantic Mastiff crossed the linoleum and put two massive paws on Aislin's chest. Only the counter and quick reflexes kept her feet under her. "Well, hello there, handsome," Aislin said.

"Oh God, I'm so sorry. Brutus pulled the leash right out of my hand."

His owner was a slight brunette, and Aislin wondered how she controlled the Mastiff at all. He must have weighed at least a hundred and forty pounds. "Down, Brutus," the woman commanded. The dog obeyed immediately. "Greet." Obediently, the dog lifted a paw as big as Aislin's face.

Completely charmed, Aislin didn't even have to crouch as she shook it. "Nice to meet you." She was rewarded with a massive tongue licking her face.

"Down. Again, I'm sorry. He's a lover."

Aislin smiled. "I wish all my patients were as happy to see me."

"They'd be fools not to." The woman smiled shyly at her.

Is she flirting with me? Flustered, Aislin stood. "It takes at least until the second visit. Then, they hate me." Unbidden, Zane immediately came to her mind but she forced herself to grin back. "Let's take advantage of our first meeting."

"Yes, let's."

Aislin turned and led the way down the hallway.

It was closing time before Aislin saw Brianna or Sabrina again other than in passing.

And the roses. How had she forgotten the roses?

The sting in her hand reminded her why. A persnickety elderly cat nipped her hard enough to draw blood while she was distracted.

Brianna made comfort noises at her bandage.

"Lester bite you again?"

"Apparently not enough kitty gas and being distracted was very bad for me today."

"Do you want me to look at it?" Brianna asked.

Aislin shook her head. "No, it's clean and I don't need stitches."

"Good," Brianna said. "Now, what are you going to do about these?" She pointed at the roses.

"What do you mean?" Aislin asked. "Why do I have to do anything about them?"

Aislin knew she was a mess. She only need look at the bandage on her hand to know she wasn't operating with a full deck. She felt defensive, annoyed, and buzzed at the same time.

What was she going to do about Zane?

The hell if she knew. Aislin hormones hadn't been this revved in years.

Brianna could read her emotions at the drop of a pin and jumped in to soothe her. "Here now, it's all right, I was just teasing. Tell me what's up."

Before Aislin could reply, the bell rang over the door and it was followed by a gaggle of giggles and feminine chatter.

"Ooh, Brianna, you're right. They're gorgeous."

Aislin shot Brianna a dirty look and hissed before she pinched the bridge of her nose and turned to face her sisters and mother.

Heather punched Aislin's arm. "You've been holding out on us."

"Have not!"

"Have too!" said Kathleen.

Aislin cringed inwardly. She was an adult, damn it. Why did she always feel twelve when confronted by her family? She had to remind herself it was fun when the shoe was on the other foot and she wasn't on the receiving end.

"Is she talking to you?" Darcy asked. "After you slipped her a doggie downer?"

The waiting room walls echoed with their laughter.

"No, we haven't talked yet."

"Oh, I don't know," her mother said. "These roses say plenty to me."

"Don't you all have better things to do?" Aislin gestured at the clock.

Darcy put an arm around her shoulder. "Nope, of course not. What could be more important than my little sister's happiness?"

"Aw," Heather said. "Tear." She wiped a finger under her eye.

Aislin pleaded with her mother silently to save her. And as always, her mother seemed to have heard.

She kissed Aislin's cheek. "We're going to the wedding planner to finalize the flowers. Do you want to come?"

"Not on your life," Aislin muttered under her breath, and then smiled sweetly at her mother's hopeful look. "I think I'd rather stay here and enjoy mine."

"Of course, your evening appointment. Come on, girls. It appears Ace can't play with us."

Aislin pinched Brianna before she could tell them she had nothing scheduled.

Sabrina, who had been uncharacteristically silent through the exchange, kissed Aislin's cheek as well before helping her mother and grandmother herd the rest of the family out the door.

Dodged that bullet.

Now that there were no witnesses, Aislin buried her face in the fragrant roses and they smelled heavenly.

She'd read somewhere that they emitted measurable positive energy into the air. She could believe it.

The bell rang again and Aislin spun around, thinking it was her sisters again. "What now?"

Zane stood framed in the doorway. The late afternoon sun had a halo effect, surrounding her with golden light.

The apology Aislin had practiced for days flew out of her mind and she couldn't think of a single thing to say.

The smell of roses permeated the air, and the scent burned into her senses. It was a weighted moment, one she knew she'd remember forever.

Aislin took a step forward, then another.

Shannon looked at Granny. "Do you think they'll get together this time?"

"Let's hope so. The flowers were a nice touch."

Bella nodded. "I'd like to think Zane learned from me." She patted her perfect chignon. "I always loved getting bouquets."

"I used to bring Aislin wildflowers," Shannon said. "I remember one time—"

"Hush now, both of you. I want to hear."

The trio of women in the corner collectively held their breath.

࿐ ࿐ ࿐ ࿐

Zane had waited all day for a phone call after ordering the roses. It had been the first time she'd sent them to a woman because she wanted to, and not because she felt obligated. She'd imagined the look on Aislin's face when she received them. Would it be surprise or a quiet smile?

Her stomach sank with each passing hour. Zane had always won at the end of the day. She set her mind to something and achieved it, accepted nothing less.

She wasn't familiar with failure, and she didn't like it one bit.

Instead, at the end of the day, she found herself here, in Aislin's clinic, looking for an answer. Insecure and defensive, knowing her usual best offense—her voice—would fall short.

She stood and waited for Aislin to step forward, then moved closer and wrapped her arms around her.

Finally. Zane stared down into Aislin's eyes.

"Am I forgiven, then?" Aislin asked.

Zane smiled and raised an eyebrow.

"Because," Aislin continued. "It truly was an accident and—"

Zane stopped Aislin's explanation by gently drawing her lower lip in and nipped. A quick intake of breath, and Aislin's arms came around her waist.

Her soft mouth spurred a bolt of pure desire. Instead of backing Aislin up and taking control, Zane trembled at the gentleness of her kiss that bred a sweet expectation that wasn't at all rushed.

Until Aislin's fingers tightened and drew Zane forward forcefully, her tongue battling with hers. Zane felt herself losing balance and gripped her hips tighter, leaving not an inch between their bodies.

Zane rode the sensation and emotion forward, lost in the moment until Aislin pulled away. She tilted before steadying herself and drawing in a difficult breath. The pleasure she saw mirrored back from Aislin's eyes nearly undid her control. She wanted to lay her on the counter and take her right there.

She laid her forehead on Aislin's while they

caught their breath. The after-hours line rang, harsh in the silence between her heartbeat and Aislin's.

"I have to get that," Aislin said. "It's an emergency."

Zane took another step back and nodded. As the space between them grew, she became more aware of their surroundings, and the odor of various animals and disinfectants was obvious. Jesus, she hated that smell. She hadn't noticed when she came in.

Aislin had put a fancy Irish spell on her. There could be no other explanation why she was behaving so out of character.

Zane's blood cooled several degrees, and she half-listened to Aislin's side of the conversation while the voices in her head argued with her heart and libido. She'd only really caught the last line.

"Uh, huh. Well, keep him calm as you can. I'm on my way." Aislin hung up the phone and talked over her shoulder as she headed for the double door to the infirmary. "I'm sorry, but I have to go."

Zane used long strides to catch up. "What's wrong? Somebody coughing up hairballs?" She chuckled at her own joke before catching the venomous look on Aislin's face.

"No," Aislin snapped and continued to throw things in her bag. "There's a horse down whose leg is trapped and they need me there to sedate him while they try and dig him out. He's struggling and we both know what might happen if he breaks his leg."

And just like that, they were back to where they started.

Zane tried to ask more questions, but Aislin ignored her. She felt foolish running around behind her as she closed the clinic, called her sister to feed the boarders, and handed a bone to her dog.

Him, she talked to. "Sorry, Mikey. I'll be back when I can. I might be late." She herded Zane toward the door, out of it, and locked up before sprinting to her ancient truck.

Zane felt rejected, which prompted her unreasonable behavior. "Impersonating an equine vet again?"

Aislin gave her a stony look and threw her truck into reverse, leaving Zane to feel like an idiot standing by her sports car and wondering—again—what the hell had just happened.

She drove home, and even shocked herself as she kept to the speed limit. Zane was more than a little ashamed of the way she'd acted. Almost as if she'd been jealous.

Jealous of what?

How was she going to fix this?

The first thing she heard when she walked into her front door was giggling. It sounded so out of place in the house she stopped in her tracks. How long had it been since she'd come home to laughter?

And how sad was it that she hadn't noted the absence of it until she heard it?

Zane found herself smiling as she walked toward the back of the house and found her brother doing a butt-shaking booty dance that she hadn't seen in years. Louis spun around and nearly lost his balance when he spotted her leaning against the doorway.

"When did you get home?" His face was flushed with excitement and Zane noticed, really noticed, how pretty he was. Did she ever get that excited look? Had she ever let her guard down enough to wear it? Louis looked nervous and tense, as if he were on the defense from one of her sarcastic comments. Was she so bad then? That he knew she would be snarky if he were happy? It was high time to take predictably out of the equation.

She was rewarded with a warm smile when she laughed instead.

"Apparently, in time for the show. What's up with the victory dance?"

"I've got a date!"

"Since when has that been a cause for this much exuberance?" Zane lowered her voice to a dramatic whisper. "You've had them before, Master Louis."

Louis spun a circle again. "Yes, I have, Zany." He wagged his eyebrows. "But I've never had a date with an O'Shea sister before."

Her blood turned ice cold. "What?" Irrational jealousy ripped up her spine and stiffened her back. "Did I just hear that correctly?" Had Aislin really had an emergency, or was she playing games here? It happened enough in the past, women who were turned on by sleeping with twins. She knew she played them as well, but the thought of Aislin kissing her brother made her want to rip his face off.

What kind of an ass did that make her? The two of them must have laughed their asses off behind her back when she was sick. Zane's temper boiled and she raced toward the stairs.

She heard her brother yelling behind her but sprinted the last few yards to her door and slammed it with such force, the paintings shook on the walls from the impact.

"Aren't you going to congratulate me?" Louis spoke through the keyhole.

"Not on your life!"

Ath-hole.

Chapter Eight

Zane managed to avoid her brother and ruthlessly shoved her thoughts of Aislin into a dark place for the next few days. Somewhere in the back of her mind, she knew she was acting pissy and unreasonable, but dismissed it. Sometimes, Zane just loved to coast on righteous anger.

She was currently nearing the end of a big case, and conveniently spent most of the week at the company's condo in San Francisco.

When Louis managed to get around her Caller ID by using another's phone, the second she heard his voice, she hung up.

She was pissed off at his gall. At least Aislin wasn't trying to call and feed her more lies.

Then she flipped one-eighty. Why wasn't she calling?

Zane rarely felt helpless or second-guessed herself, and in addition, she hated feeling stupid.

It was the reason her temples pounded and she felt nauseated.

Utter stupidity.

Thank God the case was well rehearsed and researched because she was barely going through the motions expected of her in the courtroom.

When they won later that afternoon, she felt nothing of the intense satisfaction that always followed a triumph. She'd won the case, but in the competition with her brother, lost the girl.

Zane nodded to her colleagues she passed on her way to the underground parking garage and sat in her car. What was she going to do? She didn't want to see her brother with Aislin, the woman who'd turned her life upside down,

It was Friday. She could drive to Monterey Bay. No one would actually look for her there.

The house had everything, including extra clothes, no reason to go back and pack.

Zane turned off her cell phone and drove toward the freeway, ignored the little buzz on the back of her neck, and the tiny thought that she should go home.

෯෯෭෭

Aislin dropped the mop into the bucket and paid little attention to the water that splashed over the side from the force.

"Pureblood tease. That's what she is," Aislin said to the empty cage. She bent over to make sure she got to the back of the large kennel with the disinfectant.

She felt a gentle paw tap her face and turned to look at the Siamese cat who wanted her attention. Wise blue eyes stared at her then blinked slowly.

Zane's eyes were blue.

Aislin's mental scream nearly blinded her. The cat meowed and purred, reaching through the cage again to touch her.

Enchanted Aislin dropped the mop to scratch under her chin.

"Here I was, Simba, minding my business, when Zane barged into my office and laid one on me. Did I ask for it? No, I did not. I was kind of expecting her

to slap me after that whole doggie downer business."
Aislin waived the thought away.

"Where was I?"

Simba purred.

"Oh yeah. Not one word from her. Nothing.
Nada, zip, zilch. She just sneered at me when I got the
emergency call, then left."

Simba's faceted eyes never left Aislin's.

"You're right," Aislin said. "She's playing me."
She briefly imagined where the kiss might have led if
not for the call, then tried *not* to see Zane stalking at
her all Amazonian-like. She didn't want to remember
how the kiss left her feeling all soft and vulnerable.
And needy, dammit.

Hell, Aislin had kissed a couple of women in
the last few years. They hadn't elicited this response,
though. They hadn't even made it past Shannon's face.

Shannon. Aislin put the mop and pail away. She
considered her soul mate, but loving her hadn't been
a roller coaster ride. Their relationship was sweet and
gentle. She felt the tears coming and checked herself.

She hadn't even been on a date with Zane.

She was all messed up now. She didn't want her;
she wasn't her type.

Why hasn't she called?

She hated herself for it, but Aislin crossed the hall
to her office and found Zane's business card with her
cell number on it. Aislin looked down at her bloody
coat and pushed three buttons before she hung up. She
was probably busy.

With the exquisite leggy blonde in the restaurant.

There. That felt better. Aislin stormed back out
of her office. She'd take mad over insecure any day.

She clipped on Mikey's leash. They would walk

to the restaurant, then her parents' house. She refused to sit here and wait for a call any longer.

Maybe she could find out why Brianna had left so early.

❧ ❧ ❧ ❧

Zane turned expertly at the nearly invisible road and traveled down the long driveway. When she came around the last corner, she slowed the car to a crawl, looking forward to seeing the summer cabin.

In her family for three generations, "cabin" really wasn't an accurate term for the three-story wood and stone house. It had views from large redwood decks, a rooftop terrace overlooking the beautiful Pacific Ocean, and an infinity pool that gave the illusion you could swim right into the waves.

Zane rolled the window down and took a deep breath of the salt air. It brought back so many wonderful memories at once. Yes, this had been a good decision and a perfect place to gather herself. There had been a lot of laughter here.

She left the car in the driveway and noticed a light from behind the curtains.

What? No one came up here. It had been almost a year since she'd been.

They had the same housekeeper she'd known since childhood, and she only came in once a week.

She was pretty sure that Miss Odessa wouldn't be here at this hour on a Friday. Zane grabbed her keys between her fingers as a weapon and let herself in quietly. She'd catch the fuckers.

Whoever it was, they were upstairs.

She thought about calling the police, but the

property was so far out they would take too long, and she was already in the house. While she was debating, she heard unmistakable noises of bedsprings and soft female sighs.

A male voice groaned and Zane raced up the stairs. She didn't need to be mindful of the sixth step from the top that creaked.

The couple was making enough noise to cover it. Clothes littered the hallway down to her...

Brother's room.

Oh, my God. He brought her here? Louis brought her girl...his conquest...here of all places?

She'd kill him. That's all there was to it. Zane stomped the rest of the way to his room and threw open the door.

Louis was just rolling to his side when the door slammed against the wall. He pulled the sheets up as if in protection.

One adrenaline-fueled moment later, her brother laughed. "Jesus, you about gave me a heart attack, Zany."

Zane grabbed a large vase from the dresser, and held it about her head as she advanced.

"Whoa," Louis said. "Hey, you can come out now. It's just my crazy sister." He spoke to the lump under the covers.

"Yes," Zane said with ice in her tone. "Come out you two-timing, doctor-impersonating, drug-pushing slut."

"What?" A slender arm appeared from under the covers and Zane felt her heart might break. The sheet peeled down and the next thing she saw was clouds of...

Red hair.

A very pissed-off Brianna stared back at her. "What did you just say to me?"

Zane was shocked and opened her mouth, but nothing came out. She felt paralyzed but managed to lower the vase.

Louis cracked up.

"What's so funny?" Brianna snarled at him.

"She thought you were Aislin."

His laughter was quickly subdued when he had to lunge to keep Brianna from leaping at Zane.

"How dare you talk about my sister like that?" She struggled to get loose from Louis and elbowed him in the mouth.

Zane took a step back from her. "But Louis, you said—"

He wiped a drop of blood from his lip and adjusted his grip on Brianna. "What's wrong with you? I said an O'Shea sister, I didn't say which one. You would have known that had you answered the phone."

Still stunned, Zane looked at Brianna. "I'm so, so sorry. I have to go."

She ignored the raised voices that followed her race down the stairs, jumped in her car, and sped back down the long dirt road, correcting the wheel when she nearly clipped a large redwood tree.

She didn't know where she was going, she just knew she wanted to leave her humiliation far behind.

Zane drove for hours, and when she found herself driving on the shoulder for the second time, she pulled over to the side of the road, lay her head back, and fell asleep.

A sharp rap on the window startled her and she had to shield her eyes from the rising sun. One of her neighbors, a man she'd gone to school with, was staring at her with a grin on his face.

"Hell Zany, ten more miles and you'd been home to sleep it off."

"Shut up, Beau, I wasn't drinking. I drove all night and was nodding off at the wheel."

He held his hands up in mock defense. "Okay, fine. I was just checking. It's not every day I find a beautiful woman on the side of my road. I thought you might need some help before I fix the barbed wire fence that went down."

Zane felt bad for being rude. "Thank you. I just need to get home."

Then she had a sinking feeling it had been Aislin's emergency. "Was it Night Ryder?"

He nodded and looked down. Her heart sank. "Aw hell, Beau, I'm so sorry. He was a beautiful horse. Who was the vet?"

"Doc O'Shea. She held his head and cried with me."

Zane was irritated. "Where was the real vet? You do know she's not a horse doctor, right?"

"What's your problem, Zany? We've always used her. Her partner Shannon brought her up all the time on house calls. We all can't afford a live-in like you."

She already regretted her harsh words. She wasn't angry at Aislin, she was ashamed of herself. A lot. She felt small.

"Right," Zane said. Maybe she could get more information. "I fired ours for drinking on the job again. Maybe I could use this Shannon person."

"Don't play me for stupid," Beau said. "Word is you know exactly who Doc O'Shea is and she delivered your newest. I'll see you later, I got work to do."

Zane started her car and headed home.

Again with Shannon. The veterinarian on the business card.

Who the hell was Shannon?

⁂

Aislin opened her eyes slowly. Mikey was snoring next to her head and Merlin was purring loudly on the other side. She untangled her hair from the cat, and patted both of their heads in turn.

It was one of her rare days off during the week. Even more uncommon, it was a Friday.

Merlin jumped up immediately. Mikey continued to snore. "Get up," Aislin said. "You sound like an old man in my bed."

Memories of wonderful, lazy mornings slipped into her consciousness. Aislin rubbed her eyes, then where her chest hurt. "Enough," Aislin scolded herself.

She got up and crossed to the window. The sun was just coming up over her street and the day whispered it might just be beautiful, or could be, if she let it.

After waiting for her coffee, Aislin stepped out onto the back porch while Mikey patrolled the fence line. It was something he took very seriously, lifting his leg every foot or so.

Two of her boarders, Sir William, a King Charles spaniel, and Mad Max, a tricolor Shih Tzu, pranced happily behind him and peed over his marks, adding their own signatures.

Their owners were on vacation in Europe. She let herself dream of a time when she could see the world for herself. She grinned as she pictured a jaunty black beret on her head while she drank espresso and ate fancy cookies. She was sure she could pull it off.

She sipped her coffee while watching the Parisian pedestrians bustle by her table at the sidewalk café, and turned to talk to her companion.

Icy eyes framed by blond hair stared at her from across the table.

Who invited her to this fantasy? Aislin shook her head to dispel the daydream. She clearly needed a distraction. She thought about going to the restaurant but only for a split second when she remembered the endless talk of the wedding and its myriad of details. She didn't want to talk, and frankly, was still upset about the dress her sister picked out.

She weighed different ideas, then dismissed them. She didn't want to do any of them alone.

Why hadn't Zane called?

Who the hell did she think she was up there in that mansion on the hill? It hurt to think that after kissing her, Zane would, in her own words, get over her self-described crush.

Aislin felt her face burn and her blood simmering to a boil. The nerve! She had half a mind to tell her off. She would stand up to Zane and tell her she couldn't play with her emotions like that. She was not to be played with.

Ha.

Pissed off, Aislin whistled for the dogs, then got ready.

It was pure temper that got her to the Whitman Ranch and up to the front door. Aislin rang the doorbell. And because she wanted to feel confident, stood with her hands on her hips in Supergirl fashion waiting for someone to answer.

When no one did, Aislin swung at the door with

her fist.

⁂

Zane had heard the truck come up and was on the other side of the door in panic mode. What on earth would she say to Aislin? *Sorry I haven't called, but I thought you were banging my brother? Or how about, sorry I called your sister a slut because I thought she was you?* Zane leaned her forehead against the door.

She could do this. She'd faced rooms full of angry, bloodthirsty sharks in business suits for a living. She could certainly handle a small, pissed-off woman, right?

The trick was to be fast, like when you ripped off a Band-Aid. She opened it swiftly, and then a bright light exploded in her head when she fell backward onto the marble tile.

And landed flat on her back.

Again.

She felt Aislin kneel beside her.

"Let me see it," she said and tried to pry Zane's hand away from her face.

"You hit me!"

"I didn't mean to. I'm sorry, let me see it."

"You. Hit. Me," Zane repeated slowly.

"Here now," Aislin said in the tone that Zane associated with her I'll-humor-you voice. "Let's get some ice for it. I barely tapped you. One of my sisters could take that punch, get up, and try to kick my ass."

Zane's shock ebbed and she peeled herself from the tiles. "Third time's a charm?"

Aislin had already started down the hall toward the kitchen. "Come again?"

Zane followed and waited until she pulled out an ice pack, then picked Aislin up, and set her on the counter where she trapped her with her arms.

"I have to go."

"You came to see me," Zane said.

"Now I have. Let me up."

"You can't just come here, hit me, and leave."

"Why not? You came to my office, gave me a crazy kiss, and left." Aislin pushed against her chest. "You didn't answer my calls."

Zane didn't budge and locked in a stare. "You only called me twice."

Aislin kept her gaze, and stopped pushing. "No return calls," she said between her teeth.

Zane didn't want to tell her that she thought Aislin was sleeping with her brother because now that she remembered, it made her look ridiculous. "I'm sorry, I was stupid."

"Oh." Aislin blinked first. "Wow. I don't know what to say now. I thought I would come in here and we'd argue…"

"And you'd make a grand exit," Zane said. "Or try to. I know I haven't had much luck in that department. So, why don't we skip that part and get back to where you assaulted me." She took the ice and held it against her cheek. "How do you plead, vixen?"

Aislin smiled wickedly. "Not guilty, Counselor."

"Oh," Zane said. "I think you are. Try again." She leaned closer until Aislin's torso was backed against the cabinets and she heard her sharp intake of breath.

"I was framed."

Zane laughed. "There's no one else here." She put the ice down, placed her hands on Aislin's cheeks, and watched her eyes widen.

"No contest?" Aislin asked. Her voice squeaked.

"That'll do," Zane said, and lowered to kiss her. The way Aislin trembled against her spurred her on. Zane wanted to kiss her deep and hard, but kept it gentle and soft instead.

It was Aislin who took it up a notch. One of her hands tangled through Zane's hair and tugged, while the other lightly scratched Zane's back, digging in her nails. She nipped Zane's lower lip.

And it was Aislin who broke the kiss. "I can't breathe."

The tension in Zane's stomach was painful, her frustration near boiling. She had to have her. She pulled the hem of Aislin's shirt up, and intended to pull it off.

Aislin grabbed her wrists. "No."

Zane would have insisted but for the tears filling Aislin's eyes. She stopped cold. "What's the matter?"

Aislin's hands went to her stomach and rubbed. "I have a powerful need for you."

"And?" Zane was confused. "I want you right back, just as much."

They stared at each other for a moment and the space became awkward with silence. One of the gardeners started a lawnmower nearby and the angry buzz of a weed trimmer followed.

"You don't understand." Aislin's voice hitched. She pushed Zane aside and hopped down off the counter.

"I really am sorry."

Aislin shook her head. "I don't know what I expected by coming here. You hurt my feelings, and I just threw myself at you. There's something wrong with that."

Zane felt a moment of panic. "There's nothing

wrong with the way you kissed me." She reached for Aislin's hand.

Aislin backed up a step, then shook her head when Zane stepped closer. "Please don't."

Zane felt a lump begin to form in her throat. "Why?"

"Now I'm sorry I left this mark on your face. Put the bag back on," Aislin said.

The pain in her cheek was fine, but the thought of Aislin leaving hurt. Maybe humor would help. "Is that an insult?"

Aislin laughed. "Good one. Look, it's not you. And I'll give you the truth." She picked up the ice from the counter. "I haven't done this in a long time."

"It's like riding a bike," Zane said, then flinched when she held the bag against her face again. "You were doing just fine." *And I don't want to let you go.*

Zane pulled her in for a hug and when she didn't resist, she felt a small measure of relief.

They rocked back and forth for a moment before Aislin stepped back. "I have to go."

"Stay, please," Zane said. "Let me make it up to you."

"I have animals to take care of."

"Go out with me tomorrow." *I want to see where this can go.*

"A date?"

"I'll give you the words you gave me back and give you the truth then. I don't want to just sleep with you. I would love to spend time with you."

"God, I hope I won't regret this, but I'm an impulsive creature. I'm on call for the evening. How does a picnic sound? Leave the details to me, and you can pick me up at noon."

Zane watched Aislin walk down the hallway and out the door.

She sincerely hoped that tomorrow wouldn't involve any accidents and the only time she would be on her back was if she chose to and Aislin was on top of her.

Chapter Nine

What on earth possessed her yesterday, asking Zane on an afternoon date?

More disturbing, Aislin had come close to telling her why she hadn't been involved with anyone for such a long time.

And it was so much more than remembering how to ride a bike.

Aislin's heart couldn't take a casual affair, and she knew it.

She ran around the kitchen, checking and rechecking the picnic basket she'd packed.

It had only taken her the better part of half an hour to find it. She'd have to go through the catch-all that was the spare room and straighten it up, maybe even have a garage sale.

If anything was in that room, chances were she simply didn't know where else to put it.

Then again, if she *had* cleaned it, she wouldn't have found the picnic basket Darcy had given her for Christmas a few years ago.

She hadn't had the chance to use it.

Which is the whole reason for a junk room anyway. See?

Hoarders unite.

Not that I have anything against—

"Omigod, shut up!" Aislin yelled at herself and scared Merlin, who had been weaving through her legs meowing pitifully for her to feed him again, as his tone implied he was wasting away.

Mikey sat at what he must have thought was a safe distance and stared at her, hope eternal.

Aislin put a hand to her chest. "I'm so sorry. I'm yelling at me, not you." She crouched down and gave them both scratches and cuddles, and because she felt bad, slipped each of them a tiny piece of cheese.

She pointed. "The doctor says no people food, so don't tell on me to me."

God, I run myself in circles like no one else. She was still chuckling when she heard the sounds of very loud motorcycle turning the corner.

The kind that caused a clench of excitement low in her belly,

It was a beautiful day for riding. Her father had a bike for one glorious summer until her mother put her foot down. Dad did triple duty taking them all for a little spin.

An unfortunate accident in the rain caused him to skid the bike into a bush. That took care of that, and her mother made him sell it.

Then her parents spent the money on a midlife honeymoon they both enjoyed immensely.

She still heard the muffler and was more than surprised when it pulled into her driveway.

Please don't let this be an emergency. Then she wondered where the hell the animal was hiding.

Sun speared off the chrome and danced along the cherry-red tank. One long, black-clad leg swung over to kick the stand. The rider reached up to take the helmet off and a cascade of platinum hair fell from its confinement.

Aislin was reminded of an old Pantene

commercial where a sexy woman comes out of a swimming pool and swings her hair back.

Yes, it was exactly like that. Except different.

She was delighted when Zane strode up to her door. Her leathers made a weird juxtaposition to her corporate suits.

Maybe Zane wasn't as staid or stuck up as Aislin had presumed. There seemed to more than a couple of facets to her.

Where were they going to put the picnic basket?

Zane knocked and Aislin nearly danced to the door. Who the heck cared?

As all her mother's warnings about riding a motorcycle surfaced. Aislin battled them down. "Shut up," she murmured.

❧❧❧❧

Zane walked down the pretty pathway to Aislin's door that was painted a vibrant peacock blue.

The yard and flowers told her Aislin enjoyed gardening, much as her mother had. It didn't have the rigidity of a planned landscape design; rather, it was wonderfully eclectic.

Just like her, she thought when the door opened. Aislin smiled at her and it about knocked Zane over.

She wore royal-blue harem pants slit up the side, the kind that give a glimpse of heavenly bare skin, a cute white shirt that laced up the front, and she'd put her hair in a high ponytail.

I Dream of Jeannie, anyone?

Anyone?

Before she could laugh, a large—make that very large—ball of fur came barreling around the side of the house.

Zombie cat. But after learning her lesson the last time she'd met him, she crouched down to see what he was about.

Through the corner of her eye she watched Aislin pause and wait, probably to see her reaction. The cat's weight nearly knocked her off balance, but she cautiously pet him, and the loud purr that followed was kind of nice.

His cheeks rubbed against her chaps and he— *gross*—drooled all over them.

She must've passed the test, because he meowed once and went running to Aislin on his three legs.

Zane watched her pensive expression turn to pure love for the cat, Merlin was it? What would it be like to be the recipient of such focused adoration? Not because Merlin was pretty, or wealthy, but just because he was.

Great. Am I talking about animals, or myself?

Her mother had matching Siamese cats and Afghan Hounds, but they considered themselves royalty and above playing with her as a child.

She shook her head and brought her attention back to Aislin's face.

"You didn't say we'd be on a bike."

Zane pretended indignant shock. "Bike? Woman, this is a machine, not a toy."

Aislin sighed. "I'm not dressed for it, I have a large basket, and I, uh, wanted to bring Mikey."

As if perfectly timed, Mikey raced past Aislin's legs and straight down the path. Zane hadn't been fast enough to catch his collar.

"Hurry, we have to catch him before he gets hurt." She took off after him. Zane noticed the pretty gladiator sandals slapping against the concrete and hoped Aislin wouldn't slip.

She's quick, Zane thought, and then raced the other way to cut him off.

Mikey appeared to be having great fun and ran back and forth between the two of them. It was after one of his mad dashes that Zane finally caught the harness and lifted him up. He settled happily against her chest and covered her face with kisses.

"He's a terrible flirt." Aislin took the dog, stood on her toes, and kissed Zane's cheek before she turned back to her house.

Zane covered the spot with her hand, a bit stunned at the sweet gesture.

And more than a little awkward in the wake of it.

When she realized she was standing in the middle of the sidewalk with her mouth hanging open, she walked up to the door and into the house.

From the entry, Zane saw an explosion of color. The living room lived up to the shade on Aislin's front door. The scent, clean and floral, hit her first, which surprised her as the clinic was attached and right next door.

Original woodwork gleamed from a recent polish and the biscuit walls set off the art: Waterhouse prints, dreamcatchers, and a lovely painting of what looked like the coast of Ireland steeped in a dreamy mist. Old windows and iron grates hung alongside fairy paintings and dragon sculptures. Gorgeous sheets from India, a riot of reds, oranges, and blue, popped against the light furniture.

Again, Zane was reminded of a genie bottle, and fascinated at the way Aislin's personality seemed to jump into her surroundings.

It was as far a cry from hers as she could imagine. Then again, she'd hired a snooty decorator to design the mansion when she took it over from her father.

This is a home, Zane thought. *A comfortable one.* "I love your place," she said. "It looks happy."

Aislin laughed. "I like it. It's much smaller than what you're used to."

The remark pinched. Was that another social crack? She didn't want to believe it and she wondered what it was exactly that Aislin held against her money.

Aislin sat on the wide couch, the split in her pants exposing her thighs. Was she aware of how subtle the move was? How sexy? Zane wondered if her skin was as soft as it looked, and appreciated the titillating view of Aislin's breasts, barely peeking over her shirt.

Zane swallowed and found her voice. "You look lovely. Have I said that yet?"

"No," Aislin said. A whisper of a smile appeared with just a wink of her dimple. She pulled her ponytail to the side and fiddled with it. "You look rakishly sexy pulling up on that...machine."

Zane took a step then nearly tripped when Mikey raced between her legs. "I can't keep my feet around you."

"He's been acting weird all day, barking into corners, chasing things I can't see, growling at nothing."

A small chill stirred the hairs on the back of Zane's neck. "Ghosts?" She might have missed the brief distant look in Aislin's eyes had she not been staring at her.

Mikey jumped up next to her on the couch and Aislin rubbed his belly. "I've often wondered if my place was full of them, animals who have passed that we've treated and couldn't save. There was this gigantic banana boa…" Aislin must have seen the fear on Zane's face. She laughed. "Never mind."

Safe from the horrid thought of banana boa ghosts, Zane walked to the fireplace where more things glittered, and looked at the framed photos.

Amongst the family photos, one stood out. She couldn't say why, but it appeared more focused, brighter than the ones around it. A younger Aislin stared out with a full-on, knock-you-dead smile, and the woman next to her was looking at Aislin with adoration. She turned to ask her about it but Aislin wasn't on the couch.

She'd moved silently and stood in the hall. "Are you ready to go?"

Zane wanted to ask who was in the picture but Aislin's expression stopped her. "I know the perfect place. You won't have to change, and you can bring Mikey."

"It seems a shame not being able to ride your, um, machine."

Delighted at the innuendo, Zane smiled and followed Aislin into the kitchen and saw the red and white checkered basket. "I promise you a ride soon. How about we load your truck and you can follow me back to the house?" She tugged Aislin's ponytail and drew her close for a quick kiss.

What she hadn't expected was how Aislin melted into it. *Mercy.* She'd assumed the fire, but sweetness she was completely unarmed for.

Aislin pulled back. "Okay, raincheck on the ride. Let me get Mikey's leash."

She was gone before Zane could catch her breath. How could such a simple kiss destroy her so? Because it was real, without guile, genuine. And Zane had been thinking of another ride altogether.

The anticipation was likely to kill her. Aislin blew back into the room. "Are we going or what? Oh, and where to?"

"My place," Zane said.

"Your place?" Aislin clipped the leash and picked up the basket.

"We have a lake."

Aislin blinked slowly. "Of course you do."

❧❧❧❧

"How come I didn't know she had a l-a-k-e?" Aislin spelled it out for Mikey. "It seems a lot to have overlooked that."

As they drove the now familiar route, she continued to talk to him. "I mean, I know the first time I only saw the stables, the second, I, uh, made a house call."

It might take a couple of years to laugh about how she'd dosed her with doggie downers. Aislin chuckled. *Maybe not.*

"What? It's not like you needed the pills or anything."

"The third time," she went on, "I knocked her on her fine ass. Well, I didn't mean to. Stop looking at me like that." Mikey lay on the passenger side and tilted his head this way and that as she talked to him. It was freaking adorable.

She racked her brain for any memory of the layout of the property, and finally decided she'd just have to see for herself. The sight of Zane on her motorcycle was totally hot, and she had to admit, exciting as she took all those turns in the road with her knees barely above the concrete.

She told the practical side of herself to shut up while she enjoyed the sexy view.

The Beast popped and groaned but made it up the driveway. She might just have to look for a newer vehicle sooner than she'd thought, and because it upset her, Aislin shoved the reminder down, down, down to rest with all the other stuff she'd yet to deal with.

Nervous anticipation had taken over and she was nearly dizzy with it. Zane had taken a little road to the left Aislin hadn't noticed before. Not surprising, as it was on the opposite side of the house. Not that she could ever call it a house. "Mansion" was a better fit.

Her truck sputtered along the narrow path through the tangle of well-manicured trees. When the view opened up, she could only gasp at the wonder of it.

Yup, it was a lake. In her mind, she thought maybe it might be just bigger than a pond, but the reality was more than she'd imagined.

And absolutely stunning.

After she kicked the stand down, Zane walked over to where Aislin had stopped and opened her door. Aislin had a moment of wonder when it did so readily—no pops or the screech of metal on metal.

She held out a hand and Aislin jumped down. She thought she'd enjoyed the entire view until it narrowed down to her current one: Zane's breasts under her white tank.

Zane smirked. "Eyes up here."

Aislin looked up quickly but there was only amusement in her eyes. She felt shy and embarrassed she'd been caught staring, but how was one not to? Zane's nipples were hard and visible, and in Aislin's opinion, just begging to be touched.

It wasn't fair for her to remember the last time she did. Zane was hardly lucid at the time.

"We have to walk from here." Zane reached out to her. "I'll take the basket, you get Mikey." Her head titled. "What kind of dog is he?"

"Heinz fifty-seven," Aislin said, glad to bring her mind off the pill escapade. "Even I can't determine what breed, and I know dogs."

Zane took her hand as they walked to the water's edge.

The sun sparkled on the calm water and as Aislin watched, a fish breeched and plopped back down with a splash.

Zane put the basket on the redwood table. "Several years ago, Dad had it stocked, though he hasn't fished here in years. It was more of my grandfather's passion."

The silence stretched, and crickets, Aislin thought, would be welcome. She never had a problem with conversation, but being near Zane made her nervous and tongue-tied. She bent and tied Mikey's long leash to the table. "If he does his business, I'll clean it up when we leave."

"Okay." Zane laughed and touched her shoulder. The spark and snap of electricity surprised them both.

"Ouch!" Aislin rubbed the spot. "Static. Here? We're on the grass."

Zane shook her head. "It's nothing like the shock you get in an office around the machines."

The tension between them was becoming painful to bear. There was a need curled up inside her that threatened her manners, her sanity. "Just one," Aislin said and stood on the bench, which made her taller than Zane and gave her an advantage.

She grabbed her collar first, then her hair, and before she could change her mind or analyze it to death, kissed her.

Zane's hands gripped Aislin's waist and held her in place. One electrifying second later, the kiss became a tangle of tongues and shared breath. Desire rocketed through her and shook her to her core.

Aislin broke away. "I can't. I'll have to tell you again, you take my breath away."

Zane lifted her off the bench, onto the grass, and held her. Aislin felt Zane's heart pound and her muscles tighten just as her own had. It was powerful knowing she'd caused it.

"Just one?" Zane asked. "Good thing. Two would kill me."

Aislin laughed and stepped away. "I couldn't think, can't think, but I needed to get that out of the way."

"Fair enough," Zane said.

Aislin turned to the basket and felt herself spun back to face Zane again.

"Here's mine."

Sweet baby Jesus. Zane could kiss a girl. Just when her knees went weak and her chest felt ready to explode, Zane gentled and ended it tenderly.

That scared Aislin to death. She'd accepted they had a physical connection, but her emotions were raw, and in order to have some semblance of control, she had to slow down. She placed a hand against Zane's chest and pushed her back. "Too much."

She couldn't help but notice Zane's expression; she looked struck as well.

The late morning sun was shifting and began to

shade the table where they would eat. Zane stripped her leathers. *Or is it armor?* Aislin thought. For a moment there she wasn't sure. She'd looked like a warrior Aislin had once dreamed of. Or maybe that was a fantasy about Lucy Lawless—she couldn't remember.

The spell was broken when Mikey jumped between them and scrabbled for the attention Aislin was sure he thought he was entitled to.

"Jealous, are you?" Zane reached down and pet him.

"He's never, um, had um, seen me—"

"I get it," Zane said. "What's for lunch? That basket weighs a ton."

Easier now, Aislin smiled. "A little of this, a little of that." She looked at Zane and thought of the possibilities. "And maybe a whole lot more."

The corners of Zane's mouth curved. "I certainly hope so."

Shannon lay on her stomach on the striped umbrella to look down at the couple. "It seems to be going well," she said. "They're not fighting, anyway."

"Sure, and I saw sparks." Granny leaned over with her.

Bella sat primly on the grass below, her dogs beside her. "I love this place. It's always been one of my favorites. I'm glad she brought Aislin here. It's a special one for Zane as well." She adjusted her large sun hat. "Time for a little privacy"

Granny sighed. "You're right."

Shannon said nothing at all and all three faded away.

෴෴෴෴

Zane studied the wreckage of fruit, cheese, fried chicken, and potato salad. They'd managed to decimate the contents of the basket, as if the food were a substitute for the sexual frustration snapping like a live wire between them. "More wine?"

"No, I have to drive home."

Disappointment rained down, and Zane reached for Aislin's hand. "So soon?"

"I've a while yet." Aislin rubbed her stomach. "I'm so full. Normally I'd need a nap after eating so much."

"The food was wonderful," Zane said. "Thank you."

"I'm embarrassed." Aislin smiled. "I didn't make it, Darcy did. I don't want you to think I can just whip up stuff like this. I rely on my family heavily for my lack of skills in the kitchen."

"It could have been from a greasy fast food chain and I wouldn't complain. This has been one of the best afternoons I've had in a long time."

"Me too," Aislin said. "The clinic takes up so much of my time."

"What made you want to become a veterinarian?"

Aislin looked thoughtful. "Our house was always noisy, full of dogs and cats. I don't remember a time when we didn't have several animals living with us. For some reason, I was the one the strays always followed home."

"Did they really?" Zane asked. "Or did you coax them? Here puppy, puppy—or kitty, kitty—come this way?"

Aislin laughed. "A little of both. I always wanted to help them, couldn't stand to see any creature in pain. When Brianna went to college and chose her major, I felt that thrill. You know, the one that you get when you absolutely know you're doing the right thing?"

Zane nodded. "I can get the same feeling when I have a case that I know is righteous or going extremely well."

"Did you always want to be a lawyer? I mean, I know that you're following in your family's footsteps and all, but did you want it?"

No one had ever asked Zane that question before and truthfully, it had been so long since she'd thought about it, she had to reach back in her memory to answer it. "It was expected from my brother for sure. My oldest sister, Pearl, had no desire, and I think I was always so caught up in doing things as well as or better than Louis, that I aimed for the same career. I don't know that I made a conscious decision about it, but really, no other path made itself known to me. I didn't want to do anything else."

"So," she said, wanting change the subject. "What's it like growing up with four sisters?"

Aislin's face lit up. "It was crazy and wonderful, and never a dull moment. We got to be our own club. But, you have more siblings, so you know, right?"

"Pearl was already in boarding school when my mom passed, we talked maybe once a year. Louis and I were close, as twins are, until my father remarried and the new stepmother—that would be the first one—sent us away as well."

"The bitch," Aislin said.

"Thanks for the solidarity." Zane laughed.

"My sisters and I check with each other daily to see who's on what list and whether we are or aren't talking to someone for whatever reason."

"Oddly, that sounds fun." Zane wiped her hands

on her napkin. "I've never had that before."

"It is a blast. But really? As much as we love each other, there was never a quiet moment in our house, mostly it was pure chaos. My mother was a saint to put up with all of our quarrels."

"What did your father do?"

Aislin laughed. "He always had, and still has, a perpetually dazed look. I imagine years of living with just women does that."

Zane stood from the table and picked up the blanket that had been tucked away in the basket.

She flicked it open and spread it on the lawn. "Want to lie in the shade with me, Aislin?" Zane watched her carefully. Surprise, need, and indecision were apparent, but it was the sadness that made an impression, the expression of a little girl lost that remained.

She'd always studied people. In her line of work she'd mastered the dance of separating pretty words from the actual truth, and become an excellent judge of what people were feeling.

But nothing she'd seen compared to the hurt she thought might live inside Aislin. She wondered what it was she could do to help soothe it, but until Aislin talked about it, she had no clue how to go about it.

She came around the table and sat cross-legged across from Zane, and when her knees poked out from her pants, Zane noticed an ugly bruise on one she hadn't before. On the other knee, she saw several nasty scars. "Aw, what happened?"

Aislin waved a hand. "Nothing major. Great Dane wanted to dance, and we fell instead."

"What about the healed cuts?"

After angling to cover herself, Aislin waved her

off. "It was a long time ago."

Her tone said it was none of Zane's business, so she let that one go. "Any other interesting scars?" Zane propped on her elbow.

Aislin grinned. "Actually, I did get bit on the butt."

Zane perked up. "What bit you?"

"A baby chimp." Aislin rubbed her backside as if remembering.

"No!" She pounced and slid Aislin to her back, Zane poised above her. Their gaze locked and held before Zane lowered her body to meet hers. "That's a hell of a segue to wild monkey sex."

Aislin laughed and pushed until Zane lay next to her. "Get off."

Zane loved the ease and comfort of the afternoon, and the fact it was her favorite place only made it more so. "Can I see it?"

"No, you can't see it."

"Now, that's just a challenge." Zane thumped a fist to her chest. "I can promise I have no scars on my ass."

"Don't have many clients who bite, Counselor?"

"There was this one time..." Zane laughed when Aislin's eyes widened. "No, I'm just kidding." She wanted to tuck Aislin underneath her again, but found she was just as pleased to get to know her.

Once, just *once*, she wanted to not have an agenda, to just lie on their backs watching the clouds.

"So," Aislin said. "How many women have you brought here?"

"Only two, yourself included. It was my mother's favorite place."

"I'm sorry. That must have been so difficult, so

hard to lose her at such a young age."

Zane felt the automatic rise. "Yes, but our best times were spent here, at this spot."

"Thank you for sharing it with me." Aislin paused. "And the other?"

"Caught that, did you?" Zane chuckled and turned over to look into Aislin's eyes. "The other was my very first kiss."

"You never forget your first."

Zane shook her head. "No."

Aislin grinned and flashed a dimple. "Still think that one would get me out of your system?"

"No. I can say in all honesty that was wrong."

"And stupid," Aislin added.

"Well..." Zane dipped closer and watched Aislin's lips part in anticipation. It was easy to sink into the kiss, harder to keep it gentle, and more difficult yet to rise up from it. "Nothing foolish about that."

Aislin shook her head but stopped Zane when she would have kissed her again. "We don't seem to be at odds now."

Zane wondered what that had to do with anything, but smiled anyway. "We spend a lot of time there."

"We do."

"Why is that do you think?"

Zane didn't answer and the moment was lost when Mikey once again decided he was left out, wriggled between them, and rolled over to show his belly.

"You're shameless," Aislin said.

And a horrible wingman, Zane thought, but he did look cute all sprawled on his back with his tongue lolling out. She could see the appeal. The saying "so ugly it's cute" came to mind.

"Can we walk?" Aislin asked.

"Sure." Zane got up, then held out a hand to help Aislin.

"Thanks. Where does that path go?"

"Up around the stables. Want to see the horses?"

"Will they mind Mikey?"

"I don't know. I haven't had a dog in years. My mother's would never have deigned to walk to the stables, and my father's second wife only had an ankle biter that never touched the ground that I saw."

"That must have been awkward, having your father bring another woman into your home."

More than awkward. Zane nodded. "Which one? The first who convinced Dad to send us away? I know it was her idea. But, by the time we came home, that wife was gone, and my father moved his third wife into a new house they had built."

Aislin shook her head. "Isn't he on his fourth marriage now?"

Zane didn't mind Aislin's questions about her family. It was common knowledge that the Whitman men either had bad luck getting married, or were dogs. It depended on who you talked to. "Yes, Imelda is his latest. We went to college at the same time."

Aislin's indignation was clear. "Are you kidding me?"

"No, I'm not. Imelda and I were in calculus together. I had brought her home one holiday, and unbeknownst to me, they had an affair. When he divorced—again—she was waiting in the wings, and after only a few months, they formalized it."

"Didn't that piss you off?" Aislin asked. "It's kind of creepy."

"I was more stunned than mad. I'm used to it now. As long as she stays out of my way, we're good."

"You're nicer about it than I would be," Aislin said. She held Mikey's leash, and Zane held her hand. "My parents have been together since they were teenagers. I can't imagine growing up as you did."

"I turned out okay," Zane said. "I didn't know any other way."

"I get that. But it still seems so sad." Aislin stared at the ground.

Zane didn't want to talk about her parents anymore. It wasn't something that she did, and really, there was no purpose rehashing things she'd had no control over. She did, however, wonder briefly how different her life might have been if her mother hadn't died. Zane dropped the subject, and wanted simply to enjoy Aislin's company. "So, how about those Forty-Niners?"

Aislin laughed, as Zane hoped she would.

The path was a winding one and designed to be meandering. Zane could almost see her grandparents holding hands and walking as she and Aislin were. Something about being with her brought up all kinds of emotions.

She remembered walking here with her mother, asking a thousand questions about flowers along the way. It was a distant memory, one that rested with those that had been buried when her mother died, but one that still had tremendous impact. She never had much cause to come here often after that. It made her miss her too much.

"Where did you go?" Aislin paused for the tenth time while Mikey raised his leg. He looked supremely happy with all the new scents.

"I was walking down memory lane, literally. My brother and I used to run like hooligans up and down here."

"It must have been wonderful. It's like a park, not a backyard."

"I suppose it is." She'd never thought about that before, either. Aislin was like a little can opener, peeling off emotional lids Zane hadn't known were there. But there was no denying she was enjoying the easy pace of the day, holding hands with a pretty girl and walking a dog—a pretty snapshot in her mind, something she never knew she always wanted.

Zane tried to picture Giselle or one of her predecessors strutting down the dirt path in their spiked heels. It was an amusing thought that she wisely kept to herself.

As they turned a small curve, a beautiful gold and black monarch butterfly crossed in front of them. She heard Aislin sigh when it turned back and flew in circles around them.

They stopped and watched as two more joined in. A shaft of sunlight shot through the trees and they continued their graceful dance in the spotlight.

"A sign of joy and change," Aislin said. "Of our loved ones' spirits saying hello."

"That's a nice thought," Zane said. Wouldn't it be cool if she could believe one of them was her mother? It wasn't logical of course, but she wanted to believe, if only for a minute, because it made Aislin look happy.

"I see them all the time," Aislin said. Mikey pulled at his leash, jumped at them, and then barked maniacally when they disappeared into the trees, but Aislin easily distracted him with a finger snap.

They turned another corner in the path. "Oh,

look how gorgeous she is!"

The foal was beautiful, and the spitting image of her mom.

"What did you name her?" Aislin asked, and laughed as Mikey nearly tripped her in an attempt to hide behind her legs.

"Crimson and Clover."

"You did not."

Zane laughed. "Did too." She watched as mother and daughter turned and headed back to the stable along with several others. "Feeding time."

"I've had a wonderful afternoon, but it's also time for me to go." Aislin started to turn back along the way they'd just come, but Zane tugged her hand.

"It circles back around."

Mikey barked at the retreating horses. "Oh, now you're brave?"

"How about you? Are you brave, Aislin?" Zane didn't know the last time she'd been shy or pursued someone who was as expressive as Aislin. Whether she voiced it or not, she wore her emotions on her sleeve and broadcast them in her eyes, yet she remained a marvelous enigma to Zane. She couldn't wait to see her again.

"Am I brave?" Aislin repeated the question. "Hmm. Depends on your perception. Are we talking about large animals with fur or having to poke them in dangerous places?"

"Are you going to poke me in dangerous places?"

Zane had to smile as Aislin cracked up before she answered. "Maybe...might...could be. I don't know yet."

The walk ended too soon in Zane's opinion, and together they packed up the blanket and basket. After she loaded it into the truck she walked over to Aislin's door. "Thank you for the date. Can't say as I've ever had a picnic one before."

"Aw, that's just sad." Aislin reached and tucked a lock of Zane's hair behind her ear. "You have the perfect place for it."

"I'm glad you're my first," Zane said.

"And, we're back to you never forget." Aislin smiled. "Give me a kiss good-bye, Counselor."

"Okay, Doc," Zane said and began, she hoped, to knock Aislin's socks off. She kept her hands on Aislin's shoulders and enjoyed the moment, despite the ache of frustration and the fact that she was now eyeing the truck seat as a potential bed.

This time, she was the one who pulled away and was pleased to see Aislin's eyes were a little unfocused. Maybe, just maybe, she felt as dizzy as Zane did. She closed the truck's door and waited for Aislin to roll down the window. "Will you go out with me again tomorrow?"

Aislin shook her head and Zane tried not to let her disappointment show.

"Dinner at my parents' on Sundays. One could, if one wanted to, make a fine impression and get on my good side if one were to brave the family on a Sunday evening, if one were so inclined."

"One is," Zane said. She was nervous already. She knew Aislin's sisters of course, but was apprehensive of the last time she'd seen them all together.

When she'd been on her knees and hiding in a circular clothes rack. *God.*

She managed a weak smile and hoped Aislin wasn't also thinking of that incident.

"Five o'clock. Don't be late."

Chapter Ten

Aislin's parents lived in a nice middle-class neighborhood on a rising hill above San Rafael. The outside was 1970s classic stone, but with the update of black paint and super white trim, it looked modern again.

Zane parked and set her emergency brake. She was sweating. How pathetic was that?

How on earth did she got roped into this? Sex, that's how. Really incredible sex, Well, the hope she'd get the opportunity for some, anyway.

The curtains parted in the front window and a tiny face peeked out, and, from the wide open mouth, appeared to scream.

Kids, too. Awesome. Zane had been around her cousin's baby when she'd been little but only held her a handful of times, and it had been years since then.

The front door opened and Aislin stood in the entry.

Yes, Zane thought. *This is why I'm here.* Her insides did a slow roll from nerves, but she got out of the car and opened the trunk to grab the two huge flower arrangements. The roses she'd gotten for Aislin, the Star Lily plant for her mother, and the good manners she'd learned from her own.

When she looked back up again, Aislin's mother stood next to her and both were smiling. Zane had a flash of what Aislin would look like in the future.

It was immensely pleasing. She walked to them and was surprised when her mom gave her a huge hug and thanked her. No fake air kisses here.

"Zane, this is my mother. Mom, Zane."

"Nice to meet you, Mrs. O'Shea."

"Fiona, please. I'll go put these in water. They're gorgeous, thank you."

"You're welcome," Zane said as she disappeared into the house.

"Here's my gratitude." She handed the flowers back. She reached up and with both hands pulled Zane down to kiss her, long and slow. When she pulled back, Zane remained motionless, mostly because she was thunderstruck. She'd never had the occasion to think she was, thunderstruck that is, but it was a good description.

"Ah…" Aislin laughed, took her flowers back, and grabbed Zane's hand to pull her into the house. When they went past what must be the garage door. Loud music was playing.

"Who's that?" Zane held a finger in the air.

Aislin stopped. "The music? Metallica. My dad loves them. Why?"

Zane noted the defensiveness that had been missing the day before. When her eyes narrowed this time Zane caught the warning and waylaid it. "Cool." She may have said it a little quickly, but it took that look off Aislin's face and the moment passed.

"Dinner will be ready in just a few moments. Go have a seat."

"Aren't you going to officially introduce me?"

"Oh," Aislin laughed. "They all know who you are." She disappeared into the kitchen.

Zane ascertained the men must be in the garage

because the living room was empty. She sat on the couch and folded her hands in her lap.

Thank God it was only a few minutes before Aislin's mother yelled out that dinner was ready. Her eyes widened at the stampede coming through the door. Men, little men, and a small pack of various sized dogs.

"Come on, dear. Come sit at the table."

It had been so long since Zane had heard a motherly voice, it almost hurt. She crossed and sat down next to Aislin, the only empty chair.

Zane was certain she'd had easier times facing a court full of criminals. The O'Shea clan, complete with children and spouses, were all staring at her like a bug under a microscope.

Sitting across from her was the youngest, Heather, and if she remembered right, the one getting married soon.

Points for me.

She'd been observing their dynamic and noticed the entire family catering to Kathleen. She was very sweet, smiled often, and rubbed her pregnant belly frequently. Her husband, Bernie, seemed attentive. They were the quiet couple, letting other, more boisterous family members take center stage. Zane smiled hesitantly at her across the table.

"Where did you get the shiner?" Kathleen asked.

Direct and right to the point. She appreciated that. "Your sister," Zane said. "Can you believe it?"

"Oh, that's nothing." Kathleen waved her hand. "She broke my nose once."

Bernie leaned over the table. "She broke my arm."

Aislin gasped. "It was second grade, and you hit me first."

"Stop it children, you're scaring our guest." Aislin's mother chuckled.

Everyone at the table was shouting injuries they'd received from Aislin over the years, during different squabbles. Zane felt like a stunned bunny. Raucous laughter filled the house, small boys yelled and ran like bandits from each other. She wondered at the lack of little girls; Sabrina had been the only one she'd met. Everyone was talking at once and over each other.

It was absolute chaos.

She felt a sharp punch to her shoulder, and she looked for the threat. Sabrina smiled at her. "A bit more than you're used to, I'm sure," she said. She stopped two of her little brothers from leaving the table, and shoved them back in their seats.

"Just a little." *Okay, a lot.* Zane rubbed the spot and looked over at Aislin. *But so worth it.*

She could get used to this. In a decade or so. In spite of being overwhelmed, Zane felt good.

A splat of mashed potatoes sticky with gravy flew out of nowhere and hit her in the face. Zane felt the glob run down her chin and land on her blouse. She was shocked, and didn't know how to react. She'd never had food thrown at her before.

"Sean!" Aislin's father yelled. "You've slimed our guest. Apologize."

Aislin grabbed a cloth, cleaned the mess up. "There," she said. "All better. We'll pay to have your blouse cleaned."

"At this rate," Zane said, "we should wait to see if there's to be more."

Aislin looked puzzled for a second or two, and then laughed. "The pants, yes."

Zane whispered to her. "Is it always like this?"

Aislin looked around the room. "Pretty much." Ferocious loyalty and love was evident in her expression.

This was so far out of her world it may as well have been a different planet. Zane considered the extravagant, elegant, country club atmosphere which hid sharp claws beneath designer dresses, and the cold, calculating social climbing.

There was warmth here and laughter rang often and easily. Love was freely offered and returned. She saw Kathleen's baby boy—Patrick, was it?—offer up a messy face to his mother for a kiss, and get one. A small tug on her sleeve got her attention.

"Mom says I hafta 'pologize for flipping my tatoes at you," Sean said.

Zane looked down at his freckled face, solemn expression, and big blue eyes. Tufts of red hair stood out in stubborn cowlicks even though gel was obviously trying to tame them. He was adorable, she thought. "It's okay," she said, then grinned. "Great shot."

He smiled back, showing the gap where his front tooth had recently fallen out. He shifted closer, then looked to each side. "I was aiming for Angus," he whispered loudly.

It surprised a laugh out of her.

There was a flurry of sound at the front door, and seconds later Brianna came through the arch into the dining room, holding hands with Louis. Zane froze in her seat.

Brianna pointed at her. "What is *she* doing here?"

Aislin looked at Zane, then back at Brianna. "What?" The room fell silent, and all eyes rested on Zane to see what would happen next.

"She's our guest," Aislin's mother said. "In my

house, Bri. You're being rude."

Zane noticed how the family all deferred to her. It was clear she was the law in the household.

Brianna stopped in her tracks, still several feet from Zane, and far, far away from her mother. "She called me a slut!"

Zane had forced the memory of her little fit at the cabin into a little box, and now she sincerely wanted the floor to open up and swallow her. Should she leave? She tried to catch Aislin's eye.

Everyone was waiting for a reaction, and to Zane it was as if a year passed.

Finally, Darcy laughed loudly. "Well, Bri, there was that phase in high school when they called you 'easy-breezy.'" Several family members echoed her laughter.

"Shut up." Brianna's face flushed and temper flared her eyes. "That was a long time ago."

"Who is this, dear?" Fiona interrupted. "Introduce him to me and your father."

Brianna took a deep breath and the temper passed from her expression. "Dad, Mom, this is Louis Whitman. Louis, you know my daughter Sabrina, and the rest is my crazy family." She went around the table clockwise and rattled off names, and managed to give Zane a dirty look as well.

Zane envied her brother's easy charm and how he appeared to slide right into the down home atmosphere without a hitch. She felt Aislin's tension next to her and whispered, "I'll explain later."

Sabrina punched her arm again. "You better."

The conversation lulled and Zane was terrified Brianna would bring up her behavior at the cabin again. She racked her brain. What would she say to her country club acquaintances in the same circumstance? Not at all the same. She would have had a pithy remark and walked away. Zane liked these people, and more important, she wanted them to like her.

She heard an announcement coming from the television that had been left on in the family room, and grabbed the life preserver. "So," she nearly yelled as she took another biscuit. "How about those 'Niners?"

There was two seconds of silence before the entire table erupted into football conversation. The O'Shea dogs came running into the room to see what the commotion was but no one ordered them to leave. Hope must spring eternal, as they hid under the table for what Zane imagined would be scraps the toddlers dropped.

"Good save," Aislin muttered under her breath. "But you're not off the hook."

Zane looked down at her plate, went back eating, and hoped the subject was dropped.

That was dashed when Sabrina leaned behind her to whisper to Aislin. "It must have been last weekend when Mom was gone with Louis."

Aislin pushed Zane forward so she could whisper back. "Where were they, and hey"—she poked Zane in the side—"why were you there?"

Zane was out of potatoes to shove in her mouth, so she forked up the green beans, and she hated green beans. "Can' tok wif my mouf fuh."

"Hmm," Aislin said.

With caution, Zane sat up straight again. She dared a quick glance across the table and saw the sweet way Brianna smiled at her brother. If he screwed this up for them, she'd kill him.

Same goes for you, Counselor. Zane turned but

no one had been talking to her. It had sounded as if it were right next to her ear. Who said it? Zane hadn't spoken out loud, she was sure of it. Who or what read her thoughts? She looked around the table, but no one was paying attention to her at the moment.

Patrick banged a spoon on his highchair with one hand, waved a baby fist in the air, and broke out into infectious baby giggles. Zane was transfixed as everyone around the table caught it until they were all laughing. She'd never heard anything like it.

He pointed at a corner in the ceiling by the picture window and rattled off a few sentences that Zane thought could not be English. Then he was quiet, as if listening, and his little body wiggled with laughter all over again.

She was just about to ask what was going on, but Patrick grabbed a handful of his mother's hair.

"Ow, baby." Kathleen cried out and untangled his little chubby fingers. His little face scrunched up and he began to cry as he looked to the corner, back at his mother, then the corner again.

Kathleen unbuckled him and gathered the toddler close. "Hey now, Paddy. Granny will come back later tonight and sing to you."

Granny? Zane checked out the family's reaction. Aislin patted her leg under the table. "She's passed on but she visits the little ones. They always see her."

Let's say, even if she managed to stretch reality for a second, and tried putting the fact that ghosts didn't exist to the side: had that been who she'd heard in her ear? Zane was a little freaked out. She'd faced the entire clan down only to find out she had deal with the O'Shea ghosts as well?

She was interested, fascinated, and definitely

wanted to ask more questions, but underneath the desire to know was a little ball of terror. She couldn't have possibly heard that right.

"Can I have some more mashed potatoes?"

"Well, Bella," Granny said. "Neither of us was expecting a two-fer." Her rocking chair went back and forth without a sound.

Bella's laugh sounded like tinkles of expensive crystal. "No, I don't imagine we did, but isn't it wonderful?"

"Come back here, Shannon. Quit poking at Zane."

"I think she heard me."

"The whole spirit world heard you, dear," Bella pointed out. "You're forgetting she's my daughter. It won't do for you to threaten her."

Shannon's face feigned shock. "I did no such thing."

"Oh, Patrick is upset." Granny waved her fingers at him and fresh giggles broke out. "I miss Sunday dinners."

Shannon sighed. "Me, too. Though there are two more redheaded babies since I've sat at that table. More boys. I can't believe Kathleen is pregnant already. Patrick is just past his first birthday."

Granny laughed. "Aye, they've been busy."

"I want grandbabies." Bella pet the dog floating next to her.

Granny immediately soothed. "Of course you do, dear. Just think, you're going to hold the little spirit first. Won't that be wonderful?"

Bella smiled. "Yes. I had so hoped. But with the women Louis married...no."

"Well." Granny preened. "I might know a thing or two about what may happen."

"*Really?*" *Shannon moved gracefully over to the rocking chair. "What gives?*"

"*Now, now. Settle down. You both know it's free will, but I can see some reeeeally interesting possibilities.*"

Below them, a large brown dog started barking furiously. The hair on his massive back rose in an impressive ruff, and two more joined in.

Bella snapped her fingers at the Afghan who was teasing them. "Heidi, stop it!"

The racket had everyone at the table trying to quiet the dogs.

"*I have to go,*" *Bella said, then faded along with Heidi.*

Shannon turned back to Granny. "You can tell me."

"*Well, let's just say there might be more redheads at this time next year or so.*"

"*Ooh,*" *Shannon clapped her hands. "That's wonderful.*"

"*Or.*" *Granny laughed. "Maybe a brunette.*"

Shannon's attention turned to Aislin. "She always loved babies. Is it her?"

"*We'll see,*" *Granny said, then cooed at a tiny little infant spirit swaddled in pink in her arms. "See baby?*" *She pointed at Kathleen and Bernie. "There's your mama and da, and your brothers who will always protect you. But, you have some time yet.*"

Granny faded along with the rocking chair.

"*Well, I'm not leaving until Aislin is happy,*" *Shannon said, then squeaked when a hand appeared and pulled.*

"*Leave them be,*" *Granny said.*

And the corner was empty again.

❧❧❧❧

By the time they got the dogs calmed down and outside, dinner was pretty much over. The men and children helped clear the table, then disappeared into the family room.

Aislin, her mother, and her sisters all filed into the kitchen.

Zane smirked then snorted.

"What was that for?" Aislin asked.

Zane laughed. "Your father and brothers-in-law are all in there, and Louis is dating Brianna, therefore subject to the third degree."

Aislin chuckled and waved an arm behind Zane. She turned and saw the line that started with her mother at the head, all four sisters, and Sabrina at the end. "You were saying, Counselor?"

She felt the blood drain from her face, and she swallowed before she cleared her throat and managed a weak smile.

"I'll let you on a little secret," Aislin said. "The women in this family are much harder. We broke Daddy years ago."

"I, uh..." Zane stuttered and pulled at her collar which had become much too tight.

Aislin's mother interrupted the growing tension. "Okay girls, let's give her a break. It's her first time." She took Zane's arm and motioned for her to sit at the table. When Aislin would have followed, her mother pointed at the sink. "Go load the dishwasher, Ace."

Zane folded her hands neatly. God, she felt sixteen again. She honestly couldn't remember the last time she'd met a date's parents. Giselle's family was a figment of her own imagination, so it hadn't been a possibility.

And the long line of women before Giselle? Zane had probably already known theirs. She'd grown up with them. They always, most always anyway, curried favor with her for her father's sake.

All hail the Whitman name and legacy.

The models and fledgling actresses were too focused on their careers and networking, and it had always been understood the goal was to see and be seen—meet people who could further their interests.

Zane knew she wasn't blameless. Her firm had picked up quite a few lucrative clients from her hookups as well.

Her stomach rolled along with her internal confession.

The happy chatter, raised voices, more than a few sarcastic remarks, and yes, the laughter, let Zane know she was far, far from Hollywood, courtrooms, and stuffy boardrooms.

Two cups of coffee were placed between them on the table. Zane smiled at Sabrina. "Thank you."

"Black?" Fiona asked.

"How did you know?"

"Years of observation. Your type always drinks it black."

Stunned, Zane wondered if it was an insult. It certainly was when Aislin had said it. She searched her face, but her expression remained open and friendly.

Fiona patted her hand. "Business woman, long hours, remaining tough in a man's world."

Zane blinked and relaxed. "That's astute."

She tapped the side of her head. "As I said, years of observation."

Tongue-tied, Zane waited to see where the

conversation would go, though really, the racket in the kitchen made it hard for her to think. Babies crawled, toddlers toddled then fell, and both were picked up by whoever was nearest.

She was still clueless about who belonged to whom, but she hoped to come around more and find out. That in and of itself surprised her.

Ear-shattering screams preceded the little Sean into the kitchen. Darcy wiped her hands on the dish towel she'd been using and crossed to him. "What's the matter?"

His little chest hitched as he sobbed. "Junior pushed me and I fell down!"

At which point Junior screamed back, "I did not!"

Zane filed away the names and faces for future reference and watched in amazement, as if choreographed, mothers, aunties, and fathers appeared magically, diffused the situation, and the house became somewhat quiet again.

Always, Zane heard laughter above and through each conversation.

"Not quite what you're used to," Aislin's mother said.

"No ma'am."

Aislin's mother laughed. "Oh, please. You make me feel ancient."

"It's from total respect, believe me," Zane said. "Observation tells me you're the queen of the kingdom, all of this says everything about how you raised your children. You're fierce, and incredibly strong."

"Now who's paying attention?" Aislin's mother's cheeks flushed prettily. "Thank you."

Zane looked up. Apparently, the sisters were done and lined up again. Aislin, Darcy, Brianna, Kathleen,

Heather, and Sabrina all faced her like a firing squad.

It can't be all that bad, right? Zane knew she was charming and great in social situations. But never, she told herself, had it ever mattered so much before.

Aislin winked at her and Zane relaxed a little, even if they were staring her down.

Her brother rushed in holding his cell phone. "Dad called. All hands on deck. The partners are on their way to the city office."

"Right now? Can't one of the junior associates take care of it?"

Her brother shook his head. "It's the Ito merger, and it's falling apart as we speak. Dad says we may have to go to Japan for damage control."

A spike of anticipation lit her up. Usually, Zane thrived on situations like this. International clients worth billions, corporate battles—it was exhilarating. But right alongside it was disappointment she had to leave Aislin.

She'd been enjoying herself in this chaotic family gathering, but she couldn't help but be a little relieved as well, as she'd miss the third degree.

Go figure.

She got up and Aislin took her hand. "I'll walk you out."

Zane learned you couldn't leave the O'Shea home on a moment's notice, or at all quickly. Everyone hugged everyone else. She was almost sure Angus had wrangled two from her.

"So, you survived," Aislin said as Zane got in her car. She leaned in the open window and kissed her.

For Zane, it went quickly from pleasure to the ache of longing. There was so much more she wanted from Aislin.

When they parted, Zane tugged Aislin's ponytail. "I'll call you when I know more details."

Aislin nodded. "It's okay. I know how emergencies go."

Yes, I'm sure you do. "Go get 'em, Counselor." Aislin rapped the hood and stepped back.

Zane turned the car around in a driveway up the block, and when she passed the O'Shea house again, they were all waving.

The warmth of the gesture spread through her chest and she couldn't have stopped smiling if she tried.

Totally alien, but oh, so welcomed.

Chapter Eleven

Y ou've got to help me tonight, Ace!"
It was her sister. No hello, no how ya doing.
"Slow down, Darcy. What's wrong?" Aislin looked at
the ceiling while she listened. And they called *her* a
drama queen. Well, even if she was, she'd learned it
from Darcy.

"The doctor put Kathleen on bed rest and now
I'm short on help Friday night for a fancy party I'm
catering. A referral from the Whitmans. This is another
fantastic opportunity and I don't want to screw it up."

"Wait," Aislin said. "Back up. What's wrong with
Kathleen that she needs bed rest?"

"Oh, Kathleen is okay. The doctor doesn't want
to take any chances. She's been really tired with this
one, and has cankles."

"What did Kathleen say? She hates to miss these
affairs."

Darcy laughed. "She says it better be a girl, and
if lying down means she'll have one, she'll wait flat on
her back until the baby is born."

Aislin sighed. *How cute.* She would help Darcy,
she always did. But this time, it would cost her. She
calculated quickly. "Okay, I'll do it."

"Oh, Ace. Thank you. I—"

"On one condition."

"Anything," Darcy said. "Name it."

"I'm not wearing a black and white uniform. I

haven't had much luck with those. I'm choosing what I want, and it will be nice, I promise."

The silence told Aislin that Darcy was hesitating and near refusing her request, so she jumped back in to the conversation. "What was Kathleen going to do at this event?"

"Hostess," Darcy answered. "But—"

Aislin grinned. She'd already won this round. "I'm wearing what I want, and I get to hostess instead of working in the kitchen."

Silence.

"Take it or leave it."

After a few seconds, Darcy finally answered. "Okay, deal. But you have to be here early and help set up."

"Fine, see you then."

"Thanks, Ace. I really mean that."

"Bye, sweetheart." Aislin hung up the phone. She would make sure she didn't let her sister down.

Brianna walked into her office. "What did Darcy want?"

"She's shorthanded tonight for a big bash. Kathleen is on bed rest." She held up a hand to waylay the question. "She's fine, just tired and it's precautionary. Hey, how come she didn't ask you?"

"She did," Brianna said. "But I have a date. You were her last resort, Ace."

Aislin tried not to let the remark hurt her feelings. Had she really been so difficult to work with? She wasn't a slacker by any means. A rush of memories of the last few years came to mind. She'd been heartbroken, prone to panic attacks, and unpredictable. She couldn't blame her sisters for that. All she could do now is make it up to them

"So," Brianna interrupted her walk down Guilt Lane. "How's Zane?"

They'd kept in constant contact, talking and texting all week. Aislin smiled to herself when she recalled the exchange that started with a simple, "So, what are you wearing?" She didn't repeat it to her sister. "She's fine, still in Japan doing her thing." And because she could tell Brianna was percolating with questions, she cut her off. "Don't ask. My eyes glazed over. I smile and nod, say uh-huh at appropriate times. But I'm sure she does the same when I elaborate on a broken bone that needs screws to set or a particularly nasty skin condition I've treated."

"I would be bored stiff," Brianna said.

Aislin was curious. "Isn't Louis the same?"

"Blah, blah." Brianna laughed. "Who would have thought"—she waved her fingers at Aislin—"the O'Shea sisters would be dating the Whitman twins at the same time?"

They looked at each other and burst into giggles as they did when they were much younger and gushing over the Backstreet Boys.

"Do you want deets?" Brianna asked.

"Eww, no. That would be too weird."

Brianna nodded. "Wouldn't it though?" She waved and left the office.

For Aislin, the day went quickly, and before she knew it, she was doing kennel rounds.

After bedding down the animals for the evening, Aislin started to get ready for her sister's catering gig. She was disappointed Zane hadn't called, but she'd sent a text saying she would be home the next day if there weren't any additional problems. Who knew corporate espionage could be so cutthroat?

Too bad for her, Aislin thought as she slipped into the only little black dress she owned. It had pretty rhinestone straps and matching pumps her sister Heather had made her buy that glittered. Delighted, she turned her ankle this way and that so she could see the lights shimmer when it caught the light just right.

It felt like forever since she'd dressed up for anything. She went into the bathroom to straighten her hair, and surprised herself. The dress didn't cover as much as she remembered. Aislin glanced at her watch. *Oh crap. Well, there's no time to change now.*

It took her a few minutes to find the sweater that matched before she ran out the door.

Darcy ran her business like a marine drill sergeant, and heaven help the employee who was even five minutes late.

Aislin was ten. She tried sneaking in behind Heather to act as if she'd been standing there, but her little sister ratted her out without a qualm.

Darcy came storming across the kitchen and stopped short of Aislin. "Oh, honey, look at you. You're gorgeous."

Aislin picked at the short hem nervously. "Really? I mean it's been a while since…"

"Yes, Ace, I know." Darcy pulled her in for a hard hug. "I'll let you slide this time. Now get to work. The seating chart is on the counter along with the clipboard and table diagrams for the hors d'oeuvres."

Aislin saluted her and then gratefully left the busy kitchen.

An hour later, the mansion was filling up and buzzing with multiple conversations. Aislin marveled at the breed. Women decked out in silk, diamonds, and other precious jewels. Men in nothing less than suits, and she'd spotted more than one tuxedo in the ballroom.

They gravitated in small groups of people, some holding their own courts, and others flitted like butterflies from one gathering to another, seemingly unable to land in any one place.

Aislin could relate. The energy in the room was palpable and she could feel her A.D.D. gathering momentum. If she wasn't careful, she could become manic. She was almost sorry she'd wanted the hostess position tonight. What was she thinking?

At least everyone was civilized, nothing like her family gatherings. It all seemed so fake. She'd take dirty jokes and raucous laughter any day of the week over this polite tittering.

The room fell silent and Aislin turned to see why or who had caused it.

A woman posed in the arched doorway wrapped in a—was that a gold toga? It showed off her long, tan legs and a generous cleavage. *Good God, those can't be real.*

She looked sort of familiar and Aislin finally placed her as one of the newest models for the Victoria's Secret campaign. She knew that because she had the catalog. Not that she ever ordered from it, but she would freely admit she received them for visual pleasure.

No shame in her lack of game. *Ha!*

Giselle Royce—yes, that was her name—swept into the party with an entourage of gazelles behind her. Gold spiked pumps tapped on the marble in a staccato rhythm while she marched over to Aislin, looking for all the world to be strutting on a Paris runway.

Giselle picked up a stuffed date off the tray Aislin

was holding, and popped it into her mouth. She didn't make eye contact, and didn't move out of Aislin's way, forcing her to step around her. It was an excellent reminder why she had a hard time liking the people at these kind of events. She found them rude.

When Aislin had arrived this evening, she'd felt beautiful in her dress, but now she felt dowdy in the fancy atmosphere. *Oh, that's right,* she reminded herself. *I'm working, not attending.*

Aislin could almost hear the bubble when it popped.

And that was that.

She headed back into the kitchen to refill her tray, and when she came back through the servants' hallway, she had a dead eye view of the entry. Her stomach did a little flip when Zane stepped into the room dressed in a black tuxedo with a white silk tank she'd substituted for the stuffy long-sleeved shirt.

God, she's sexy.

Wait a minute.

What was she doing here? She'd told Aislin that she wasn't coming home until tomorrow.

She didn't know Aislin was helping Darcy tonight.

Zane had lied to her.

Was it because she wanted to attend a fancy party without her or was embarrassed to be seen with her?

What else didn't Aislin know?

Her thoughts were interrupted by a long squeal and the noise of running heels. Giselle flew across the room, hurled herself at Zane, and covered her face with noisy kisses.

Her stomach dropped to her feet. Aislin turned and hurried away as fast as she was able in her high heel shoes back down the hall. She didn't have Giselle's grace. A bumpkin fool, just as she was in high school. She shoved her tray at Sabrina, and then ran out the kitchen side door.

Aislin kept running until she came to the stone retaining wall out of range of the outdoor spotlights and sat on it. A pail of freezing water wouldn't have made her feel worse.

She didn't hear Darcy until her arms came around her. "Was that...?"

"Yes."

"Then she doesn't deserve you, not one little bit. Want me to put cayenne in her food?"

"Would you?" Eternally hopeful, Aislin turned.

"In my heart I can, honey. In reality, I need the business contacts this party is going to give me."

Aislin sighed. "I know."

"I can, however, wait until I see her on the street sometime." Darcy winked at her. "But I think you should go back inside and see if there is a reasonable explanation before we race down that road."

"Yes, of course," Aislin said. "She might not be a two-timing snake."

"About that," Darcy began. "Honey, did you talk about exclusivity? You are aware of her reputation, right? Did she make a commitment?"

Aislin thought for a moment. "I just assumed since we were, you know, together, there was one."

"Well, there you go. Ace. If it's not said, it's not heard, and I hate to say this, but you can't be mad, either."

"I can be anything I want," Aislin said. "But, you're right. Go on back to your kitchen. I'll be right in, I promise."

Darcy kissed her cheek. "Okay, I really do have

to hurry, but we can talk later if you want."

Aislin nodded and stayed seated. Of course it was her fault. She hadn't even thought about it. She'd fallen into thinking they were a couple after the picnic. The only other significant relationship she'd had since the failed asshat—*whose name will never be mentioned again, Amen*—was Shannon.

She felt so naïve. Had Zane even been in Japan at all? Or did she and her brother construct the excuse beforehand to escape?

But then again, that little voice in her head said, *You're not really part of her world anyway, are you?*

In an instant, she was the little girl in pigtails with scraped knees and droopy bobby socks, an O'Shea girl from the wrong side of the tracks.

On the heels of that Aislin felt familial pride. Hey, she *was* an O'Shea girl and she never backed down from a fight. She knew she was impulsive, and she'd always been quick to jump to conclusions before she had all the facts. It was in her nature, and most of the time, she couldn't help it. But she could, and would, take back her pride. That she could do.

Aislin walked back into the kitchen with her head high and back straight. She did a quick makeup fix in the bathroom and then marched back into the ballroom to pass out more champagne.

Brianna waved a finger at her. *What is she doing here?* She was supposed to be on a date with Louis. Her sister looked lovely with her hair in a smooth chignon and a pretty green dress that matched her eyes, and Aislin was happy to see her.

"She's a vision, isn't she?" Louis appeared at her elbow to take two of the crystal flutes.

"She is," Aislin said. "And if you're playing with

her, I'll kill you."

"Whoa," Louis said and held up a hand currently sloshing liquid. "Where did that come from?"

Aislin sighed. "I'm sorry. It's not you I'm mad at. It's just that she's my sister, you know?" She studied his face and saw his features soften.

"Yes," he said simply. "I do know." He cut expertly through the crowd and handed Brianna her drink. She noticed how her sister leaned closer and smiled at him, and the pain in her heart eased a little. But, she promised herself if Louis took that look off Brianna's face, her threat would hold. Both of the Whitman twins had less than sterling reputations.

Aislin felt strong, the gloves were on, it felt fabulous, and she was itching for a fight. She passed out the rest of the glasses without seeing either Zane or Giselle before going back into the kitchen for another tray.

Darcy nodded her head to approve her selection and went back to preparing more hors d'oeuvres.

Aislin went through the swinging door, caught a glimpse of long platinum hair out of the corner of her eye, and her stomach flipped nervously.

Time to have it out.

※ ※ ※ ※

Zane searched the crowd and finally spotted Aislin. She started toward her but was stopped by a bony hand grabbing her biceps.

"No, *bella*, don't go," Giselle whined in her fake accent. "We have much catching up."

God, she hated it when she called her that. She'd already broken up with her. What did she have to do to make that clearer? Zane tried to extricate herself but every time she made progress, it seemed Giselle grew another hand that clawed at her.

When Aislin was closer, Zane noted her narrowed eyes and the blush high on her cheeks.

Uh-oh. She knew that look well already.

"Giselle," Louis said loudly as he and Brianna walked over to join them. "How's the world traveler? Looking gorgeous as always."

Always ready for attention, Zane thought as she watched Giselle preen, prose, and finally let her arm go only to clutch at Louis with her dark red claws. She rubbed her arm where it burned, and straightened her jacket.

"Shrimp?" Aislin asked sweetly.

Her tone didn't match the temper in her eyes and Zane was grateful it didn't seem to be aimed at her.

Yet.

"You certainly are." Giselle looked down at her and laughed at her own joke.

"That's my sister, you freak." Brianna took a step closer to Giselle, and Louis closed his eyes.

"And she's my girlfriend," Zane said.

"Zis'ees your girlfriend? The maid?"

"Please, drop the phony accent." Zane's defense was as quick as Brianna's, who placed herself between Louis and Giselle. "You're from New York for Christ's sake."

The conversation in the room died down as their raised voices created a hushed silence all around.

Zane pulled herself up to her full height. "She isn't the maid."

"Slumming, Whitman?" All trace of the accent disappeared, and only Bronx remained.

Zane took a step forward, but Brianna beat her and pretended to trip while she flipped the entire tray of shrimp out of Aislin's hand and into Giselle's cleavage.

Giselle shrieked at the obscene mess of cocktail sauce and pink morsels sliding down and into her dress.

"Omigod!" Aislin yelled. "You feed those?"

From the back of the room, there was a small titter.

The soft laugh had a domino effect until the entire ballroom was lit with laughter. Giselle's entourage scooped her up and headed down the hall, leaving a trail of red sauce and shrimp behind her.

Darcy appeared out of nowhere, and competently cleaned the mess while muttering she better not have lost new clients over this.

When she was done, Darcy stood, dropped her mad pretense, and giggled. "Did you see the look on her face?"

Zane reached a hand out to Aislin. "Surprise!"

"You knew I was here?"

"Of course I did, it's why I came, Ace. Oh, wait. You thought I came with her?"

"Well, she *was* wrapped around you like foil on a Hershey's kiss."

"It was totally uninvited," Zane said.

The band started playing a slow Eric Clapton song and Zane took Aislin's hand. "Dance with me."

"Fraternizing with the help?" Aislin asked.

Zane merely smiled and tugged.

"What if I can't dance and have two left feet?"

"I'll try not to step on your little fairy toes."

"Fairy?" Aislin laughed.

"Queen of them all. Dance with me, Aislin." Zane whispered in her ear and twirled her expertly. "Us mere mortals simply worship at your tiny throne, content to live in the fairy mound for a hundred years."

"Is that romance, Counselor? You're singing to my Irish."

"Might be." Zane spun her again. "And I know."

"My heart goes pitter-patter."

"Hearsay. Let me feel the facts." She pulled Aislin closer.

At the edge of the dance floor, Zane twirled her again, then pulled her close. Aislin's curves fit her despite the height difference. A soft sigh blew across her breasts and caused an intense chill that instantly flamed and heated her blood.

The beat of Aislin's heart echoed against hers until they began to beat in unison with the music. Funny how she'd never noticed a tiny detail that meant so much before.

They danced across the floor in a graceful dance that had guests moving out of their way to stand back and watch.

It was intoxicating and heady. Zane felt drunk but knew she hadn't had more than a sip of champagne since she arrived. It was much better. She couldn't remember the last time she'd waltzed, but silently thanked her grandmother for making her take lessons and her grandfather for making her practice.

For the first time, it felt like magic.

Nothing compared to holding Aislin, her fairy queen.

Hers?

The word slipped in like smoke and settled in her mind. Somewhere between their first meeting in the stable and this dance, her heart had been stolen.

Aislin was all fire, switching moods as smooth as mercury at the drop of a pin and then back again. She was hot, and wanting her was easy. That adorable smile with the dimples and little crooked tooth had taken over her thoughts, and the heat between them blistered long after they left each other.

She didn't want to let go, but the music stopped and the guests were clapping politely.

Zane continued to sway with her a moment before stopping to kiss her. She'd intended to devour her parted lips, but felt Aislin's tension. With great restraint, she kissed her gently instead.

Aislin pulled free. "I have to go back to work."

Zane smiled. "Better get more shrimp circulating."

She turned and started to walk away.

"Wait," Zane said. "Thank you for the dance."

Aislin looked over her shoulder and smiled, but it didn't reach her eyes. Zane watched her back until she disappeared behind the door.

Zane fought her first instinct, the one that wanted to beg her to stay. She wasn't accustomed to vulnerability, and really, it wasn't the time or place to put herself out there.

Not in the pool of sharks already circling to ask questions. Zane smiled politely, prepared to deflect and verbally spar with them.

It was a behavior she was well acquainted with and skilled at.

Still, in the back of her mind, a question circled round and round.

Now what the hell had she'd done?

Chapter Twelve

Aislin hid in the storage closet and cringed inwardly. After the confrontation with Giselle, she'd wanted to keep the moment light because she was uncomfortable with the jealousy that simmered below her temper.

When she was in Zane's arms, which she could still feel, all her racing thoughts stopped, just stopped. She felt as if she were dancing in a fairy tale, and had felt a rush of love so powerful, tears came to her eyes.

But when the music was over, she'd panicked. That voice came back that told her she wasn't good enough, and dear God, if she fell in love again—and she would—she'd never survive the fallout when it ended.

Zane's lips had vibrated against hers, and she could still feel that as well. She'd wanted to laugh at Zane's shrimp comment, but the mirth couldn't make it past the lump in her throat.

Instead, she rushed back here to hide. The kitchen was comforting, and her sister's presence helped steady her further.

Every instinct in her body said to turn around and return to Zane's arms.

She shook her head. She had responsibility here to Darcy, and after another deep breath, her legs almost stopped shaking.

The door opened and her sister stood there. No

spatula in sight, thank you. "You've caused quite a stir tonight, love."

Aisling smiled absently. "It was wonderful, Darcy."

"Oh, honey. It was, it is, and you deserve it. We're a little backed up in here. Can you come out now and talk?"

"Of course, I'm sorry." Aislin couldn't shake the anxiety. She walked back into the vast kitchen. "They don't get richer than this."

Darcy didn't look up, but expertly plated a tray and sprinkled parsley on it. "Mmm?"

"I mean really," Aislin said. "They're not the same, you know?" She knew her sister was aware of Aislin's aversion to the country club set.

Darcy pulled another platter toward her. "What are you talking about, Ace?"

"Take a look around. We *work* for them. Brianna may be dating Louis but we're still O'Sheas and they're still Whitmans."

She was comfortable voicing her opinion to Darcy. She was the one she ran to when the asshat— *whose name will never be mentioned again, Amen*— broke her heart.

But it wasn't sympathy in Darcy's expression, it was annoyance.

"Ace. I thought you were over that crap. You really have to get over this discrimination of wealthy people. They're not all like—"

"Asshat blah blah." Aislin lowered her eyes so her hurt wasn't obvious to her sister. "Whatever."

She felt the words Darcy wanted to say. But now wasn't the time, and they were working. Aislin picked up the tray to circulate through the ballroom.

See? She was right. Nobody she knew had a ballroom. Who was she fooling? Since when did the granddaughters of Irish immigrants mingle socially with the blue-blooded Whitmans, Hearsts, and the like? It was much better for her to back away now, before she got hurt. She allowed her insecurity to blanket her like a familiar friend.

It wouldn't stay, however. It lit a spark of indignation instead. She was a doctor, she'd gone to medical school. She was hardly wearing a potato sack with her hand held out.

Aislin jutted her chin and walked briskly into the party, and felt a pang when she didn't spot Zane immediately, but put a bright smile on her face before she continued to circulate.

❧❧❧❧

Zane watched the door like a hawk, and saw her enter. Damn, she was so pretty in that black dress. She felt magnetized to her, and her body hummed in response.

"Are those stars in your eyes?" Louis asked and elbowed her. "I never thought I'd see the day."

She ignored him and waited for Aislin to reach her side of the room so she could pounce, maybe get her out of here early and take her home.

"Hey, Zane. Taylor called and said she'd be here earlier than expected and to get her room ready."

She turned her attention to Louis. She loved her cousin and Taylor's daughter, and they were always welcome. "Thank you," she said. "She'll want to ride with the other women tomorrow."

With company coming she could hardly play out

her cavewoman fantasy with Aislin. She'd have to take a cold shower instead, and put her libido to rest for the night. *As best as can be expected*, she thought with Aislin's smooth thighs coming closer.

Louis appeared to have given up on trying to pull her into the conversation. "Brianna and I are leaving now. Don't wait up."

Zane snorted. "As if I ever do."

"Damn. Heads up. Dad's here."

Zane looked over to where he'd pointed just as Aislin stopped in front of her father. She'd better intercept him, as her father and brother's sense of humor was usually off the wall, and she prayed her dad wouldn't offend Aislin before she could get there to run interference. He would accost her and think she was after something other than Zane. It was insulting and damn hypocritical, as his wife was a money-grubbing...

She let the thought go. It only pissed her off.

≈≈≈≈

"That was some waltz young lady. Where did you learn to dance like that?"

"My Da can dance circles around everyone, he taught me." Aislin turned to look at the silver-maned man who introduced himself as Peter, Zane's uncle from Palm Springs.

Aislin knew it was malarkey. She'd recognized Zane's father immediately, but because she was curious, she'd play along.

He sighed and whispered loudly. "I feel sorry for the woman who settles down with her."

"Why?" Aislin widened her eyes in mock

innocence. "Would she beat her?"

He looked confused for a moment, and Aislin thought maybe she shouldn't be playing with him. Maybe he retired because of Alzheimer's and it was a well-kept secret.

Her uncle John had been afflicted, and when he waxed on her family didn't at all take it personally, they just went along with him. It made him happy and why would they want him to not be?

"It's a shame she's so bad with money. That branch of the family is all a little bit crazy."

The vast difference in class slapped at her again. He wasn't sick, he was trying to chase her off. Still, she kept her mask of naïveté in place to see how far he would go. "Really?" Aislin asked. "Good thing it was just a dance and not a marriage proposal and all. You're such a dear to warn me off."

"Indeed." He nodded. "You wouldn't want to get mixed up with that bunch of loonies." He squinted at her. "You look like such a nice girl." He went into a tirade about Zane and Louis.

Amused, Aislin listened before she turned up her brogue and patted his arm. "Well, put your fears to rest, darling. I have no interest in the Whitman girl."

"That's good. Whew, you dodged a bullet. Make sure you warn the lovely woman Louis brought, would you?" He smiled at her, then walked away into the crowd.

Aislin's cheeks burned. Everything he had just said proved her right once again. She didn't belong here. They certainly didn't want her unless she was circulating food or giving their dogs shots, though this time she was warned off with sugar rather than just shown the door.

Louis appeared at her elbow and steered her in the opposite direction of his father. "Whatever he said, you can ignore it."

Aislin smiled sweetly. "Your uncle Peter said wonderful things. Though I was bit surprised when I'd heard you'd been committed last year. You seem so stable."

Zane reached them. "I'll apologize for him." She paused. "Then I'll strangle him."

It was hard to keep her resolve around Zane. Even if she didn't think it was feasible or a good idea, she let her off the hook. "It was kind of cute. I imagine he thinks my sister and I are after your money."

Louis groaned. "He was trying to be funny."

"And I should believe you," Aislin pretended to be shocked. "You who were so recently sprung from the funny farm?"

Zane laughed. "He's been so good we're going to let him play with his very own crayons tomorrow."

Louis huffed good-naturedly and then excused himself. "I have to find Bri before our father does."

"Dad's a bit eccentric," Zane said. "Please don't take it personally."

How could she not? It was eerily similar to what she'd been through years before. She nodded slightly, but stayed silent. "Go out with me tomorrow, please?" Zane asked.

"Well," Aislin said. "I don't know if I want to be seen with the looney Whitman girl."

"Walked into that one," Zane said. "Dinner tomorrow?"

She felt her earlier resolution to stop seeing Zane dissolve further by the minute. "Maybe."

"Are you going to play hard to get now?"

Zane's hot breath against her neck gave Aislin chills. "Could be."

"Mmm," Zane said. "Let me catch up on the jet lag. I'll call you. But please make sure you come and see me before you go."

Aislin nodded again, then almost lost her balance when Zane kissed her chastely then let her go. "I have to catch Dad and let him know the latest on the Ito merger."

She sighed and watched her walk away. It was late and she needed to help clean up.

The time it took passed quickly. Most of her mind was on Zane's heat against her, the imprint of her body etched into her skin and memory. The band had stopped playing nearly an hour before, but Aislin swore she could still hear strains of the melody they'd danced to.

Aislin picked up the last glasses remaining in the ballroom when she spotted Zane in the back hallway, near the entrance, with yet another glittery blonde wrapped around her. Her head was thrown back while she laughed as she swung the other woman right off her feet, spun her in a circle, then kissed her.

She stopped in her tracks. *Seriously?* Aislin was weary, tired of the emotional labyrinth she'd been in all night. And her feet hurt, dammit.

It was painfully comical how many red flags she'd seen that night. She didn't belong here, and honestly? Right now she didn't want to.

She was so done with this.

By the massive stone fireplace, Shannon was visibly upset. "She's crying. I hate it when she cries."

"She's healing, but she'll get over it," Granny said.

"Oh, wipe that shocked look off your face. You know as well as I do how impulsive and insecure our girl is. She's going on a false conclusion, and a simple conversation will take care of it. Someone needs to give her one of those fat red buttons the hardware store hands out."

"Still..." Shannon argued.

"Look at my husband, that pompous ass. His wife is younger than Zane." Bella pointed. "What?" She laughed. "It's said with love."

She flicked a finger and the glass Imelda was reaching for slid a couple of inches to the left. "Watch," Bella said. "She's trying to get his attention and he's patronizing her, patting her head."

As soon as he looked away, Bella slid the glass to the right. Imelda's face scrunched up.

"Stop that!" Granny snapped. "That poor girl is going to scream."

Bella sighed. "Fine. You're no fun, Granny."

"Really?" The glass lifted then hovered before it smashed. "Let 'er rip, Imelda!"

Shannon gasped when Imelda did scream and caused a great commotion from the straggling guests.

"Oh look," Bella said. "Now he's giving her there-theres."

"I may be the newest, relatively speaking, at this table, but aren't we supposed to be all love and kumbaya now?

Granny laughed. "We are, but girl, we're allowed to stir things up now and then."

"I thought Robert was an ass before I died. Now, don't look all stricken, Shannon. If I had stayed married to him, he would have still had his mistresses, each younger than the previous one." Bella preened. "And every one of them a miniature me."

"Yes," Granny agreed. "But none of the class."

"Thank you," Bella said, and continued to explain. "Not that it's at all morally right, but at a certain level, men of wealth can feel wrongfully entitled to have both a wife and mistress. They can certainly afford it."

"But, no," Shannon said. "I don't want Aislin or Brianna to be hurt that way. We can't do this."

"Oh, they have enough of me, their mother, in them to not," Bella said.

"Louis has married three times already," Shannon pointed out. "And Zane has never had a serious relationship."

Bella shook her head. "My children are not blameless and have made poor choices. Some of it was ego. Some, I'm sad to say, was shallowness on their part. But a lot of those decisions were made because the people who professed to love them, loved their money more."

"Aislin doesn't care about it," Shannon said.

"Of course she doesn't," Granny soothed.

Below them, the stragglers had left and Darcy's crew packed up while the cleaning crew followed behind, clearing the rest.

Shannon blew out a breath. One she didn't need at all, but did so purely for effect. "Round five?"

Ding, ding.

"Something like that," Granny said. "Our work is done for the night."

Chapter Thirteen

After she'd come home, showered, and climbed into bed, Aislin stared at the ceiling. The full moon lit the corner where a dainty glass fairy flew on an invisible string.

Her imagination ran away with her as she saw an army of tall, flawless models lining up in front of Zane, ostensibly waiting for their turns while they high-kicked and fluttered their feather fans.

Bitches.

She fell into sleep somewhere between the cha-cha and striptease.

The phone rang and Aislin felt the two deep creases between her eyes, as if even in her sleep she knew she was going to have the nightmare again.

Aware now of being split, she observed her dream-self walk to the bedroom window and part the curtains to see the highway patrol's vehicle pull into her driveway, the crazy spinning lights bouncing off her walls like a demented disco ball. Her dream-self walked to the phone.

"Don't answer it." Aislin saw her arm reach for the phone. "No!"

She sat up in bed, her heart thundering in her ears. Aislin could almost see her own shadow at the window, frozen there since that devastating night.

The blankets had twisted around her legs and she kicked furiously to free herself. She pulled off her sweat-soaked tank top and felt the dry tracks of tears on her cheeks. Both Mikey and Merlin came to her and pressed as close as their bodies would allow. *Her sentries*, she thought. She checked the clock, and noted the time: three in the morning.

Like clockwork and on time, as always.

Aislin lay back down. From experience she knew she wouldn't go back to the dream, so she may as well try to get some more sleep. She wondered if the nightmares would ever stop.

When the phone rang again, Aislin looked quickly around the room. No, this one was real, and the Caller ID said it was her mother, likely angling for another hand in the wedding favor preparations. Sighing as she answered, Aislin mumbled one excuse after another until her mother gave up. "Call Bri," she said. "She's not busy." She supposed she shouldn't feel so delighted throwing her sister under the bus, but hey.

"Well, I would Aislin Marie, but I can't find her."

Aislin said good-bye and hung up. She almost felt guilty for not helping, but good God, she was not up to Heather's crocodile tears today.

The phone rang yet again. Aislin groaned, then answered without looking to see what number it came from. "I said no!"

"Excuse me?" the female caller said.

Crap. "I'm sorry, let's start again," Aislin said. "Hello?"

The woman's voice sounded amused. "I'm trying to reach Aislin O'Shea?"

"This is her. How can I help you?"

"I know this is terribly forward of me, but I was in with my dog, Brutus?"

"Yes." Aislin shuffled her memory to find the

woman's name. "Uh."

Feminine laughter bubbled. "Laura Chavez."

"Yes, of course." Aislin recalled the pretty brunette, her distressed jeans that showed beautiful, tanned skin, her casual shirt, and versatile flip flops. She'd been right after all—she had been flirting with her. "Brutus. Awesome dog," she said. "How can I help you?"

"Well, I was kind of hoping you'd have coffee with me today. I'm new in town..." Laura's voice trailed off.

Aislin thought about it for a moment. The silence must have embarrassed her because Laura jumped right back in. "Oh, God. I sound needy, don't I?"

She sounded adorable and so like Aislin herself that she laughed. "No, really, you're fine." Well, she could mope here the rest of the day, go to her parents' house, or have coffee with a gorgeous woman. She certainly wasn't calling Zane—or waiting for her to call.

Why was she even thinking about it? "I'd love to."

"You will? Um, great! I saw a little café on the corner of Main and Third Street. Can you meet me there? Say, in about an hour?"

"Sounds good. I'll see you there. And Laura?"

"Yes?"

"Thank you."

"No problem. I'm looking forward to it."

She smiled when she disconnected, but the happy feeling ran away rapidly. It was either feast or famine, Aislin mused while she rubbed Mikey's fur. She had a date with Laura, who radiated kindness, seemed to be honestly interested in her, and was her type right down to the toes.

It baffled her as to why she was so sad to realize it.

Aislin picked out casual clothes and firmly put Zane out of her thoughts each time she entered them. After taking care of the animals, she locked the door and looked, really looked, at the ancient Chevy parked in her driveway. Recently, it seemed to grow new rust freckles every night. Aislin thought it looked tired.

Her clinic did modestly well; it wasn't as if she couldn't afford a new vehicle. She'd refused to replace it solely because it was Shannon's.

Aislin held a hand to her heart, expecting the stab of pain she usually received when someone mentioned retiring it. The flash had dulled, and it felt nowhere near as uncomfortable as she thought it would. There had been a time Aislin thought she might feel the agony forever.

She shook her head. If it wasn't there, it wasn't there, and she didn't want to analyze right now for fear she just might create more grief to soothe her guilt.

Aislin patted the hood before she opened the sticking door, got in, and made the decision to at least look at a few options.

It couldn't hurt to look, right?

Aislin parked a block away from the coffee shop, and the walk helped her to clear some thoughts.

She waved when she spotted Laura waiting for her outside. Aislin felt sad and guilty even while she was struck by how lovely Laura looked.

It was the weirdest sensation. But here, at least, she felt she was on even ground.

Laura gave her a brief hug. "I'm so happy you came. I was so nervous about calling you."

"I was nervous, too," Aislin said. "So, please, don't be."

≈≈≈≈

Zane studied the four women that the crisis clinic volunteers had brought up from the city while they were lining up in the barn.

She'd met Marcie and Selma before, and had in fact handled their legal problems and been instrumental in wrestling them away from their abusers.

The two new women, Stacy and Keisha, were a study in contrast of before and after next to the others. Whereas Marcie and Selma were laughing and eager to ride the horses, Stacy was hunched over as if she were trying to be invisible, unable or unwilling to make eye contract. Keisha's hair hung over her face, hiding a nasty swollen bruise and a cut on her cheekbone.

Zane's cousin, Taylor, clucked around the newcomers and regulars like a mother hen, encouraging, soothing, and smiling at them. Blue appeared over the top of her stall when she heard Zane's voice, and leaned into her to nuzzle her neck and snorted softly.

"Do they bite?" Keisha asked. "What is she doing?"

"Nah. She's just looking for some sugar. This is Blue, two-time champion and new mother."

"She's so big." Stacy folded her arms across her chest and took two steps back, visibly fearful.

This is where the therapy began, to help them begin to face things larger than themselves and have some control. It had a wonderful trickle-down effect, empowering the women to gain some confidence in their lives once more with help from a loving and gentle horse along with a group of supportive women.

"Auntie Zane," her niece, Perry, yelled as she ran into the barn. "I heard Blue had her baby. Boy or girl? What's its name, can I see it? Can I..."

"Slow down, turbo." Zane swept her up and hugged her. "How's my girl?"

"I lost another toof. See?" Perry smiled wide, and Zane could see the gap then nodded enthusiastically.

"Well can I, Auntie?"

"Of course you can. Blue had a girl, a filly, and we named her Crimson and Clover."

Taylor opened the door and ushered Perry in to join the four women.

Zane excused herself for a minute and heard their nervous and excited sighs as she walked down the hallway to the office.

As if one more phone call would make a difference in Aislin's unexplained silence, she left another message anyway. Zane didn't want another disaster such as the colossal misunderstanding at the cabin. She really, really hated this. Falling for Aislin was easy. Keeping up with her moods was hard.

Zane returned to the group and wished she didn't feel so uncertain. It bogged down her shoulders with invisible weight and kept her stomach roiling intermittently.

Perry intercepted her. "Guess what I got you for your birfday?"

Zane smiled. "It's not for another two weeks, little one."

"I know," Perry said. "But we can't be here that day, and I can't be late with it."

"Okay," Zane said. "Another race horse?"

"No, silly." Perry giggled. "I can't 'ford that."

"Um, a box of candy to share with me?"

More giggles. "No, but that's a really good idea." Perry looked back at her mother, who shook her head. "Wait here. The gardener's keeping it for me. I'll go get it."

"Just so you know," Taylor said. "I tried to talk her out of it. She's so stubborn."

"Should I be worried?" Zane asked.

Her cousin laughed a bit nervously and sighed. "Probably."

"Cover your eyes, Aunt Zany."

Zane resisted opening them to peek when she heard grunts and groans. Perry was obviously scuffling with something large.

"'Kay, you can open them."

Zane made a show of opening them slowly and found she stared back at a pair of golden eyes as big as her own.

"Woof!"

She jumped back but not in time to keep the very large dog from leaping. She was immediately covered with sloppy, enthusiastic kisses.

"Down, Fifi," Perry said.

Fifi? The absurdity of this Shetland pony being called such a prissy name had Zane laughing, then she choked when the dog's tongue went down her throat.

She finally wrestled him off with Taylor's help pulling on the pink rhinestone harness. Good Lord, what was she going to do with a dog?

Fifi sat back on her haunches, the gemstones in her collar blinking in the sun. Fresh hilarity bubbled from Zane's throat. Maybe it was hysteria.

The hundred-plus-pound dog looked at her with adoration, a foot-long pink flag hanging from the side of her mouth.

Her muzzle was closed. "How come her tongue is hanging out like that?"

"She's missing teef, like me," Perry said. "Thee?" Her niece opened her mouth again and pointed.

Zane pinched the bridge of her nose. "Is she part horse?"

"No, silly. The vet in the city said she was a Indeeterma."

"Indeterminable," Taylor automatically translated for Perry, then stood behind her as if protecting herself from Zane.

"I wanted to keep her, but my mommy said we didn't have the room. Then I remembered your birthday coming up and I just couldn't *think* of a better present than Fifi."

Zane shot a look at Taylor, who dropped her gaze to stare at her shoe.

"'Sides," Perry continued, "Mommy said you were lonely out here and you needed company."

"Mommy said that?" Zane lifted an eyebrow at Taylor.

Perry looked at her with wide, wide eyes. "Uh-huh."

Zane peered back at Fifi. She was the ugliest dog she'd ever seen in her life. Her fur couldn't decide if it wanted to be curly or straight, so it stood out in odd clumps, the color of mud. One ear was mangled and hung at an odd angle. A fresh-looking scar on her muzzle ran down from her eye to the tip of her nose, another straight across the huge neck. The yard-long tail was also bent in the middle, obviously broken at some point in her life. It apparently didn't faze Fifi at all; she was wagging it a mile a minute.

Zane couldn't help but make the correlation

between Aislin's butt-freaking-ugly cat and this dog.

Her niece looked so proud of herself, hope shone from her eyes, and Zane melted. She crouched down in front of the dog and Perry.

"Okay," she said simply and was rewarded with a huge exhale of relief from Taylor.

"We had her checked out, she's all up on her shots, and she's been groomed."

Dubious, Zane looked closer at Fifi. "Really?"

"Perry, why don't you bring Fifi up to the house and set up her things. Have Kiki help you."

"Who's Kiki?" Zane asked.

Taylor looked at her strangely. "Your housekeeper?"

"Right," Zane said, and reminded herself to go and meet the new staffer. Zane had lured Esther back with a huge salary increase after the flu fiasco, and one of the conditions was she'd have to hire additional help. She'd left that in Esther's more than capable hands.

"C'mon, Fifi." Perry picked up the leash and ran. The dog happily pranced beside her, while exuberant barks sounded like broken foghorns exploding in the air.

"What's wrong with her voice?" Zane asked.

"Listen," Taylor said. "Perry and I found her lying on the side of the road with her throat torn. Someone had thrown her out of a moving car." Her eyes filled with tears, and she wiped at them briskly. "They threw her away."

Zane knew full well what buttons that pushed for Taylor, and let her finish.

"I called a neighbor who has a truck to come and help us. As battered as that dog was, she kissed my little girl's hand and wagged her tail as if she were trying to comfort us for being a bother. We took her to the emergency. Zany, he said she'd had almost every bone in her body broken at one time or another. There are scars on her from things I don't even want to contemplate. What she's been through…"

Taylor stopped and composed herself. "Perry didn't need to know the details, but shit."

Zane felt her eyes widen. Taylor never swore.

"My baby looked at me and said, 'That dog was broken by her daddy, huh?' I about died of grief in that surgery room. That Perry would make that connection with what Blake did to me…" Her eyes pleaded with Zane's. "I couldn't Zany, I just—"

"Of course not."

"I couldn't refuse her."

"I get it." Zane pulled Taylor into a hug.

"I can't keep her in the city anymore, and it would break Perry's heart to give her away after we nursed her back to health."

"Hey, it's okay." Zane comforted her. "She can come and visit anytime, even more now."

"Oh, Zane. Thank you, thank you for being so understanding."

"Okay, but have you convinced Esther? I'm still on really thin ice with her."

Taylor laughed. "It's all good. She likes me better anyway."

❧❧❧❧

"Hello?"

"What?" Aislin shook her head. "I'm sorry, what did you say?"

Laura's smile looked a little sad. "You're just not

into this, are you?"

Aislin was a bit confused after being caught daydreaming. "Into what?"

Laura twirled a finger in the air. "This. You, me, this awesome cup of coffee…"

Aislin didn't know what to say. She liked her, she did, but couldn't push Zane out of her mind. Her stomach was in knots. She knew she wasn't present and it was hardly fair to Laura sitting so prettily across from her.

"Who is she?"

"Pardon me?" Aislin asked.

"Aislin," Laura said then smiled gently. "I'm very attracted to you and would love the idea of this maybe going somewhere. But I'm not blind, and I can see there is someone else at the table with us."

"Oh." Aislin was embarrassed by her own inattention and apparent lack of focus, but before she could say anything, Laura continued talking.

"It doesn't mean we can't be friends."

Grateful that she was being let off the hook so graciously, Aislin couldn't help but feel worse, but it made her like Laura even more.

"So, tell me about her."

❧❧❧❧

"So, tell me about her."

"That obvious, huh?"

"Zany, I have never seen you like this, not ever. You're, I don't know, softer somehow."

At one time that would have insulted her right down to the bone, but right now, Zane didn't mind. Even though she hadn't been able to get ahold of Aislin, the sun was brighter, the birds a little louder, and the harsh edges that used to color her thoughts blurred and became—wait for it—softer. All of the illogical details were cliché. But really, didn't things become cliché for a reason?

"I would have introduced you to her last night, but she disappeared."

"Was that before or after your father's crazy uncle routine?"

Zane laughed. "After. How did you know about that?"

"Louis told me after he introduced his date, Brianna. What a breath of fresh air she is. Glad to see he got rid of that great white shark of an ex-wife. What was her name, Muffin?"

Zane tried to keep a straight face. "Muffy."

"Whatever," Taylor said. "Who is she?"

"Aislin O'Shea. She and Brianna are sisters."

Taylor raised an eyebrow. "Really? Didn't that end badly for you two before when you dated the Leonardo sisters?"

Zane swallowed. "Only after I slept with both of them."

"Good Lord, Zany," Taylor said, then laughed.

"What? They were twins as well. To be fair, I didn't know at first I was studding both, or I would have done them at the same time."

"No!"

Zane refrained from telling Taylor that she'd done just that with another pair of sisters in college later that same year. She judged her too innocent for the details. Zane still didn't know how she'd passed her exams that year, let alone made the dean's list. It was all a blur of female flesh.

Alas, the sisters graduated and it took Zane her entire sophomore year to recuperate.

She put it back in the past. "I have to call Aislin, I'll be right back."

Taylor nodded. "The women are coming back from their ride, go ahead. I'll do their counseling session, and see you later."

Zane hummed to herself happily while dialing the numbers. No answer. Zane disconnected the call. She wanted to confront Aislin in person, but didn't want to leave her cousin and niece while the therapeutic riding session was going on. It would have to wait.

When she did catch up with her little fairy they were going to have to have a serious talk about this whole hot and cold thing. It really bothered her that she felt unbalanced most of the time.

If this didn't stop, the relationship was going to end before it really started.

❧❧❧❧❧

Aislin pulled up in front of her parents' house. Her coffee date had been a disaster, and even though Laura had been amazing, it really only served to make her feel worse. She hadn't wanted to talk to her about Zane, but managed to have a brief conversation about what to do in Marin County before excusing herself with lame but genuine apologies.

Now her dad, that was someone she wanted to talk to.

She parked and entered the house. None of them ever knocked, the door was always open to everyone. Aislin had wanted the distraction that even the annoying wedding talk could provide, but the

loud classic rock of Heart came from the direction of
the kitchen, and her father was singing falsetto about
never running away along with Ann Wilson. No never.

Amused, she followed the noise down the hallway
and found her father grumbling at the stove.

When he saw her, his face lit up. "Hey, Ace.
How's my girl?" He reached over and turned down his
station.

"Did you just call that appliance a sumbitch?"

Her father's face turned pink while he ran his
fingers through what was left of the hair on his head,
leaving red clumps standing straight up.

She adored him, though he always looked a bit
dazed to her. He said it was because he lived in a house
full of women but Aislin knew her father wouldn't
have it any other way.

"Since the remodel, I still can't figure out how to
use the damn thing."

"Um, Dad?"

"Yes?"

"That was two years ago."

He looked up from the stove and smiled. "Really?"

"Where is everyone?" Aislin asked.

"Honestly, baby, I don't know. They told me,
I'm sure of it, but all I can remember is smiling and
nodding when they ran out the door." He shook his
head.

She plopped onto a counter stool and wrapped
her feet around the legs. "Right?"

"Want a grilled cheese sandwich?"

Aislin knew her father never made any other
kind. "Sure."

His disappeared into the refrigerator. "Where's
the damn cheese?"

"Top drawer, left, Pops."

"That's right." He buttered the bread and they enjoyed a comfortable silence for a few moments while he cooked.

Her father cleared his throat. "Darcy said the party went well for her."

Aislin looked down at the counter.

"Despite the fact that your sister shoved shrimp down some bimbo's dress."

Aislin felt the corner of her mouth twitch.

"She also said that you turned quite a few heads last night dancing with Zane." His voice was gentle.

Aislin looked up and saw him staring at her with that loving and patient way he had.

"Ace, I just want you to be happy again. It's been so long since I've seen my baby's face joyful."

Tears threatened to fall, but she held them in while he continued.

"Of all my girls, you're the one who's walked the hardest path." He waved the spatula. Thank God it was never a weapon when he held one.

"Something's burning."

Her father spun around to the stove and turned the burner off before sliding a very dark sandwich onto her plate. She chose to ignore the burnt crust and eat it anyway.

"I liked her."

"She's not my type," Even as she said it, Aislin's throat closed around the bite she was swallowing.

"What do you mean? She's successful, and she made moony eyes at you at Sunday dinner."

"She likes the tall, cool blondes, daddy."

Her father looked pensive. "Did she tell you that?"

"They wrap themselves around her at every opportunity, like burritos."

Her father guffawed. "And what does that have to do with anything?"

Aislin sighed. "Okay. I'm not her type?"

"Does this have anything to do with—"

"Asshat-whose-name-will-never-be-mentioned-again?"

"I'm serious, Ace. The jerk, Tad, who dumped you in high school?"

"Maybe."

"Honey, you have to let that go. He was one stupid selfish boy, don't let him determine your value today, or any day. Knock that chip off your shoulder."

A bucket of ice water thrown at her wouldn't have woken her up more effectively. *Oh God, he's right.*

"What's really going on here, honey?"

Aislin looked down again. "She's nothing like Shannon."

"Ah." Her father picked up the empty plates then loaded them to the dishwasher. "And there it is."

"I mean, Shannon was everything, Daddy. We never fought, or even argued."

He was silent, as she knew he would be. It was a trait of his, always knowing his daughters would rush to fill it.

"Everything was so easy with her, you know? It was comfortable, sweet, and I loved her with all my heart."

"We all loved Shannon, baby. And there is no one else in the world just like her."

The tears came back. "When I'm with Zane, Daddy, I feel like I'm on a carnival ride going double speed—up, down, sideways. I can't catch my breath before another dip and roll. I'm never sure of what's she's thinking, or what's going to happen next."

"Huh," her father said. "Did I ever tell you that the first time I met your mother she slapped me silly?"

"What?" Aislin was brought out of her state, immediately intrigued. She leaned closer. Her parents argued, of course they did. But she'd never seen them raise a hand to each other.

"Senior year in high school. There was a keg party at Billy O'Brien's house on Lake Street." He smiled, Aislin assumed at the memory. "Anyway, Billy's girl Amanda shows up with her new neighbor, your mother, who just moved here from back east." He held a hand to his heart.

"There she was, clouds of black hair and the bluest eyes I'd ever seen. She looked Fae, impossibly beautiful. She smiled at me and the world stopped, Ace. It just stopped, and I thought, there she is, the girl I'm going to marry and have gorgeous babies with."

"Aww. That's so sweet, Daddy, but—"

"Let me finish. So, I'm standing there with my mouth hanging open, looking like an idiot, I'm sure. Which at seventeen, I was. Totally struck dumb. I couldn't say a word, so I followed her around all night, getting more tipsy by the hour, and more stupid."

"Drinking at seventeen, Pops?"

"Hey, things were different in the seventies, really. Everyone was still a little crazy from the sixties. Anyway, quit interrupting. Your mother was getting ready to leave and I panicked, grabbed her arm, said something cave-man-stupid that I will not repeat to my daughter. I thought I was being cool in front of my friends. She stopped, and smiled at me. It was a very scary smile, you know the one she gets before the boom falls?"

Aislin laughed. She did indeed know the one. Thankfully, they were usually reserved solely for her father, but she and her sisters had been the recipient of a few.

"She pulled back her shoulders, and put her purse between her feet before asking me, very sweetly, mind you, if I'd said what I'm not going to repeat to you. And like a dumbass, I said it again, and before I finished the sentence that girl slapped me and had her purse back in her hand before five seconds had passed."

Aislin tried to see it, her parents as teenagers, and found she could. "What did you do?"

"Stood there like the ass I was while my buddies hooted and hollered, and the love of my life, future mother of my children, walked out."

"How did you make it up to her?" Aislin asked.

"Ah, now that's another story, baby. The point is, we fought like cats and dogs that first year, all that passion for each other bubbled and boiled and we..." Her father blushed again. "Blah, blah."

"Dad, you got married right out of high school."

"And thank Christ she's put up with me all these years. Again, Ace, the point is, those amusement park feelings? They keep life interesting, at least for me. Sometimes you have to look and see what it is you feel under the fear you're holding."

"You think I'm afraid to love again?" Aislin asked.

"Aren't you, baby?"

She thought about it for a second. "Yes," she said, and felt loneliness drop around her in that comfortable family kitchen. Was she ready to move forward? Take a chance at something new and uncharted? Or was she going to throw an opportunity for happiness away with both hands because she was afraid?

Aislin heard the loud commotion coming from the front door before her father winked at her. "See you tomorrow."

She grinned at him and slipped quietly out the back door, knowing her father would have done the same thing if he could have.

Aislin headed for home. At a stoplight downtown she saw Zane's zippy little red car turn the corner. What really drew attention was the woman in the passenger seat, the same one who had been hanging on her the night before she left.

They were both laughing and appeared to be having a grand old time. So why was Zane leaving all the messages for Aislin? Were they amused by her and laughing behind her back?

A honk from behind brought her back. "Afraid to love, my ass." She had no intention of being another trophy or joke for Zane Whitman. She probably lied about never taking other women to the lake, too. Probably called them all fairy princesses. She felt stupid.

She hated feeling stupid.

But this time, when she wanted to hold on to the anger she'd built, the hurt leaked right on through.

She waited until she'd gotten through the front door to cry.

Chapter Fourteen

G ood morning, Ace," Brianna said.
Aislin frowned at her cheery tone. "Where were you yesterday?"

"Louis and I went into the city and stayed downtown in the condo. We had naked champagne sex."

Laughter bubbled out of Aislin's throat. "What?" She thought of several pithy remarks but she wouldn't be the one to take the joy from her sister's face. If anyone deserved love, it was Brianna.

On the other hand, if she stayed with Louis, wasn't that going to be uncomfortable for her on the holidays? *Damn Zane.* "I'm getting more coffee. Where's Sabrina?"

"Doctor appointment." She waved quickly before Aislin could ask. "Checkup, she's fine. We'll take turns in reception until she gets here."

Aislin didn't answer as she pushed through the doors to the clinic. She wasn't going to have a good morning, not if she could help it. Sometimes you just had to feel the roll of righteous anger and let it burn out.

The warmer weather brought all kinds of patients in. She gave several sets of shots, neutered and spayed two kittens, set a broken leg, and comforted the dog who had stumbled into a beehive and was staying overnight for observation.

She glanced at the clock, relieved it was almost lunch time. Sabrina must have returned hours ago as her sister hadn't called her out to answer the phones.

Aislin had just come into reception when a little girl ran through the front door.

"Please help us! Fifi was hit by a car!"

Aislin, Brianna, and Sabrina ran toward her as a unit, only to have to step back when Zane came in carrying a massive dog in her arms.

They stepped up to help her get the dog directly back to the x-ray room. Aislin couldn't help but get a flutter in her belly at Zane's show of strength, even covered in mud and blood.

"Hurry!"

"It looks pretty bad," Zane said as she gently laid the dog on the stainless steel table.

"Honey," Brianna took the little girl's hand. "Do you want to come with me and look at the new puppies born today? We're in the way, and Dr. O'Shea needs some room okay?"

Aislin saw the grateful look Zane shot to Brianna before she stepped back to let her look at the dog.

Fifi stared up at her with pain-filled eyes, yet still her tail pounded on the table. Aislin patted the massive head. "What happened?"

"We think it happened about an hour ago. My niece found her down by the main road, at the mailbox."

"She looks like she's in shock. I'll have to give her fluids but she needs an x-ray. There's blood, there might be broken bones and internal injuries."

"God," Zane said. "She's been through so much already." She stepped back and told Aislin what Taylor had shared with her about Fifi's background.

Aislin checked the dog and stamped down her

rage so she could focus on the patient. She needed to radiate positive energy for her.

"I'm going to have to operate," Aislin said while she ran fingers through Fifi's fur and gently palpitated her limbs.

"Surgery?" Zane's face drained of color.

"She has a broken hip. I'm still going to have to x-ray to be certain there aren't more." Aislin slipped the IV in and adjusted the drip before pulling the machine down from above the table. Her patient was large, so she would need several films.

"Fifi?" Aislin stroked the dog's fur, taking care not to touch her abrasions that were full of gravel.

"My niece gave her to me for my birthday," Zane said.

"Birthday?"

Zane smiled briefly as she also stroked Fifi's head. "Not yet, but it was a good excuse to bring her to the ranch because their apartment is so small. Why is she so still?"

"I gave her a little something for the pain in her IV. Any chance you're pregnant?"

"What?" Zane looked stunned.

For the first time, Aislin smiled. "I have to ask." She pointed to the machine. "Would you grab two of those vests please?"

"These are heavy, what's in them?"

"You really haven't been to the doctor in a long time have you? They're lead. Put one on if going to stand there." Aislin positioned the lens over Fifi. Normally, an owner wouldn't be back here with her, but this was a side of Zane she'd only seen briefly when she'd delivered Blue's foal, and she had to admit she was curious to see more of it.

Aislin took the film to the light box, and pointed out the fresh break. "I'll have to operate to reset that. It'll be extensive, and it will take a while. I also have to clean out these abrasions to find out if any need to be stitched."

"I'll stay."

Though her heart leapt at the quick statement, Aislin finally convinced her to take Perry home. It was going to take a few hours yet.

Sabrina rescheduled some of Aislin's and Brianna's patients and they got to work.

As she thought, it took a few hours. The break was nasty and placing the pin was tricky. Now the poor dear would likely limp for the rest of her life as well.

She tried not to think of Fifi's past but instead look forward to her future. Her vitals were good, and aside from her battle scars, she appeared to be quite healthy. It took another hour to clean her scrapes and cuts, and all that was left was a few stiches here and there.

Between the two of them and help from Sabrina, they managed to carry Fifi to a kennel where Aislin continued to fuss for the dog's comfort. When Brianna's eyes shifted to look at the clock for the second time, Aislin told her to go home.

"Are you sure? I mean this is more important than a date."

"I'm nearly done," Aislin said. "Be away with you, lass, and have a good time."

Brianna smiled as Aislin knew she would at their father's saying. "Call me if you need me."

Aislin waived her off and patted Fifi's head.

She was starving, as she hadn't time to eat lunch. She wanted to keep an eye on the dog, so she walked to the clinic's small kitchen to see if there were any leftovers. Darcy usually sent food for them to test out weekly from her ever-changing menus.

Aislin had just pulled a white Styrofoam box from the fridge and was contemplating the identity of its contents when she heard the bell over the front door. She peeked around the corner in time to see Zane, Perry, and that woman come in loaded with Chinese food cartons.

"How is she? Can we thee her?"

Aislin crouched down to Perry's level. "She's going to be just fine. She's sleeping now, but we can go wish her sweet dreams if you like."

"Did you hear that Mommy? Fifi's going to be just fine!"

"This," Zane said and took the woman's hand, "is my cousin Taylor. You've met my niece."

Oh, Aislin, you freaking dumbass. This is her cousin?

Zane must have seen the look on her face. "You thought—"

"Of course not," Aislin said, already feeling the heat in her cheeks. She grabbed Perry's hand. "C'mon, sweetie, let's go check on Fifi."

She heard Zane following behind her. "Is that why you didn't answer your phone?"

"What are you talking about?" Taylor asked.

Dear baby Jesus, let me fall through the floor. Aislin quickened her pace.

Zane pulled at her elbow, and let Perry and Taylor go ahead to Fifi's cage. "Slow down. I don't know whether to be relieved or angry with you, at your obvious lack of trust in me."

"I know," Aislin said. "I'm sorry."

"We're going to have to have a serious talk later."

Aislin nodded and crossed to the others. She had misjudged Zane again, and again, she was embarrassed and felt small. She couldn't help but notice Taylor's and Zane's obvious relief and concern—no rich bitches in sight. She really was going to have to quit judging others by events in her past.

Time to knock that rich bitch chip right off my shoulder.

The short visit with Fifi put all at ease. Aislin let Mikey in to play with Perry while they sat at the small table and ate. The food was spicy and delicious, and the conversation was easy.

Aislin looked at Zane from under her lashes from time to time, but she didn't catch her looking back. She really hoped she could fix this last misunderstanding.

Zane grabbed the last pot sticker that Aislin was eyeballing and laughed. "What'll you give me for it?"

She didn't have time to respond as the reception bell rang again. Aislin excused herself and left to take care of a regular client who'd stopped in to pick up some vitamin supplements for her toy poodle.

By the time she rang out, Zane was in reception with Taylor and Perry. "While you're standing there." She pulled out her checkbook and smiled. "Maybe you'll take this one without throwing it back at me?"

"I haven't even done the paperwork yet."

"That's okay, I'm sure this will cover it. What's left can go to the next person who needs help."

"Thank you. It's always appreciated."

Taylor shook Aislin's hand. "It was nice to meet you," she said. "Let's go wait in the car, Perry."

"Thank you, Dr. O'Shea," Perry said very politely. "Good-bye, Mikey." She threw her arms around the little dog's neck, and he wiggled enthusiastically back at her.

When she'd gone, and they were alone, Aislin found she couldn't quite look Zane in the eye. "Your cousin seems very nice."

"Yes, she is." Zane lifted Aislin chin with a finger. "And we need to talk about this later."

"Okay." Aislin took the check and felt her mouth drop open. "This isn't for an operation, this is for a trip to Hawaii."

"Not quite," Zane said.

Aislin couldn't help but think she would owe her if she accepted it. "I can't—"

"Sabrina would."

Aislin laughed. "Yes, she would." *And I should to learn to be gracious*, Aislin thought, remembering her conversation with her father. "I was really obnoxious that day."

"So was I," Zane said and touched her cheek. "You're worth every penny, Aislin. You helped Blue, you saved Fifi, and you made the people I love very happy. I told you to put the rest to a need you might have in the clinic."

Aislin felt the warmth of her words spread under her skin, and tucked the check under Sabrina's desk blotter. They could do a happy dance tomorrow on the way to the bank.

"Go out with me tomorrow night, Aislin. Let's go into the city."

Aislin's thoughts raced. She supposed she could shift things around and have Sabrina do nightly chores and take care of the animals. "Okay."

"Just okay?"

"I mean, I'd love to." Aislin's heart thudded as

Zane leaned over and touched her lips against hers. It was a soft, gentle kiss, but this one felt full of promise.

Throughout the evening, her thoughts never strayed far from Zane. How silly was it that she'd been tripping thinking Taylor was another girlfriend?

A couple of mere weeks ago, she hadn't known anything about Zane Whitman that hadn't been printed in the paper. Now her thoughts seem to go and wrap themselves around her, nearly to the exclusion of all else. The more she knew, the more Aislin realized she hadn't seen, really seen, all of Zane. She'd been hung up on a cardboard cutout of who she thought Zane was, and what she thought of her class.

No one besides Shannon had ever held that much space in her mind.

Her father's assumption was right, and Aislin knew it. She and Zane weren't as far apart as she'd believed. Fear had Aislin building the railroad tracks between them.

It wasn't social standing that kept her on the wrong side; her boundaries were fear based.

She had loved Shannon with her entire being, and to love someone again not only made her feel disloyal, but she was scared to death of losing it.

After she was in bed, Aislin recalled the way Zane's body had felt against her, the amazing way her lips felt against her own, recalled how her heat melted the chills her breath against her neck had caused.

All the feelings she'd locked behind protective barriers that had been frozen and in stasis for years were now wide awake and screaming. That night, Aislin dreamt she was on a small rowboat in the middle of Shasta Lake, one of her favorite places. The water was like glass, Mikey barked happily, and the birds were chirping happy songs. The sun was on her face, and she smiled at the beautiful, serene scene.

"Beautiful, isn't it?"

Aislin looked behind her and saw Shannon in the back of the boat. Her long hair stirred in the breeze as she steered the outboard motor.

"Babe?" She stood on shaky legs and tried to make her way to her but a cloud covered the sky and the water rolled violently shaking the boat. Dismayed, she fell back onto the seat and held on to the sides to keep from falling out.

There was a shout and Aislin turned toward the sound. Zane popped her head out of the choppy, blood-red water. "Come on in," she yelled. "The water's fine."

Aislin startled awake, opened her eyes, and stared into the dark. Mikey was at the foot of the bed, and Merlin hadn't come up yet.

The empty side of her bed seemed to mock her, and she curled into a ball around her stomach and rocked herself back to sleep.

.𝔄.𝔄.𝔢.𝔢.

The next day was another busy one at the clinic. Aislin wondered since it was like this more often than not, if she should hire another veterinary assistant.

Sabrina never said a word about the large check, but when Aislin picked the corner of the blotter up, it was gone, presumably in the green deposit bag in the bottom drawer.

After they were officially closed and she and Brianna checked on Fifi and fed the rest of the boarders and patients, they went over to the main house.

Every other word out of Brianna's mouth was

Louis this and Louis that, said in the same reverent tone that had been reserved solely for the New Kids On The Block group.

The anxiety she felt was making Aislin a little queasy, which brought up the uneasy dream she'd had the night before.

Her sister went immediately to the house phone, leaving Aislin to get ready for her date with Zane.

What was she going to wear? She ransacked her closet to look for something halfway dressy. Zane had already seen her in her little black dress, and that was her best outfit.

Her eye caught something shiny in the back. Aislin moved the hangers full of T-shirts and jeans out of the way, and took it off the rack.

When she unzipped the clear garment bag she gasped. She had bought this particular dress for her anniversary party that was never held. Blue and shimmery, she traced the shiny embroidery and opaque beads along the neckline before holding the cool material to her cheek.

Aislin was totally conflicted. The dress was stunning, but damn, now what? She turned quickly when she thought she heard a voice in her ear.

She could have sworn it sounded like Granny's.

It's a sign, dear. It's a sign.

She'd never had a chance to wear it and must have overlooked it when her sisters helped her clean out the closet just last year.

Was it a sign?

A barely perceptible cool breeze fanned her face, her lips tingled, and was that Shannon's Lauren perfume she smelled?

She didn't know whether to take it as her blessing,

or that she was doing the wrong thing by going out with Zane.

Aislin swallowed her indecision and stepped into the dress, which clung to her waist and was a little shorter than she was used to these days. She turned to look in the mirror and was surprised at the woman that looked back at her. This was a side of herself she hadn't seen in a very long time. Date pretty, not I'm-catering-an-event pretty.

She caressed the silk for a moment, and then went into the bathroom to find her straightener and see if she could beat her hair into submission.

By the time the doorbell rang, she was ready, but still hardly recognized herself.

Who was the stranger reflected back at her? Who was that woman in the mirror with sparkling eyes? She looked happy.

Mikey raced past her ankles and nearly tripped her as he tore down the stairs waving his tail in a frantic helicopter motion.

Brianna beat her to the door and Aislin stopped halfway. On the other side, the twins stood there and, in her opinion, resembled matching Greek gods.

Her sister dragged Louis into the kitchen

"How come you're not dressed up?" Aislin heard Brianna ask Louis.

Aislin didn't hear his answer, her focus was absolute as she looked at Zane. And even though she knew it was corny as all hell, she felt time slow down and she drank in the sight.

Zane looked impossibly tall in her heels, and was gorgeous in black pinstriped slacks and a shimmery silver camisole that showed more cleavage than it didn't. Her long hair was loose around her shoulders, and in the glow that streamed into the open doorway, appeared to be spun from the moonlight.

Drop. Dead. Fine. And she's going out with me.

The temperature in the hallway increased a hundredfold. She wanted to fan herself, and the butterflies in her stomach transformed themselves into the frantic beating wings of hummingbirds.

She was terrified but convinced her feet to move.

Chapter Fifteen

Through the open door, a late spring breeze wafted in and brought the promising scents of beauty. The early crickets sang into the silence.

Zane's necklace felt too tight around her throat, and she was certain all the blood rushed from her head south to play the drums in interesting places.

Aislin's dress had a slit in the side, and with each stair she descended, Zane was rewarded with a teasing glimpse of Aislin's ivory skin.

She was struck mute by Aislin's appearance, but finally managed to clear her throat. "You look..." Zane struggled for the perfect adjective, because they all applied at this moment.

"Nice?" Aislin asked.

Zane shook her head. "I was going to say exquisite."

A faint blush appeared on her cheeks. "Thank you, and so do you."

Aislin reached the landing, and when she looked up at her, Zane kissed her lightly.

The jolt she received in return had her body humming with electricity and radiating heat. Aislin leaned into her body for a moment and her clean scent teased her senses.

"You smell fantastic," Zane said.

Aislin smiled up at her, and the light in her eyes made Zane feel powerful. That sensation lasted only for a second. Though she'd planned the date to the last tiny detail, she hadn't taken into account she'd feel so unsteady and unsure.

Brianna giggled in the living room. "Have fun, kids!" she said loudly.

Zane took it as their cue to leave. Louis put in his two cents. "Don't do anything I wouldn't do."

"Is there anything on that actual list?" Zane asked.

Her brother laughed. "Pretty much, um, no."

She took Aislin's hand and drew her outside to the porch. "Goodnight. Don't wait up, Brianna."

"Wouldn't think of it," Brianna replied. She started to say something else but Zane shut the door behind her, cutting off the laughter from the living room.

Zane heard Aislin's sharp intake of breath. "Are you freaking kidding me right now? A limo?"

"I'm trying to impress you. How am I doing?"

Aislin smiled. "Not bad."

The chauffeur held the door and Zane was treated to the sight of more skin as Aislin slid across the long, leather seat.

When Aislin was in and the door was shut, Zane knew she was nervous by the way she tugged on the bottom of her dress to cover her thighs, but when she turned her head to look at her, Aislin was staring right back.

"It's hot in here," Aislin said. "Are you hot?"

Zane nodded. "Going to get hotter."

Aislin laughed. "Is that your best line, Counselor?"

Zane ran a finger lightly down the side of Aislin's neck, and the shiver it caused made it difficult to concentrate. "Nope, just the opening argument." Zane pressed a kiss at the pulse of her throat, and nipped

Aislin's earlobe.

Her sigh of pleasure shot heat straight to Zane's core and threatened to put her into overdrive in an instant. She was bombarded by the sexual tension, uncertainty, and insecurity she'd felt over the last several weeks. She barely kept herself in check, trembled with the effort to not to slide Aislin under her and assert her dominance, to feel confident again. She wanted Aislin more than she'd ever wanted anyone.

Whoa, slow down, she told herself. With regret, she pulled away and sat up straight. She'd planned a great seduction, not a teenage hormonal tryst in the backseat of a car.

A very nice ride, yet still a car.

Zane looked away and inhaled sharply. It didn't help much because Aislin's breathing sounded as ragged as her own. When she glanced back, Aislin's eyes reflected her lust and Zane needed to double her resolve.

"What's wrong?"

"I'm trying to behave until after dinner."

Aislin stretched her body and laughed. "This is so luxurious."

"Do want champagne or…something else?" Zane asked.

"Oh," Aislin said. "Define something else. It's a long ride to the city."

"Let me show you." Zane hit the button for the privacy screen, and then opened the sunroof. "Come here," she said and then took Aislin's hand, placed a kiss in the center of her palm before lightly running her tongue along the inside of her arm to her elbow, and pulled her closer in one smooth motion to press against her body.

Aislin's eyes were wide. "You're good at this." The movement had caused her dress to slip further up her thighs.

"Your legs are gorgeous."

Aislin laughed. "They're bruised and scarred."

"I'm the one looking at them, and they're beautiful."

"You need your eyes checked."

"Is it so hard for you accept a compliment?" Zane watched the blush spread across Aislin's cheeks and worried briefly that she may have said the wrong thing.

"No," Aislin said in a low voice. "It's just been a long time." She laid her head back against the seat and looked her in the eye. "Thank you."

Zane smiled and ran her thumb over Aislin's lower lip. "I think about your mouth during the day."

Aislin captured her hand then licked the tip of Zane's finger, drawing it in and sucking it before she drew it out slowly. "Yeah?" she asked. "And what it is doing to you?"

The gesture and her words hit Zane and her blood went from hot to boiling. She shifted her weight to cup Aislin's face in her hands. "Very interesting things. We start here…" Zane covered her mouth with her own, pressing gently until she felt Aislin's lips soften and open to her exploring. When Aislin's teeth softly clamped around her tongue, Zane's entire body tightened in response.

Aislin hands gripped her shoulders, combed through her hair, and then fisted. Zane couldn't move anywhere except deeper into the kiss.

Which was fine with her. She didn't want to stop anyway.

She leaned closer, and without breaking the kiss,

nudged Aislin to ease back, once again thanking the leather for making it easy. The sighs and little moans Aislin made were driving Zane crazy. The subtle rocking of her hips against her spurred her to want, and take, more. She straightened and then kissed the vivid marks on her knees before separating them languidly, giving her time to stop if she wanted. Zane kissed the smooth cool skin of Aislin's thighs, and her sound of pleasure nearly undid her resolve to go slowly.

Zane glanced down at the damp black lace panties and felt the growl deep in her throat. Aislin's eyes were hooded, full of mysteries, and Zane wanted to solve every single one of them.

She felt how hot her own breath was as she blew across the fabric then pressed her lips over Aislin's mons. Zane grew dizzy from the scent of her passion. She ran her tongue along the sensitive strip on the inside of each thigh, marveling in the taste that was uniquely Aislin. When she covered the material with her mouth and sucked, Aislin stiffened and Zane was rewarded with her ecstatic cry as her panties soaked.

Zane pulled the fabric to the side and blew softly against her sensitive flesh before firmly pressing her lips to her and holding still until she felt Aislin's pulse beat wildly. Zane entered her and stroked gently and excruciatingly slowly until Aislin came again. When Aislin opened her eyes, Zane licked her fingers.

"Oh." Aislin pushed her hair out of her eyes. "That was ferociously sexy."

Zane reached into the bar, and took out a small towel. "And you," she said, "taste delicious." She stroked the cloth along her thighs and labia, and in mere heartbeats, Aislin's hips began to dance again. Zane's own passion throbbed and cried out for release, but she concentrated solely on Aislin's. It gave her great pleasure to give this to her, and she would give most anything to have Aislin continue to look at her in just that way as she was rewarded with another orgasm.

"Enough, I can't take any more right now. God, what you must think of me."

Zane slipped off Aislin's wet underwear and put them in her pocket. "I'm thinking I'm the luckiest woman in the world right now." She helped Aislin sit up, framed her face, and brushed her lips gently against hers and then sat back.

The limo smelled of sex, blistered with heat, and Zane etched the encounter into her heart. Aislin was passionate and held nothing back. It both humbled and melted her. A wave of tenderness rolled through her and she wanted to wrap Aislin up in love, give her the world on a silver platter.

She blinked rapidly to dispel the tears she felt gathering. Where the hell did that come from? She'd never, ever, been this overcome with emotion after sex.

Making love.

Zane felt Aislin's small hand cover her breast and her thumb brush across her rock-hard nipple. She held her wrist back. "Later, love. We have all night, and we're almost there."

"All right." Aislin smoothed her hair, reached into her purse, and checked her face in the mirror. "Wow, I don't look any different."

"Why should you?"

"I haven't done anything remotely sexual in almost four years."

Stunned, Zane could only stare. No wonder she'd been so receptive and responsive. Now, in addition to the pleasure she received from pleasing Aislin, she also felt some righteous pride that she'd been the one to break her celibacy. "I don't know what to say. Will you tell me about it?"

Aislin smiled. "Later."

"Touché."

❧❧❧❧

"Good evening, Ms. Whitman."

"Thank you, Charles." Zane swept into the lobby and held her hand.

Aislin's built-in insecurity barked at her. "I've never been here," she said.

"One of San Francisco's finest," Zane said.

Aislin tried not to gawk and the huge fountain, gorgeous marble, colored glass sculptures—was that a Chihuly? She'd bet it was.

Although she'd never seen one outside the pages of a magazine, she knew. The formal social setting made her painfully aware she had no panties on. It had seemed like a such sexy idea at the time, But she clearly hadn't been thinking when she let Zane take them. "It's like something out of a movie set."

"It's been used in quite a few," Zane said.

A slightly built man dressed to the nines in a tuxedo hurried over to greet them. She couldn't help but think he was the perfect stereotype of a maître d'.

"Ms. Whitman, so nice to see you. We have your table ready." He smiled at Aislin and held his arm out. "This way, madam."

Madam? Amused, Aislin wondered how much more of this night would seem as if scripted. It had certainly felt dreamy on the way over.

A tall woman walked toward them and she

noticed the predatory way she looked at Zane. The redhead took a deep breath, as if she wanted her breasts to be noticed.

The maître d' cleared his throat, and Aislin waited to see if Zane had been affected.

She didn't even break her stride.

Aislin grinned at the woman and couldn't help feeling a little smug as she strolled past her.

He led them to a small, intimate table at the back against a wall of windows. Candlelight flickered and red roses graced the center. A bottle of champagne cooled in a silver bucket. Aislin was once again struck with a sense of Hollywood glamor. But, instead of watching the movie, she was starring in it.

He held out her chair and bowed to Zane before he left the table.

Aislin looked out over the wharf and the lights over the San Francisco bay. It was gorgeous.

"You look stunning in the candlelight," Zane said.

Aislin smiled at her. "My gran used to say anyone looked good in candlelight."

"I'm not here with just anyone, I'm here with the most beautiful woman in the room." Zane licked her lower lip.

"No, I think that distinction belongs to me," Aislin said. "I feel like Cinderella."

"Do I get to be the charming prince?"

Aislin laughed. "Of course."

Zane snapped her napkin before placing it on her lap. "Then, I accept." She lifted her glass. "To the prettiest princess of all the lands."

Warmth spread through Aislin and she tapped her glass to Zane's. The bubbles tickled her nose, but the taste was unlike any she'd had before. It must have been expensive. Certainly not a bottle of the screw cap variety. *Shut up already,* Aislin told herself. "To the charming prince and a fabulous date." She tried not to stare at Zane's long, slender fingers, attempted even harder not to blush when she'd remembered how they'd made her feel.

Zane made it all happen, this perfect fairy tale date. She felt special, already a teensy bit tipsy from the marvelous champagne, and...oh my God, the ride over. Her body was still thrumming, she continued to feel Zane's hands on her thighs, and...

A nearby foghorn snapped her out of it and she was grateful. There was so much to take in, and she was sure, mostly, that there would be more...loving, later.

She looked out the window at the tourists and the bay. Aislin had always loved San Francisco but was always happier to be home.

She stared at Zane from under her lashes. What on earth were they going to talk about? She certainly wasn't going to ask about her social life, or talk about the lack of hers.

Not a conversation she wanted to have.

When she dared to look, Zane's eyes were level with hers, and the intensity made Aislin even more nervous. Didn't her kind go to charm school or something? She felt shy and a little afraid she was going to say something stupid.

She wasn't hungry. Nervous how the evening would go, yes. That and more than a little flustered over her behavior in the limo. Plus, she'd eaten most of the artichoke dip and all of the tiny pieces of brown bread already. All that and, well, she had no panties on.

No. Panties.

God, I'm a mess.

Aislin had the unnerving sensation of being watched. She felt the tingle on the back of her neck.

She had to look. Had to.

She tried to be nonchalant but after searching left, then right, Aislin couldn't imagine any of the other diners having any interest in her at all.

She did however, notice the redhead trying to catch Zane's attention.

Bimbo. Aislin smirked at her, even if it did make her feel a little mean. Zane was her date, and after having been so intimate in the limo, she felt closer to her, and—she'd admit—possessive tonight.

She was feeling guilty too. Maybe that's why she had the sensation of being stared at.

She ordered herself to relax.

Then the lecture in her head started all over again.

Damn, she wore herself out.

At least I'm consistent. Aislin grasped at straws.

She should be focused entirely on Zane, on how delicious she looked, and so much more interesting than her food.

It was a good thing her appetite was more than a little distracted by her libido. Her plate, though arranged exquisitely, wouldn't have sated a Chihuahua.

A small—make that really small—medallion of meat, three asparagus spears, and a teaspoon of what looked like rice pilaf. A lovely little stripe of wine reduction looked lonely on the stark white plate.

Aislin loved to go out to dinner, and she would have been happy with a big plate of messy nachos. Her racing thoughts stopped on a dime when Zane lifted a bite to her mouth and her lips parted.

She flashed on where those lips had been and shifted in her seat. Aislin felt the flush begin on her chest and move up.

Zane licked the tiny bit of sauce from the corner of her mouth and Aislin dropped her fork.

The sound reverberated like a shot in the hushed environment, and now people *were* staring.

At her.

Aislin let her hair fall forward and hid her face. This atmosphere was so...what? Too civilized, she decided.

She hoped she wouldn't have to far-, er, fluff in this place.

They would probably throw her out.

As if on cue, her stomach rumbled.

Oh God.

Then twisted.

Sweet baby Jesus.

Aislin felt the bubble descend.

Oh, no.

Sweat broke out on her forehead and she clamped her thighs together and prayed feverishly her stomach would calm down.

The food was too rich for her system.

A painful cramp nearly doubled her, and she held back a whimper. "Excuse me," she said. "I'll be right back."

She rose from the table abruptly and had to hold the chair from falling over. She knew Zane was asking her something, but she couldn't, wouldn't, stop to ask her what she'd said. Aislin pulled the bottom of her dress down. How could something she thought looked so pretty be so dangerous?

Mortification had her certain the patrons were

staring.

Probably laughing at me.

Aislin walked as fast as her heels would allow, headed toward the front of the restaurant, and prayed the restrooms were close.

The hostess pointed to a discreet door.

Hallelujah, it was empty. She hurried into a stall and locked the door.

And wanted to drop into the abyss each time she heard the door open. The comments she heard weren't kind, embarrassed her, and there was no way on God's green earth she was coming out until she was sure she was alone.

No one seemed to take much time at the mirror that she could tell, they were too busy running back out.

The guilt returned with a vengeance. Maybe this was punishment for being happy. What right did she have for it after what she'd done? Aislin realized keeping busy at the clinic kept most of it at bay, but the sheer contrast of Zane's life against hers brought it to the surface.

But when Zane smiled at her, something turned inside, and as much as she wanted to deny it, Aislin knew she was falling—no—*had fallen* in love with her.

It scared her to death.

And right now it was turning her inside out.

Literally.

❧ ❧ ❧ ❧

Zane checked her watch again. Aislin had been gone for almost ten minutes. Maybe she hadn't gone to the restroom as she thought. Maybe she left.

Zane heard a breathy voice next to her. "Aw, did you get stood up?"

It was the redhead. Of course Zane had noticed her, and she had deliberately ignored her because one, it was rude, and two, it was disrespectful to Aislin.

She knew the type well. This woman reminded of her Giselle. "No," she said. "Have a nice evening." Zane dismissed her.

She stared at her for a second, her mouth moving like a guppy before she turned and huffed off. Zane felt sorry for the man having dinner with her. *Snake.*

The champagne was still cold, but her glass was nearly empty. What was taking her so long? Just as she decided she was going to check on her, she spied Aislin walking back, holding a hand over her stomach.

She looked a little pale, and the sexy little strut she'd had on the way in was gone. "Are you okay?" Zane asked when Aislin reached the table.

She slid into her seat and slumped across from her. "Yes. I'm sorry."

"Don't be sorry, what happened?"

"I'd rather not tell you," Aislin said. "I'm utterly embarrassed."

"Again, don't be." Aislin's discomfort was obvious, and Zane only wanted to put her at ease. She leaned forward to whisper. "I should have warned you about the dip."

Recognition flared in Aislin's eyes. "How did you know?"

"Regretfully, it's happened to me too."

"You're not going to tell me about it, are you?" To her relief, Aislin's shoulders appeared to relax.

Zane smiled. "Not a word."

"Good, and neither am I. Not a date, dinner-type

conversation. Ever."

"Okay. Do you want dessert?"

"Are you kidding me?" Aislin's eyes widened.

"No, but I'll take that as you don't."

"Change the subject, please. Talk about something else, anything."

"All right." Zane sipped her water. "Have you traveled much?"

"Not much, I stay close to home. We did go to Ireland. Shannon and I—" Aislin paused. "Went a couple of times."

Shannon Riley, Zane thought. *The picture on the mantle in Aislin's home. The wall between them.*

"Is Shannon an ex-girlfriend?"

"No, my wife."

Zane nearly spit out her drink. "You're married?"

"Well, not technically with a fancy piece of paper. But we hadn't needed one."

"Where is your…" Zane just about choked on her next words. "Your wife now?"

Aislin's eyes looked sad and distant as stared out of the window. "She died almost four years ago."

"I'm so sorry." Zane immediately felt stupid for the irrational stab of jealousy she'd experienced. Deep down she'd known it was something like this, and sincerely hoped she had the ability to make it past her wife's ghost. No wonder Aislin was skittish. "Was she sick?"

Aislin shook her head.

Zane reached out to take her hand, hoping the contact would comfort her.

"Sometimes it feels like a lifetime ago, and others like it happened yesterday. My family closed ranks and carried me."

That explains quite a bit, thought Zane. "What happened, if you don't mind me asking?"

"It's painful," Aislin said, and took her hand back.

Zane's heart clenched. Aislin had averted her eyes. She had a hundred questions, but left them unasked in the silence at the table. It was apparent she'd touched a raw nerve.

"Now is not the time to tell you, and really, not the place either. I'm sorry."

"We have all kind of taboo subjects tonight."

"I'll apologize again. We can go home now."

"That's not what I meant." Zane had the entire night planned, and she didn't want to end their time together, regardless of ghosts and bad bathroom experiences.

Aislin looked surprised. "You still want to be out with me?"

"Of course. Why would you think otherwise?"

"Um, because I got sick?"

"Easily fixed," Zane said. "How are you feeling now?"

"Much better, it's just that I'm not used to this." Aislin waved her hand to encompass the room.

"As opposed to what?" Zane was curious. "Restaurants?"

"Fancy schmancy places."

Ah, Zane thought. *Aislin's aversion. Again.* She thought they were past that. Rather than get into that now, Zane put it to the side and changed the subject. "So," she said. "Do you have any hobbies?" She filled Aislin's glass.

After taking a sip, Aislin smiled. "I love my yard, and planting flowers. I do crafty things, putter around the house, and change things around. I don't get to do as much as I like because we're always so busy at the clinic, and most weekends I help Darcy, or work at my parents' bar."

"There's a lot on your plate." When was the last time Zane had worked outside? She couldn't remember. As far as puttering around the house, her family had always hired someone to do that. After thinking about that for a second, Zane was sure their furniture and art had been in the same place for decades. *Boring.* There were some rooms she'd never spent any time in, and she would have been apprehensive to sit on anything at all. They had antiques that had belonged to royalty.

She loved Aislin's happy little house; it was comfortable, and colorful. A house where laughter would be right at home. She wanted that, and until now, didn't know how much. She let herself imagine cuddling with Aislin on her soft couch.

"It's a new endeavor for Darcy," Aislin said. "I'm sure it will take off. But until then, we'll all pitch in. Until we were able to hire my niece Sabrina, there were plenty of times that my other sisters helped Brianna and me."

"I know that she's very popular right now for events," Zane said. "She shouldn't have any worries." *And I'll make sure she stays as the go-to with my friends.*

Aislin smiled. "That makes me happy. She's wanted it and worked so hard. How about you? What do you do in your spare time?"

Zane emptied the last of the champagne in her flute. "Well, like you, I work insane hours at the firm. I don't have much left for hobbies per se. I guess the horses are my passion. My cousin runs a program at the ranch for abused women. I helped her start that, it's something I can stand behind."

"Wow," Aislin said and leaned forward. "I didn't know that."

"I might have a few mysteries left."

Aislin batted her eyelashes. "I bet you do."

Zane could only be relieved to see her perk up again, that whatever had been bothering her had been put to the back burner.

The wine sparkled, as did Aislin, and she found it hard to take her eyes off her. Talking to her, Zane couldn't deny her own life had been ordered, organized, and predictable. There had been little time for fun. Aislin made her want to laugh and explore new possibilities. How on earth had she thought Aislin wasn't her type?

She was becoming everything.

The seduction in the limo was only the beginning. Zane knew how to enchant, charm, and flirt, but Aislin was guileless and seemed oh-so vulnerable. What you saw was definitely what you got. Even more, there was this incredible shy innocence that Zane treasured. It was an extremely rare commodity in her world.

❧❧❧❧

While they talked, time passed in a blur. Aislin was grateful she hadn't time to remember her embarrassment over her upset stomach. She looked down at her glass, surprised it was empty. Just how much had she drunk?

Zane came around the table. "Ready for the next portion of our evening?"

The whisper in her ear sent chills along her spine. Along with the impact it had on her physically, it also

triggered her fear. "Was it your plan to get me tipsy
and have your way with me?"

"You weren't drinking in the limo."

Aislin felt a hammer of lust strike her between
her naked thighs and she tried to swallow. "Okay, that
worked." She took her hand as they left the restaurant
and returned to the lobby.

"This really is a beautiful hotel." With her new
perception of Zane intruding into her loathing of what
she thought of the wealthy, Aislin was able to admit
she'd never been here because she never chose to go,
not that she couldn't go. She was certainly worth it.

Take that, asshat.

Zane nodded. "The rooms are beautiful, too."

Aislin shivered. "What's going on?"

"This way," Zane said and tugged her arm gently.
"Trust me."

Aislin laughed. She couldn't help it. "Never say
those words to an Irishwoman. They are sure to have
the opposite effect."

"Good to know."

When they got into the elevator, Zane pushed the
button and Aislin's heart did a slow roll in her chest. It
could be the champagne, the ride, or Zane's predatory
look. There didn't seem to be an invitation in her
expression, but a summoning that indicated she'd be
willing to take what she wanted. It was incredibly hot,
and when Zane smiled wickedly and pulled the panties
out of her pocket to stroke against her cheek, Aislin's
desire rocketed to an unprecedented level.

The elevator stopped and another couple got
on. Aislin tried to grab at her underwear, to hide
the evidence, but Zane easily deflected her. She was
mortified and turned on simultaneously.

The bell sounded for the fourteenth floor, and they exited holding hands over the small swatch of silk.

Zane stopped and unlocked a door with a swipe, and gestured her in. "After you."

Aislin's hand went to her throat as she looked around. It was, simply put, the most luxurious suite she'd ever been in. She stepped into the small parlor where candles flickered and the open drapes framed the lights of downtown San Francisco and Fisherman's Wharf.

There were more red roses in a crystal vase, and another bottle of champagne in a silver bucket. Music played softly through hidden speakers.

She turned to face Zane. "What if I'd said no?"

Zane's arm circled her shoulders. "Then I imagine the maids and porters would be having a party without us."

Aislin laid her head against Zane's chest and mumbled.

"What's that?" Zane asked.

She pulled away a little. "I said, 'thank you.'"

"Oh, honey, why are you crying?"

Embarrassed, Aislin wiped her eyes, taking care to remember her mascara. "I'm Irish, my bladder is close to my eyes." She sniffled. "You make me feel special."

"Must be because you are. Come here." Zane held her and started swaying slowly to the current song which happened to be the number one love song when Aislin was a teenager. She felt humbled by the effort Zane had made, certainly to seduce, but this much attention to detail was above and beyond. She pushed herself closer and loved the way her body molded to Zane's.

When she kissed her, Aislin was determined then and there to finally put down all the freaking baggage she'd held since she'd met Zane. Better yet, to throw it out the window and into the bay visible from the huge windows.

Zane's lips pressed softly against Aislin's neck, and she felt her pulse speed up before she covered her mouth with hers. Instead of being fast and furious, the kiss was erotically gentle and slow. The close dance took them around the room in each other's arms. Aislin pulled away first when the song ended, and kicked off her shoes. Zane had planned this perfect romantic date, and now, Aislin wanted to lead her to the bedroom and seduce her.

She tilted her head, smiled, and wanted to trust it looked provocative, but she had no damn practice doing any of it. Aislin sashayed backward to the nearest door, and attempted what she sincerely hoped was a come-hither look. She bumped the entry with her butt.

And ended up in the bathroom.

"I meant to do that. I'll be out in a minute." Humiliated at her faux pas, Aislin went to the sink to wash her hands. "Yeah, that was slick, Ace," she said to her reflection in the mirror. "We're going to have to practice that whole seduction thing."

She pulled the clips from her hair to let it fall loose around her shoulders. Her lips were full, still tingling from Zane's kiss. Her thighs slipped against each other deliciously, the silk of her dress clinging to bare skin, which reminded her, once more, that she had no panties on.

Even if she had little to no game, she felt sexy, dammit. She smoothed her dress down. "Go get her."

Aislin knew she'd remember this night for the

rest of her life, and she promised herself in the mirror she would make sure Zane did as well.

She hoped.

She stepped out and Zane was waiting with a smile. She pointed to the other side of the room.

The correct door. *God.*

Aislin met her and cupped her hands around Zane's neck to pull her down then stopped a whisper away from Zane's lips, and reveled when she heard her sigh of anticipation before she gently nipped her lower lip, and pressed her body against hers.

When she felt Zane's knees give a little, she walked her backward, in the right direction this time, toward the bedroom. She felt a hand tug near the zipper on her dress but deftly deflected her fingers. "Uh-uh," she said. "My turn." Zane appeared to have trouble breathing, and that suited Aislin just fine.

"I'm not used to giving up control," Zane said. "And I've been completely off balance since I met you."

Aislin smiled at her, Zane's confession pulling at her heart. "Trust me," Aislin said and laughed wickedly. They reached the end of the bed, and Zane sat abruptly. Aislin put a hand on her chest. "You're flushed, and your heart is beating really hard. Are you sick?"

Zane's laugh was cut off as Aislin stepped between her thighs, wound her fingers through Zane's hair, and deepened her kiss. Aislin found Zane's mouth irresistible.

When Zane gasped for air again, Aislin let her go, then straightened. With Zane seated and Aislin standing between her legs, they were now perfectly face to face.

She took advantage of Zane's breathlessness and

using the element of surprise, removed Zane's chemise in one smooth motion. Aislin was mesmerized by her beauty and dazzled by the way Zane's breasts filled her white lace bra. It could be the champagne, but Aislin was dizzy with desire.

She dropped one strap down one smooth, tanned shoulder and then the other, slowly reaching around her back to unhook it.

Aislin snapped two fingers and Zane raised an eyebrow.

"College," Aislin said, grateful she didn't fumble. Maybe she had a tiny bit of game left after all. She went down on her knees, keeping eye contact while she slipped Zane's pumps off and threw them over her shoulder.

She flinched a little when she heard one hit the dresser, but she didn't slow down. Aislin tugged at the hem of Zane's trousers. "Off," she said and smiled when Zane leaned back to unbutton them, marveling at the way her muscles rippled with the motion.

Zane lifted her hips, slid them down, Aislin took care of the underwear, and threw them in the general vicinity of the shoes. She stood to drape the slacks over the chair where they immediately fell off. She left them on the floor.

"Oh God," Aislin said. Zane looked like a Nordic goddess lying on the black duvet. She'd inched back to the center of the bed, her hair fanned out as she arched her back, one leg bent at the knee provocatively, giving Aislin a view of her smooth sex.

Zane's skin glowed in the candlelight, her eyes looked like blue fire, and her gaze followed Aislin's every move.

"Are you kidding me right now?" Aislin asked.

"You look like a Playboy model."

Her doubts spiked dangerously as she remembered Zane *had* dated, and slept with more than a few.

Aislin knew she certainly didn't look like them.

Her expression must have given her thoughts away. "You're beautiful," Zane said. "And I never lie on my back for anyone."

"Not your best argument, Counselor." There it was, Zane's past still between them. "Wait. Did you say never?"

Zane nodded. "Aislin, I can't stop thinking about you. I taste your lips at the oddest moments, hear your laughter, and smell your perfume when you're nowhere in sight."

And with those words, Aislin threw her doubts to the wind. She was sure they would be right where she left them and could pick them back up at any time if need be. Now that she felt bolder, Aislin let her instinct guide her. She unzipped her dress and let it slip to the floor before taking off her own bra.

Zane held out her arms, her sigh ending with a little growl. She lifted up on the bed.

Aislin wagged her finger. "Uh-uh. You don't get to touch me yet."

She lifted Zane's ankles and spread her legs effortlessly.

"You're stronger than you look," Zane gasped.

"I've had to be, some of my patients weigh more than I do." Aislin felt Zane's thighs tremble under her lips as she teased her way up to her sex.

Candlelight flickered, flamed higher, and increased the shadows in the room while the sound of Zane's soft sighs filled it. The atmosphere was perfect, and Aislin lost herself in the moment.

❧❧❧❧

Zane's hands fisted in the spread and it took everything she had not to flip Aislin over onto her back. When she felt her tongue flick against her, she arched her back again, then felt Aislin's hand come to knead her breast and tease her nipple. She'd never felt so vulnerable under a woman. Hadn't allowed herself to.

She resisted the urge to take control and instead tangled her fingers in Aislin's hair. The sight of her between her thighs, and the way Aislin never stopped looking her in the eyes was incredibly erotic.

When Aislin winked at her, the barriers came down, and Zane felt her first orgasm rip through her like thunder that rolled across the sky. Her muscles clenched and twisted a split second before she came again. When Zane felt her enter her, she cried out Aislin's name.

"I'm right here," she whispered and covered Zane's body with hers, a smooth thigh pressed and held against her, their hips rolled and bucked. Zane's arms went around Aislin's to hold her while her body shuddered with aftershocks and Zane continued to gasp for breath.

Aislin's wet sex burned against her own as they rocked back and forth, sharing breath, and Zane didn't know if the whimpers she heard were Aislin's or her own.

Fresh lust skated through her and gave her strength where just a moment before she'd felt boneless. Zane grabbed Aislin and kicked against the bed, flipping her onto her back.

Zane cuffed Aislin's wrists above her head toward the headboard, the expression on her face mirroring Zane's own desire. Aislin's hips bucked and she pulled against Zane's grip.

"What do you want, sweetheart?"

"You." Aislin arched and exposed the smooth curve of her neck. Zane followed the line with her tongue to the side of her throat, then bit her to keep her in place. She felt the instant she surrendered and her thighs opened wider to accommodate Zane. She ran her hand down from her neck to rest on Aislin's flat stomach, taut with sexual tension.

"Please, Zane."

She let go of Aislin's wrists and neck at the same time, and Aislin melted into her side and whimpered against Zane's mouth. She swallowed her cries while she entered Aislin, stroked into the pace Aislin set.

Nails scored her back and spurred her to go faster, deeper. Zane held her weight tight against Aislin's chest to feel her heart beat against hers.

Zane knew she could never be as close as she wanted, needed to be. She felt Aislin's silken walls clamp around her fingers, a velvet vice, and Zane held still while Aislin's orgasm took over. She cried out and soaked Zane's hand and the bed beneath her.

As they lay in each other's arms, Zane tried to catch her breath as she heard Aislin try to catch hers. Zane watched her face and smiled when Aislin opened her eyes.

She had no doubt she was irrevocably changed.

Aislin laughed and rained kisses on Zane's face, her eyelids, nose, forehead, and chin. "That was amazing."

"Perfect," Zane said. "Like you." She put a hand

to Aislin's cheek, then kissed her softly. The moment was exquisite and so full of emotion, her eyes burned.

She wrapped Aislin as close as she could, listened to their tandem breathing. "Aislin?"

"Mmm?'

"I forgot to look at your scar."

Her response was only a sleepy giggle. "Next time."

Downstairs near the chandelier that graced the lobby, Granny and Bella congratulated themselves.

"So, at last our girls are together." Granny danced around the glass in the air.

Bella wiped a tear. "It's been so long since Zane's been happy. I've never seen her like this with any of the others. As excited as I am right now, I can understand why Shannon isn't here to celebrate."

"I know she wants Aislin settled and happy. Perhaps she can rest now." Granny poked a bellman in the backside, and then laughed when he abruptly turned to find no one there.

"That's not funny." Bella pressed her lips together in a tight line.

"He deserved it. I saw him pick that pocket when he thought no one was looking. And don't give me that society-lady crap. You know you want to laugh."

"You're shameless." Bella grinned and drifted toward the front desk. "What is she doing here?"

"What?" Granny asked and spun around. "Who do you see?"

"Zane's ex-girlfriend, Giselle." Bella made a little sound of distress. "And I'm sure she's up to no good."

"Oh, she just slipped that young concierge two Benjamins," Granny said. "I detest bribery. She probably

just made that with the disgusting man she's with."

"Two hundred dollars?" Bella waved her hand. "Her dress cost more than that. It may be tacky, but it's a designer label. Anyway, I'm sure there are rules against giving any information. This hotel is known for their discretion."

"Quick, Granny, get closer to see what they're saying."

Granny pulled Bella toward the desk where she pushed the man into Giselle, who shot him a venomous look. "Watch it!"

"Sorry, did you get what you needed?" he asked.

Giselle smiled with malice. "Yes, I did. Paybacks are a bitch, but I'm a bigger one. They're both going to be very sorry they humiliated me."

"Whatever," the man said sarcastically. "Let's get on with this delightful outing."

They both saw the flicker of disgust on Giselle's face before she carefully schooled her expression. She took his arm and they left the hotel.

"What are we going to do?" Bella wrung her hands together.

Granny shook her head. "I don't know. Unfortunately, we're going to have to let this play out."

Chapter Sixteen

It was early afternoon when Zane exited the elevator on rubbery legs. She'd been smiling since she woke up. Breakfast in bed, with a side of a whole lot of everything else. She didn't think she'd ever been this deliciously sated.

Aislin's ass looked like a perfect heart in her new jeans bought at the hotel's boutique, and she couldn't resist leaving her hand on it when they walked out of the hotel.

The limo was waiting at the curb and the doorman saluted as they pulled into traffic.

Zane waited until Aislin was settled back with a bottle of water before she handed her the little black box.

"What's that?" Aislin's tone sounded suspicious.

"It's a present for you." Zane's excitement deflated as Aislin's eyes narrowed at her.

"The clothes were a present. That's a jewelry box."

Zane smiled at her. "Yes, it is. For you." She opened it and turned it toward Aislin.

Aislin gasped at the brilliant diamond studs. "I can't accept those."

"Why not? I bought them especially for you." This wasn't going at all like Zane imagined it would.

"They cost too much." Aislin scooted away from her on the long seat. "Entirely too expensive."

"I have money, Aislin. I want you to have them."

"I am not for sale."

"What are you talking about? You don't like presents?" She was baffled. Zane had never known anyone to turn down shiny diamonds. She snapped the lid closed and set the box down on the plush carpet. She'd wanted to make her happy, not be spit at.

"Crap," Aislin said. "I hate that I put that look on your face. Look, it's not you—"

"Please don't finish that sentence," Zane said. "I know the chorus to that song. 'It's not you, it's me.'"

Aislin laughed. "No, I wasn't going there." She slid back across the seat. "I mean it's not you I'm angry at." She sighed. "It's a long story, and I reacted badly. Sometimes even I don't know what's going to come out of my mouth."

"I'm pretty sure I want to hear the story," Zane said. "And it's a very pretty mouth."

Aislin grabbed her collar and pulled her close. The kiss was hungry and deep, and when she pulled back, Zane only had one thing on her mind. She reached for the privacy button.

"No, Zane." Aislin laughed and pulled Zane's hand away. "We can't right now."

"Then tell me the story. Who hurt you, Ace?" Zane put the screen up anyway. "You can trust me."

Aislin looked at her, studying her, Zane thought. She continued to stare back calmly.

"Okay." Aislin took a deep breath and sighed. "When I was in high school, I fell in love and spent almost three years with a guy. He—well, his family—was very wealthy. Now that I look back, I can see that he used his status to make me feel small, like he was inherently better and I should be grateful he spent time with me all, you know? It was so subtle that as an outsider, I didn't see it right away. But, he dazzled me with other things so I wouldn't notice. Like jewelry.

"When he graduated, of course he was going to an excellent school back east, and he let me know in no uncertain terms that I had been simply a distraction and not worthy of him, his family, and certainly not his status. After all, we were as he called us, 'the O'Sheas from the other side of the tracks.' To top that off, he said cruel things about Brianna, who'd just had Sabrina out of wedlock. Another jerk friend of his who wanted nothing to do with responsibility.

"Somebody at school started a brutally cruel rumor that I'd gotten pregnant, too, and his father heard about it. He told me no child of mine—meaning me, because you know, the Irish breed like rabbits—would be welcomed into that family. Blah, blah, blah, because how would he *ever* know that this child was actually his son's. As if I wasn't trustworthy as well."

Zane's heart hurt as she watched Aislin's eyes go to the past as she remembered. She was going to ask what happened when Aislin continued.

"God, I haven't told this story in years. Anyway, he left in the middle of the night and I never heard from him again." Aislin sighed. "As if I wanted to after that. I guess I just held that experience and tied it up with ribbons of resentment for the way people of wealth can so easily ruin other people's lives. Like Brianna's. Like mine."

"What's his name?"

"Asshat. Sorry, Tad Silverman. Do you know him?"

"Yes." Zane searched her memory for recent encounters. "You might be glad to know his father cut him off when he got the pizza waitress pregnant while in college. He's been divorced at least two times since then that I know of. Now, he's alone and miserable."

The corners of Aislin's mouth turned up. "How miserable?"

Grateful for the small smile, Zane ratcheted it up a notch. "He looks absolutely tormented."

"And? Please tell me there's more."

"He's as bald as a cue ball."

Aislin inched closer to her. "Okay, I feel much better. There's even small part of me that should be grateful. It was because of that horrid experience that I threw myself into my studies. I wanted to show them I wasn't worthless, and that he didn't matter."

"And did you? Show them?"

Aislin's smile lit her face. "When I met my Shannon, everything changed." Her smile turned into a knowing smirk. "I knew I hated sex with him."

Zane was uncomfortable, and wasn't sure she wanted to talk about Shannon right now. She felt shallow and selfish, but after last night she wanted Aislin to think of her instead. She picked up the jewelry box and slid the window open on her side. "It's a shame that you don't want these. They're half a carat larger than the ones my brother bought for your sister."

Aislin's hand moved so fast it blurred. "Oh, well," she said. "In that case, gimme." She sighed. "They're beautiful, thank you." Aislin popped out her tiny opal studs, then had Zane help her with the screw backs on her new ones.

Zane closed the window, and leaned in for a hug.

Aislin's hand to the middle of her chest stopped her "You need to know it's not why I'm with you."

"I know that, honey. As many times as you've thrown my checks back in my face? My intention is selfish. I simply want you to think of me when you wear them." She kissed Aislin's cheeks, then the tip of her nose. "I pictured you wearing these and nothing else." Zane kissed her eyelids in turn.

Aislin's hands came to either side of Zane's face, and she looked her straight in the eye. "Well then," she said. "I guess I should probably thank you properly, huh?"

Then she did.

☙☙☙☙

When they got back to clinic, Aislin motioned she was going to the house.

Zane walked her to the door. "I've got an early trial, but I'll try and cut out early." Silently, she hoped for an offer to stay.

Aislin smiled at her. "Oh, okay. So, I'll see you tomorrow then?"

No invitation, she thought as she nodded. Zane was disappointed but she didn't want to ask either.

"Spay and neuter day," Aislin said and made snipping motions with her fingers before she pulled Zane to her for a quick kiss, then laughed when Zane leaned her against the door to deepen it.

It opened behind them and Aislin nearly fell in the door.

"Geez," Louis said and bumped Zane with his hip. "Get a room."

"Did." Aislin laughed and shut the door.

Zane stood outside the door, dumbfounded at the abrupt gesture. *Didn't we just have the most excellent date ever?*

Aislin's moods were becoming legendary. She

shook her head and walked back to the car with Louis.

∂‿∂‿∂‿∂

Aislin stood with her back against the door. She didn't mean to shut it in Zane's face, though she had to admit her parting line was kind of witty.

She hadn't wanted to face the wall of emotion she'd experienced at her bright blue door.

After the amazing night she'd spent with Zane, and God, breaking a years-old celibacy with unbridled passion, it was a little unsettling to go from that experience to the home she'd shared with Shannon.

It wasn't logical, but for a minute, she felt like she cheated on her.

The tears were going to come, and she'd didn't want to cry in front of Zane.

These tears belonged to Shannon. She hadn't known how difficult it would be to reconcile how she felt about both of them in those moments walking up the path.

Brianna called her from the living room, Aislin swallowed the sorrow and joined her.

She didn't think Brianna would ever leave. She'd demanded details, compared the sparkly diamond earrings, and didn't say a word about the size difference. And because she'd gotten such a kick over it in the limo, Aislin felt small that she'd thought Brianna would.

A soft voice in her head that sounded very much like Darcy told her to grow up.

By the time she did leave, Aislin was exhausted and after last night, sure she was well used and bruised.

Not that she was complaining. She just wished she knew what to do with the distress she'd felt at the door when she got home.

The one Shannon was never coming back to.

Aislin turned on the television and pulled a small coverlet over her legs. She searched the DVR and found the latest episode of her favorite vampire series. It would be a welcome distraction from the tornado of emotions rotating inside her.

Mikey refused to leave her side. She knew it was because she'd never left him alone overnight before. Merlin did not live up to a cat's stoic personality either. He complained loudly as he climbed into her lap.

His weight was comforting and she felt herself relax a little.

"Oh, you guys are so neglected," she said. "What are you going to do when I leave again?"

Whatever she did, it would be damn near impossible to live up to last night's date.

She found herself nodding, and turned off the television as a cute little teen was about to scream.

"Shouldn't have walked into the dark alley with the guy," Aislin said and turned out the lights on her way upstairs, taking care as Mikey and Merlin tumbled under her feet.

Aislin pulled the comforter up around her ears, her animals beside her, and her last thought before she drifted off was of Zane's look of passion as she hovered above her.

It started with the phone. It always began with jarring ring of the damn telephone. Once more, the oppressive nightmare descended.

As always, Aislin was the reluctant and unwilling observer, watching and never, ever, being able to change the outcome.

She heard herself whimper, the sound coming

from far, far away as if in a dark tunnel and the events of that night unfolded.

"Aislin, honey? Where are my keys? Martinez has a horse down."

The warm comforter held Aislin in a drowsy state. "I'm sorry, babe. The Beast is out of gas, I forgot to stop and fill it."

"Again?" Shannon asked. "I swear, if your head wasn't attached…"

"Take mine," Aislin mumbled. "Do you want me to go with you?"

"No, honey. Go back to sleep, I'll be back in a couple of hours. And just for the record, I hate driving that roller skate you insist is a real car."

"Sorry." Aislin turned over and pulled the covers over her head.

Her observant dream-self watched the digital clock on the nightstand flip forward two hours to three o'clock.

Dread and grief were weights on her chest. "Wake up, oh please, wake up." She tried to hold back the sobs that were choking her. She was powerless, forced to watch the night repeat, a demented Groundhog Day.

She didn't want to watch, but she had no choice, and when the lights came through the cracks in the drapes, the colors were just as vivid as they had been years ago.

Aislin didn't have the strength to call out to herself as dream-Aislin walked to the window. It never helped anyway.

She became aware of the sirens a short distance away and recognized the fear on her face when the realization began to dawn.

The phone was ringing again, and the pounding

on the door was louder than it had ever been. Aislin watched her slow trek down the stairs, observed her shaking hand turn the knob and open the door.

"Ms. O'Shea?"

Aislin watched the tears run down her face and remembered the terror, the absolute disbelief that choked her even before the officers had told her what happened.

Her heart had roared in her ears, time slowed to a crawl, and she sagged against one of the uniforms.

She saw herself turn to look down the street where several vehicles had spinning lights. She recalled having the strength of ten men as she pushed away from them and ran over the landscaping rocks and down the road in her T-shirt and shorts.

Only when she was observing the nightmare did she notice that her bare feet left bloody prints along the pavement.

She didn't know how she'd gotten past the tape and various people who'd been called in an official capacity to the accident. She only knew she'd managed it.

It took her one second to register the man blowing into a plastic box as he sat in the back of an open ambulance, another to notice the big Suburban which sat at a crazy angle with a headlight dangling from its bumper.

One excruciating heartbeat later, Aislin saw the wreckage of her cherry-red Mini Cooper.

Heedless of the debris, the glass under her feet, she ran to the crumpled shape under the sheet laying on the ground.

There she *was* stopped, and couldn't get past the people who stood guard.

A long lock of red hair showed from under the sheet and lay on the street. In it, sparkles of glass shards glittered in the harsh glare of the streetlights.

Aislin fell to her knees where the windshield had shattered into a thousand pieces and cut her to the bone as she screamed and screamed until her anguish echoed off the houses that lined the pretty street.

And the lights came on, one by one, in the wake of her devastating loss.

It was Mikey's loud barks that finally woke her in time to experience her heart being ripped out again and being handed back to her in bloody pieces.

If Shannon had driven the Beast that night, the drunk driver wouldn't have killed her. The old truck would have protected her.

How on earth could Aislin think she had the right to move on with her life?

It was all her fault.

❧ ❧ ❧ ❧

The sky was just beginning to lighten when Aislin woke, and in the morning light, she could let some of the heartbreak go.

Time didn't heal the wounds, it only gave some distance.

Something she'd never been able to get a hold on because she relived the horror of that night over and over again.

The vividness of the nightmare had been so real she could almost touch it, almost feel herself kneeling on that blood-soaked street.

She took a deep breath, and another. Logically, she could assume it was because she'd felt so vibrantly alive with Zane.

Being with her was such a contrast to her normal life. The guilt resurfaced to remind her it wouldn't be feasible, or even possible, to love another.

Though she did.

Aislin felt torn in two and if she could have, she'd go back and put gas in the truck and prevent the horrible accident.

But she couldn't.

Then there was Zane. The epitome of everything she thought she hated.

But wasn't.

Aislin couldn't pinpoint the exact moment she'd fallen in love with Zane, maybe she wasn't supposed to. She was scared of becoming completely attached to another person. The loss would be more than she could bear and stay sane.

She twisted the diamond studs in her ears. A symbol perhaps?

Maybe a talisman. Would loving Zane really free her, or would she always carry the guilt to the exclusion of her own life and happiness?

The best thing, she decided, would be to get up and into her routine. It had always helped in the past. Work had been her salvation.

The alarm kicked on and Aislin recognized Eric Clapton's unique voice singing to her about heaven.

It had to be a sign. Aislin listened to the rest of the song and let her tears fall. When it was over, despite how sad the lyrics were, she felt lighter as she went down the stairs on her way to the clinic.

Aislin was finished with the last scheduled neuter near closing time. After carefully putting the small dog into recovery to sleep off the last of the anesthesia, she went to the empty waiting room and told Brianna and Sabrina to go on home.

"Thanks," Brianna said. "I've a date tonight and I wanted to stop at that cute little boutique downtown. I hear they have a new label."

"Oh, Mom, I want to come." Sabrina logged off the computer, picked up her purse, and they left in a hurry.

Aislin was glad she was spared the shopping trip. She went back to her office to finish up some paperwork after which she'd call Zane, if she didn't hear from her first.

She was surprised to hear the tap-tap of unfamiliar heels in the hallway. She'd flipped the closed sign over but must have forgotten to lock the door. In addition, the lights were off in the waiting room.

Mikey raced in the back dog door and barked at the stranger, who'd yet to announce their presence. When she heard him snarling, it sent prickles of fear down her spine. He'd never made that sound before, not even when the big mean dogs came in.

She picked up a baseball bat her father insisted she keep in the corner before she hesitantly called out into the hall. "Hello? Who is it?"

"Get him off me!"

Aislin turned the corner and saw Giselle backed against the wall, where Mikey had pinned her with his little body. "What are *you* doing here?"

"Call him off," Giselle ordered as she danced on her high heels to avoid him.

"Stand still," Aislin said. Mikey snapped his teeth an inch away from Giselle's calf.

She shrieked loud enough to upset the dogs in the back, and the ruckus they made got the cats yowling

And oh, please, Aislin thought. *Please let the goat scream.* She had to bite her lip again.

"Come here, Mikey." Aislin snapped her fingers and the dog came to her, keeping himself between her and Giselle, the perceived threat. "I'll ask again. What are you doing here?" Her adrenaline surged and her grip on the bat held at her side tightened.

Giselle laughed, smoothed her hair, then adjusted the short dress that had hiked up during the scuffle. "Is that how you greet your customers?"

"Why, are you a dog?"

"Good one." Giselle's tone dripped with sarcasm.

"Then again," Aislin said. "You are a bitch."

"Look, shorty, I just came to warn you."

Aislin pretended surprise. There was no way in the world this bitch thought of anyone but herself. "Really? Color me shocked. You have concern for me, the help?"

"I consider it my duty," Giselle said. "Why, I just couldn't live with myself if I didn't."

Aislin was tired of it already. "Just get to the point."

Giselle took a couple of steps and towered over Aislin, her beautiful face twisted in an ugly sneer. "What? You think you're special?" Her eyes widened then narrowed. "Zane bought you those?"

Her hand went to the earrings automatically.

"Let's be honest here, woman to woman. So, she paid you. I suppose she also took you to a fancy dinner, the high-class hotel she brings all the girls to, fourteenth floor as a matter of fact, and brought you flowers. I'll bet the candles were lit and your favorite music was playing. Am I hitting it on the head? Zane's seductions are legendary. Be careful, sister. That particular rose has nasty thorns." Giselle's expression became one of perceived triumph that turned quickly to horror.

Mikey had lifted his leg and yellow urine streamed out to puddle around her shoes. Giselle shrieked again and backed away. "These are Louboutins, you fucking mutt!"

"Get out of my clinic," Aislin snapped. "Get out right now." She waved the baseball bat.

Giselle blanched, turned on her wet heel, and cursed all the way out to the front door, which she slammed hard enough to rattle the glass.

Aislin stood still and leaned against the wall for a moment. She felt she'd been hit with the bat she held. She reached down to pat her dog. "Good boy, Mikey."

He barked and wore a look of pure adoration. Aislin could swear he was proud of himself as he strutted back to her office.

She was beyond hurt, but made her feet move in order to feed the boarders and surgery patients that were staying the night.

"Oh, that bitch!" Shannon snapped from her position on the reception desk.

"I told you she was up to something," Bella said. "I hate her kind. Always sniffing for what they can get from you, and when they don't? They just want everyone else to suffer too."

"The question is," Granny said as she continued to rock back and forth on her chair, "how much damage did she do?"

"Knowing Aislin, Giselle slammed the door, both literally and figuratively. She's always had a thing about rich bitches, begging your pardon," Shannon said to Bella. "No offense meant to you."

"None taken," Bella said. "But we should follow her and see what other wreckage she's planned."

The trio rode on the top of Giselle's BMW to keep an eye on her. No one was surprised when they ended up at the Whitman Estate, but Giselle pulled her car to the back side of the stables.

As a unit, they followed her to the front door. Granny snickered. "She keeps looking over her shoulder."

"She knows something," Shannon said. "Or it's her guilty conscience."

"Like she has one," Granny muttered.

"Ssh," Bella said. "I want to hear."

Giselle knocked and rang the bell several times. When it opened, she brushed past Kiki into the entry. They followed her in.

"Kiki! I'm so glad you're here." Giselle spun her in a circle and kissed her.

"What is going on?" Bella demanded. "She's using this poor girl to get access to the house."

Kiki froze, obviously dumbfounded.

"Oh, look at her," Shannon said. "She doesn't stand a chance against that barracuda."

"Thanks for letting me in," Giselle said. "I'll just pop up and get the things I've left here." When Kiki moved to follow, Giselle brushed her off. "No, don't bother yourself, I know the way. Don't forget our date tonight."

Kiki sighed, nodded, and disappeared back down the hall.

"Dumbass. God, you're easy to fool," Giselle said as she ascended the stairs.

"What's she doing?" Bella asked, then shot up after her, Granny and Shannon close behind.

"I don't know, but I want to slap her," Shannon announced. "Screw the kumbaya."

"She's in Zane's suite," Granny said. They hovered over the bed to watch.

Giselle peeled her panties down and kicked them under the bed. She opened her large bag and pulled out several other things.

"Now what?" Shannon asked.

"Incriminating items," Granny said. "She's putting her toiletries out on the counters, dressers, and nightstands."

Giselle snickered wickedly. "Take that," she said and spun in circles around the room. "If this doesn't cause her trouble with the little midget, I don't know what will."

"Can't we stop her?" Bella asked. "Can't we do anything?"

Granny sighed. "Unfortunately not, we can only hope it backfires."

A timid knock on the door startled Giselle from her dance.

"Someone's home," Kiki said in a loud whisper.

Giselle ran out the doorway. In the hall, she pinned Kiki to the wall. "You'll meet me later, right?"

Kiki's eyes glazed over and she nodded slightly.

"Good," Giselle said. "I'll call you."

They watched as Giselle ran down the back stairway, into the kitchen, and toward the back door. Shannon tried to trip her, but she stayed steady on her heels.

"Oh look," Bella said. "There's my boy."

"What are you doing here?" Louis asked. Giselle batted her eyelashes, thrust her chest out, and adopted a breathy baby talk. "I was supposed to meet Zane here, but I got a booking from my agent. I got a job in Paris. You'll tell her I'm sorry, won't you?" She placed a hand on his chest and beamed at him.

"He won't fall for that," Granny said.

"Well, I don't know," Bella said. "He has before with other women."

Shannon laughed when Louis sniffed the air and pushed away from Giselle. "Ha-ha! He just asked her if it was her that smelled."

Granny laughed uproariously and slapped her thigh. "It's Mikey's parting gift."

Giselle ran the rest of the way to her car and her tires spit gravel when she spun out of the driveway.

Louis watched her leave and they watched him on his way to the house while he muttered to himself. "What are you up to Zany? Taking up with that bitch again?" He checked his watch. "God, I'm going to be late to the airport."

꧁ ꧂ ꧁ ꧂

Zane went straight to the clinic after work. Her meeting had run longer than she originally planned, and her eagerness to see Aislin made the ride home seemed a hundred years long. She tried calling, but no answer.

She pulled into her driveway only see there were no lights on at the house.

"Call Aislin," she ordered the car, and tapped her fingers on the steering wheel while she waited. When the recording came on, she hung up and tried texting.

Whr r u?

Her hand tightened around the plastic waiting for a response. "Well, crap. She must be out on a call." She texted again.

Meet me @ my hs whn ur done.

With disappointment and regret, she pulled away, and spent the trip home wondering why Aislin hadn't checked in.

Upon arriving home, Zane changed out of her suit and went to the kitchen to eat, making sure her phone was within easy reach. She read the note that Taylor and Perry had gone to a movie, so she had the house to herself. She settled in and kept her mind occupied by making plans for new and exciting ways to delight her love the next time they saw each other.

Two hours later, baffled as to why Aislin hadn't called, she went to bed. It had been a long day, and she felt herself drifting off quickly. Her last thought was of the kickass time they'd had the day before. Hadn't Aislin thought the same?

In the morning, she got ready for work, and checked her phone. There were no messages, no calls from Aislin.

It only took two freaking seconds to leave a text, even if Aislin was busy. Zane was dangerously close to being pissed off.

She called again, and still there was no answer. She gave a passing glance to the bathroom counter, and saw several things that didn't belong. She made a note to talk to Perry, who loved bathing in her large tub, and have her gather them up. She was always forgetting things. That reminded her she had an entire box to give to Perry of stuff she'd forgotten on a previous visit.

The hurricane named Aislin was wearing her out. Zane resolved not to call again until she heard from her. Whatever Aislin's problem was, she'd better figure it out soon because Zane was done playing this game. It felt like teenage drama. Come here, go away. It was ridiculous. And she knew, knew she'd done nothing wrong, and she was tired of feeling like she was guilty of something.

Zane took a moment to deflate her temper. She'd reserve indignation until she heard from her. She might have a good excuse this time other than Zane's imagined indiscretions.

She better.

ȴȴȴȴ

After a long conversation with Brianna, Aislin wanted to find out for herself if there was any truth to what Giselle had said to her.

But really, she thought, *how else would she have known all the details of their date?*

She remembered the way Zane's skin felt so silky against her own, and the heat between them so hot it was combustible. When she thought of how it felt to make love with Zane, it only made Giselle's accusations hurt more.

Even though she changed her clothes three

times, Aislin told herself she was only dressing for the confrontation, not to impress her lover. She finally settled on faded Levis and a black vest that showed off her shoulders. She combed out her hair, touched up her light makeup. *Just in case, right? Look at what you threw away.*

She loaded Fifi up into the back of the truck, and during the ride the pain curled in her belly, along with wounded pride and rejection. The combination made her nauseous, but she had to deal with it now. The more time passed, the more painful it would be.

Aislin pulled up to the house, helped Fifi out of the built-in kennel, and guided her down the ramp she'd pulled out.

The front door swang open and Perry ran out at full speed. "Fifi!" She looked at Aislin. "Thank you tho much, Doctor Aithlin." Her gratitude and adoration weren't hard to miss.

Aislin's heart lurched. Perry's lisp was adorable, and she was reminded of how much she wanted children. She crouched down to receive the bear hug from the little girl, and squeezed her eyes shut against the tears of longing.

Taylor came out. "Come in, please. We were just having a snack."

Aislin looked around and couldn't decide if she was nervous, angry, or disappointed she hadn't seen Zane yet.

Taylor took her arm and chattered away. "I haven't seen Zane yet, we keep passing each other, but I'm assuming you had a wonderful time?"

The emotion she'd been searching for was rage. Zane's name reverberated like a drum in her bloodstream, and Aislin knew what seeing red felt like.

Perry skipped ahead. "We're thupposed to set up Fifi in one of the spare rooms, will you help us?" She didn't wait for an answer. She tugged Fifi's leash out of Aislin's other hand and entered the foyer. "You're the best doctor ever!"

In spite of her crappy attitude, Aislin was charmed. "I think it might be better if Fifi was in the kitchen or thereabouts, by the back door. The stairs would be too hard for her to manage right now."

"Okay, but we have to get her stuff from Auntie's room upstairs. Here, Mom." Perry handed the leash to Taylor before she dragged Aislin to the steps.

With each step closer to Zane's room, Aislin's agitation grew. When she looked in the door, she was struck again by how beautifully it was decorated, but when she stepped over the threshold, something felt off. She chalked it up to overactive hormones. Zane's scent lingered in the air, superimposed with one she associated with Giselle.

While Perry gathered up some toys, Aislin walked to the side of the bed to pick up the large dog bed. As soon as she knelt down, she saw the bright red silk. Zane had told her she only wore white, and Aislin knew damn well they weren't hers.

Aislin stood quickly and knocked a carafe of water over on the nightstand. Cursing to herself, she went into the bathroom to get a towel. She noticed a bottle of Joy and a plethora of makeup jars and other sundries she hadn't seen the last time she'd been in it. She knew they hadn't been there because her bathroom envy had catalogued every detail of the impressive space. That and she was pretty sure Zane didn't wear Rev Up Red lipstick. Ever.

The jealously she'd barely leashed surged and

jump-started her adrenaline.

Forget hurt. She was extremely pissed off.

Taylor was on the phone when Perry and Aislin got to the kitchen with Fifi's supplies. With a calm attitude she didn't even begin to feel, Aislin handed Taylor the pills along with the directions for Fifi's medication.

"That was Zane on the phone, and she wants to know why you haven't answered her calls."

Aislin sputtered and swore. "Ask her," she snapped.

"Pardon me?"

The little girl had impeccable manners, she thought. Aislin made an effort to soften her voice. "It's okay honey. I didn't say anything."

"Okay," Taylor said. "She said she has to stay in the city tonight. They're running late on a corporate case, but she's looking forward to talking with you soon."

Aislin patted Fifi and ran her hands through her fur, around her battered ears. She forced herself to brighten up and say good-bye to Perry, then motioned for Taylor to follow her out. She handed her a business card for another vet. "She needs a follow up in a couple of weeks. I've already called Dr. Fein and set it up. It's written down on the back."

She didn't wait for answer. She walked stiff-legged back to her truck, and tried not to cry.

Taylor knocked on her window. "Won't you tell me what's wrong?"

Aislin didn't trust herself to speak and shook her head. She started the engine, waited for Taylor to back up out of her way, and drove off the property.

Pain. Would she ever know the end of it? Like a

cat, Aislin just wanted to go home and lick her wounds.

ৰ⃥ ৰ⃥ ৈ⃥ ৈ⃥

Zane was weary of the reactions Aislin ripped from her. This ache in her chest felt wrong on so many levels. She stared at the phone that didn't ring and carefully began to reconstruct the wall around her heart and reminded herself this was why she didn't allow herself to care.

Who would have thought that the self-centered narcissistic models would be easier to date? At least she knew what was expected of her.

Never again, she swore. She felt a surge of pure anger and made herself hold on to it. That was better. Anger made her strong.

Who the hell did she think she was anyway? Zane's analytical mind started ticking off points to feed her mood change. Aislin's smile intruded and Zane shoved the image back, replaced it with the reality of how Aislin had hurt her, replaced her soft sigh with a sound of derision.

Zane paced the room until she had countered every moment she had treasured with Aislin into perceived transgressions.

"Mistrial," she said righteously.

On the heels of her declaration, she sat on the couch.

Why hasn't she called?

"Enough!" she shouted into the room. "I'm done."

From a place high in the clouds, Granny, Bella, and Shannon grieved.

They saw Zane harden her heart, and Aislin pull

her anger around as a shield.

"We can't leave them like this," Bella cried. "They've come so far."

"Aislin will hide again, close herself off, and not listen to reason," Shannon said. "I can't stand this."

"Hush now." Granny's voice was heavy with sorrow. "We're right where we were when we started this. We have to let it play all the way through."

Bella crossed her legs. "They love each other, I know they do."

"Neither one has said that out loud." Shannon waved a cloud away that blocked her vision of Aislin's house. "But I hope it's enough."

"Isn't it always?" Bella stroked Heidi's ears.

Granny shook her head. "Sadly, no, not when they can't or won't see clearly, and not when false assumptions run up against preconceived prejudices along with good old-fashioned, misplaced pride."

"I don't know what round this is, or have the heart to ring the bell again," Shannon said.

"Don't look so defeated, we have another chance don't we, Granny?"

"Always a chance, dear Bella. Time runs different for us, but we'll just wait and look for another opportunity to set up the right circumstances."

And from their place high in the clouds, the women watched Aislin and Zane turn in for the night.

Alone.

Chapter Seventeen

A week passed.
Then two.

On the third day of the third week, Brianna told Aislin Zane was transferring to Japan, that she was leaving. Aislin's heart broke to hear it. She hoped Giselle and Zane would be happy.

The hell she did. She wished Giselle would get a big old pimple on her—

Before she finished the thought, there was a timid knock at her door, and she got up to answer it.

She didn't recognize the young woman. "Yes?"

"Miss Aislin? My name is Kiki Stewart."

"How can I help you? Wait, do I know you?"

"Can I come inside please?"

Aislin was pretty sure she wasn't an ax murderer, but wasn't that always what they said? Anyway her purse was too small. And she was being ridiculous. "Please."

Kiki stepped into the entry and then stopped.

"Won't you sit down?" Aislin asked.

"No, and when I get done telling you why I'm here, you won't want me to stay anyway."

Puzzled, Aislin folded her arms and waited. She heard Mikey having a fit at the back door but ignored it. "Okay."

"I'm so humiliated," Kiki mumbled.

"I don't know what to say to you, or tell you not

to be until I know why you're here." Aislin's frustration began to rise.

Kiki took a deep breath. "I work at the Whitman Estate."

Instantly cold and guarded, Aislin's voice was clipped. "And I care because..."

"I, uh—" Kiki pulled at the hem of her shirt and worried a loose thread.

"Oh dear God, spit it out."

"They don't know I'm here. Please don't tell, I need this job."

"My head's going to explode if you don't get to the point. Wait." Aislin held a finger up. "Excuse me for a minute." She walked to the back door, more to steady herself than anything, but also because Mikey's barking had reached a nerve-shattering level. "Brace yourself."

Mikey raced by her and straight up to Kiki, plopped his butt on the floor, and held up a paw.

"Aw, how cute." Kiki crouched and shook it. "Nice to meet you," she said.

Aislin sighed. "Come in then and sit. You passed his test. I've been teaching him manners. Since my dog thinks you're okay, I'll listen to what you have to say."

Kiki clutched her purse and followed Aislin into the living room. She took another deep breath. "Okay, here goes. Mister Louis came home from his trip yesterday."

Aislin wrestled with her patience. She knew this already, it was all Brianna could talk about. It hurt because Aislin found it impossible to hear of Louis and not think of Zane. "Yes, go on."

Kiki's nerves were setting her own on a razor's edge. Aislin pinched the bridge of her nose and closed her eyes. "Please," she said. "All at once, like a Band-Aid."

❧❧❧❧

Zane sat at the pretty little desk in her sitting area off her bedroom and signed several documents she'd brought home from the office. The last one in front of her was her transfer documents to head the Japan office.

She'd been considering the position, and her father felt after she saved the Ito merger, she'd be perfect for it.

She recalled the lights, the frenetic energy of the city. Far busier than the San Francisco firm, a great distance away, and bonus—it held plenty of distractions.

She'd never been sick before Aislin, but now she couldn't seem to shake the flu. She'd lost weight because her appetite was nil, and she had a hard time sleeping.

Damn it.

Zane felt the familiar jab in her stomach when she thought of Aislin. She'd almost put her back behind her defensive wall.

Nearly.

But against her will, she'd pop out intermittently. Aislin was temperamental, feisty, and Jesus, she was all over the board emotionally. Zane could list the reasons she thought Aislin difficult all day long.

But really, who was she fooling?

Aislin was also loving, kind, and passionate.

Zane loved her. And she wished like hell she could put that declaration solidly in the past tense. She'd hurt her deeply by her lack of trust, her unwillingness to hear the truth.

Zane would have told her if she'd asked. Louis had called her and told her about Giselle's surprise visit. She'd put two and two together, and knew somehow Aislin got the impression Zane was still seeing her. She'd jumped to an erroneous conclusion.

Again.

She'd thought about driving to Aislin's and forcing her to hear what she had to say, but at the end of the day, Zane was tired of defending herself to Aislin when she'd done nothing wrong. It wasn't the first time, but Zane wanted it to be the last. She respected herself too much. And did she really want a future with someone who didn't trust her? Someone who always believed the worst of her?

She tapped the pen on the contract and then pushed up from her desk without signing it.

Instead, she crossed to the closet, pulled out her Diane Von Furstenberg luggage, and opened the suitcases on her bed.

She ignored the tiny flutters of panic in her belly. Leaving was the best thing for her.

Of course it was.

It was an excellent opportunity, but she wished she didn't feel sad about it.

Zane had all kinds of wishes now, and it pissed her off.

Her life had been ordered, organized, and she never lacked for companionship when she wanted it.

Predictable.

She hadn't asked for her life to be turned upside down or sideways. She certainly didn't want to make herself seem a fool in front of the tiny, mighty Aislin with the gorgeous smile.

The adorable klutz.

She hadn't trusted her, and Zane didn't know how much that would hurt.

Until it did.

She hadn't given Aislin reason not to. Zane wasn't ashamed of her past, because that's what it was—her past.

Aislin hadn't trusted her with anything. She continued to run away from her.

And she deserved better than that.

Not that she'd be open to anyone anytime soon.

Aislin had taken that tender part of Zane that she'd packed away after her mother died, and threw it away.

Zane much preferred to be in control.

She opened her drawer roughly, picked up a stack of meticulously folded clothes and placed them in her suitcase.

꧁꧂꧁꧂

After Kiki left, Aislin sat in the living room, afraid that if she moved she'd shatter. She'd handled things so badly with Zane.

She couldn't or wouldn't be mad at Kiki. Giselle had done a number on both of them, and as embarrassed as the girl was, she'd been brave enough to come and talk to Aislin.

It shamed her.

Aislin hadn't even given Zane a chance to explain. And really, since it wasn't the first time Aislin had misjudged her, she hadn't owed Aislin anything at all.

She hadn't deserved Aislin's anger or jealousy.

And how much did it hurt now, knowing she'd been so wrong about her? Aislin had done nothing but be suspicious, her willy-nilly conclusions had been nothing but her imagination.

Aislin had been so *sure* that Zane would hurt her.

It was horribly humbling to realize the only person that hurt her was herself.

The last few weeks had been a blur. She'd cruised on anger until she couldn't hold it any longer. She refused to listen to her family, and for the first time in her life, shut herself away from them and closed herself off.

More unusual, she'd had no dreams of Shannon, and the part of her that still grieved was upset about it.

Horrible as it was to relive that night, it had been the only tie she had left, and that part of her missed it.

No, instead she'd dreamed of picnics by the lake, walks on the beach, and now, it was Zane's face that haunted her.

The way she smelled, the soft sighs she made when Aislin's body covered hers.

Aislin dreamt of making her pancakes in the morning and taking off her expensive suits in the evening.

It was torture, but Aislin had managed to stand firm on the nonexistent issue, and apparently punished not only Zane, but herself. For absolutely nothing.

The knot in her stomach loosened and all at once dissolved, and emotions rushed up her throat. Aislin didn't know who she wept for: Zane, Shannon, or herself.

She felt the tears as she lay next to Mikey on the couch.

The dream phone rang. *Oh, no* Aislin thought, *not again.*

She was in her bed and felt sick to her stomach as she waited for the red and blue lights to spin. She startled when she heard Shannon answer the phone. Her heart knocked in her chest, and she was afraid to look.

"Aislin, honey?"

The pain was swift and cut like razor blades.

"I have to go."

Wake up, wake up, wake up.

Aislin turned in the bed and looked up. Shannon looked exactly the same, but her eyes were different. More aware, more vivid.

"Give me a kiss, sweetheart."

Aislin threw her arms around Shannon's neck and held her as tight as she could. "Don't go, please don't go."

Shannon pulled back then brushed her lips softly against Aislin's. "I have to. I love you, Aislin. Say good-bye now." She tweaked her nose and began to fade.

She didn't want her to leave but realized this visit for the gift it was. "Good-bye. I love you."

She watched until her eyes burned and her shadow was completely gone.

Give love another chance, honey.

It was her own sharp, desperate inhale of breath that woke her and Aislin looked at the clock on the living room wall.

Three o'clock p.m.

Of course it was, she thought. *The opposite time of all her previous dreams.*

She untangled herself from Mikey, ran to the kitchen, grabbed the keys to her truck, and sped off.

She could only hope it wasn't too late.

⁂

Zane was done packing and had already carried

her suitcases to the front door. She went back upstairs and stared at the piece of paper she'd yet to sign.

She heard the truck before she saw it, grasped the corner of the drape to peek. She watched The Beast chug and spit up the drive.

Her nerves went on high alert, her chest tightened, and her breath quickened.

God. She'd kept her resolve, and she hadn't run to Aislin even though she'd wanted to. She'd kept her pride and will intact.

And all of it went up in flames the second she saw Aislin jump from the cab and look up.

She wasn't prepared for the shock she'd feel when she saw her, or that she'd want to run to meet her.

Zane forced herself to walk down the stairs slowly. By the time she got to the entry, she might be able to swallow the lump in her throat, might be able to talk normally.

Possibly.

She opened the front door, Aislin's eyes met hers, and held. Zane forced a calm she didn't begin to feel.

Aislin looked rumpled, as if she'd rolled out of bed in her clothes. Her hair was wild, and she pushed it away from her face.

It pained Zane to see the dark circles under her eyes, the brackets on either side of her mouth. She'd recognized them because she'd seen the same in the mirror that morning.

Aislin looked at the suitcases. "So, it's true. You're leaving."

Zane didn't trust herself to speak. She wanted to wrap Aislin up and kiss the worry lines from her forehead, but she could only walk past her and in the direction of the family room. She snuck a quick glance over her shoulder to make sure Aislin followed.

She grabbed two bottled waters from the bar and handed Aislin one.

The sharp snap of electricity finally loosened her tongue. "Why are you here, Aislin? To say good-bye?" She forced herself not to react when Aislin's eyes filled.

"I had hoped that—"

Zane snapped under the pressure of pretending nothing was wrong. She hurt, damn it, and Aislin had caused it. "You hoped I would apologize—again—for something I didn't do, or maybe you hoped I would hand over my heart—again—so you could throw it in bloody pieces at my feet. Which is it?"

Aislin looked stunned. "You're right. I shouldn't have bothered you. I apologize."

"So, you're going to leave it at that?"

"I have to go. I feel—"

"*You* feel?" Zane took a deep breath. Pride had kept her voice even but the volume began to rise when Aislin stood and backed away. "As far as I can see, it's always been about how you feel. It's always been about you. What I don't or didn't see, Aislin, is you caring about how I may have felt or feel.

"I gave you no reason not to trust me. Every time you accused me in your head, you found me guilty without judge or jury. And every time I came running back to you and waited until *you* decided it was okay. I loved you and you broke my heart."

"You never told me that." Aislin's tears tracked her cheeks.

Zane exploded to her feet. "You never told me anything! I had to find out about Shannon from your sister. You didn't even trust me with the worst day in your life. How can I trust you with my best?"

"That wasn't my sister's story to tell," Aislin said quietly. "Can't you understand the loss was mine? The grief was mine, and my fault?"

"Because you won't share it," Zane said. "It's no one's fault but the drunk driver who chose to be on the road that night."

"But—"

Zane interrupted. Aislin had started it, but she'd end it. "I can't make you let it go. If I could, I would wave a magic wand and make it disappear for you. But I can't, and I refuse to live in the shadow of a ghost you won't set free and use as an excuse to keep from getting close to anyone. Hell, you won't even talk to me about it. And more, even more important than that, I will not be with someone who doesn't trust me."

"You want to know about Shannon?" Aislin's voice pitched. "Fine, sit back down."

"I'll stand."

"Whatever," Aislin snapped, then sat in the big leather club chair. She sighed. "Please sit."

To refuse now would just make her look pissy, so she sat on the ottoman opposite Aislin.

"I loved her as deeply as I can envision a person can love." Aislin looked up and to the side, and Zane imagined she was looking to the past.

She wanted a chance to be loved like that. Zane watched Aislin's hands curl as she twisted her fingers around themselves.

"I thought I'd die when she did. She was ripped from me, and our life, so needlessly. I was torn in two, the part that wanted to curl up and give up, and the part my family took care of and helped me put back together. Still, the scars remain."

"I can understand that," Zane said.

Aislin reached for her hand. "It was so damn easy to let them deal with everything. I covered myself with guilt and have had nightmares about it since."

"Why?"

"I ran her truck out of gas. I was always forgetful, but that mistake…she took my car, and I never kissed her good-bye."

"You couldn't have known." Zane's heart reached out to her. She knew how she'd felt when her mother died, and that was devastating.

Aislin smiled softly. "No, but that didn't mean I didn't use my grief as a shield, as a reason to not become close to anyone else. When I first saw you and felt that jolt, that instant attraction, I had to work very hard to convince myself you weren't my type." Aislin pulled her hand back. "As did you." She chuckled. "Don't deny it."

Zane shrugged a concession. She knew she'd put up barriers as Aislin had done.

"You were the only one, you see, that got past that shield. So, when you did, I fell back on your reputation in order to keep myself from being hurt. I wanted to believe the worst, to keep my heart safe."

"How's that working for you?" Zane had already figured as much, but her cold logic of the situation didn't begin to touch the nuances she was able to see when hearing the story from Aislin.

"Not so well, "Aislin laughed. "Today I realized that if I didn't love you, you wouldn't have had the power to hurt me, and I wouldn't have needed an excuse to stay away. I've been miserable."

"All you had to was ask, Aislin. Giselle—"

"Don't bring her to the party."

"You certainly did," Zane snapped.

"Yes, I believed her, and I can't take that back.

I can't take any of this back, and it breaks my heart."

"I loved you."

"Past tense, then?" Aislin looked defeated but waved her hand to stop Zane's reply. "No, don't answer that. I won't bother you anymore. But before I go, I want to tell you something. I love you, Zane, and I'm sorry, so damn sorry. Can you forgive me?"

"It was the monkey bite," Zane said quietly.

Aislin coughed. "I'm sorry. What?"

"It was the monkey bite. That's when I fell in love with you, at my favorite place."

Aislin's lower lip trembled and she looked down at her lap. "Please don't leave. Give me another chance."

Zane lifted Aislin's chin to look into her eyes. "My bags are packed."

Aislin nodded. "Okay, then. I was wrong, and I'm sorry. I'll go now." She stood and ran out of the family room.

She'd been so fast, Zane had been surprised. She hurried after her. "Wait!"

Aislin spun mid-stride and Fifi hit her behind the knees. She yelped and tumbled to the marble, Fifi covered her face in sloppy kisses, her broken tail wagging as hard as fast as it would go. "Get off me, you horse!"

Zane stood over her, saw the laughter in Aislin's face, and gave in to giggles herself. "Falling for me, Doctor?" She held a hand out to help her up and motioned to the suitcases. "They're packed, but I haven't signed the papers yet. There is another partner at the firm who wants to transfer."

Aislin stood motionless until Zane crushed her body against hers. "I'm still hurt."

"I know, and I apologize. All I can do is love you, and make it up to you. I owe you that."

"You think?"

"What can I do?" Aislin stood on her toes and covered Zane's mouth with her own in a blinding kiss. Zane felt every emotion she'd packed away. One by one they unfurled and opened the cage around her heart.

When her knees threatened to give way, she broke the kiss, leaned her forehead against Aislin's, and considered. "Okay, I have it."

"Really? So soon?" Aislin smiled. "Anything."

Zane tugged her away from the door. "You can show me where the monkey bit you."

Their laughter rang as they raced each other up the stairs

"I lied," Aislin said. "It sounded good, though."

Zane pulled her down the hall. "It did. And now you have more to make up."

"I promise to show you every day you're loved."

"As will I, Aislin," Zane said, then opened her bedroom door. "Court adjourned."

"Well, we're done here." Granny stood from the rocking chair and put on her cardigan. "And that, Shannon, was a wonderful gift good-bye for our girl."

Shannon nodded.

"I couldn't be happier, well, until grandbabies," Bella said, then startled when a blue swaddled infant with platinum hair and blue eyes appeared in her arms. "Oh, look! Louis and Brianna's?"

"Looks like," Granny said.

"But what happens with them now?" Shannon asked as Zane's door shut behind the couple. "Don't go on about free will and choices, I'm not leaving until—"

Granny's voice was soft and she placed a hand on her shoulder. "I have it from a higher authority they'll be just fine. It's time to let go."

As they began to fade away, Bella asked, "So that's it? They live happily ever after?"

Granny cackled. "Cheesy, isn't it?"

Their laughter blew away in the wind as they traveled through the clouds on their way home.

About the Author

Yvonne Heidt is a multiple award-winning author of paranormal and modern romance. She was born in the Haight-Ashbury district in San Francisco in the early sixties during the hippie revolution and her self-described claim to fame is that she lived in the same apartment building as Jimi Hendrix (but not at the same time).

She currently lives in Texas with her wife, four dogs, and a myriad of visiting ghosts.

Other books by Sapphire Books Publishing

The Dreamcatcher - ISBN - 978-1-943353-67-5

High school is rarely easy, especially for a tall, somewhat gangly Native American girl. Add a sprinkle of shyness, a dash of athletic prowess, an above-average IQ, and some bizarre history that places her in the guardianship of her aunt. Then normal high school life is only an illusion.

Kai Tiva faces an uphill struggle until she runs into Riley Beth James, the extroverted class cutie, at the principal's office. Riley shows up for a newspaper interview, while Kai is summoned for punching out a classmate.

Riley is the attractive girl-next-door-type whom everyone likes. Though a fairly good student, an emerging choral star, and wildly popular, she knows she'll never live up to her older sister. She makes up for it with bravery, kindness, and a brash can-do attitude.

Their odd matchup is strengthened by curiosity, compassion, humor, and all the drama of typical teenage life. But their experiences go beyond the normal teen angst; theirs is compounded by a curious attraction to each other, and an emerging, insidious danger related to mysterious death of Kai's father.

Their emerging friendship is tested as they navigate this risky challenge. But the powerful bond forged between them has existed through past lives. The outcome this time will affect the next generation of Kai's people.

In the Direction of the Sun - ISBN - 978-1-943353-65-1

"The emotions flying between the two women who tell their story here is as dramatic as the Appalachian Trail and as tumultuous as the Atlantic Ocean. These natural elements are a perfect backdrop for the revelations of love which both repel and engage them."
    – Jewelle Gomez, author, The Gilda Stories

Steady and smart, Alex McKenzie is settled into a comfortable life in her beloved hometown of Stockbridge, MA. Everything Alex thought she knew about life and about herself changes the moment Cate Conrad blows into town like a warm breeze. Alex falls head over heels in love with the free-spirited artist and sailor but there's one problem: Cate's complicated past makes it impossible for her to open her heart completely and so she does what she's always done— she runs away. Devastated, Alex tries to heal her heart by literally walking away from her life to hike the famed Appalachian Trail while Cate takes to the water. The unexpected turn of events shows Cate and Alex how fragile life is and how love is the all that really matters.

Lavender Dreams - ISBN - 978-1-943353-59-0

When Sarah Chase got on the ferry to Bainbridge Island, she left her lover, her job, and her past behind. She didn't know that in the course of one day she would meet a woman who might be the girl of her dreams, change her career path, create a new family, and find herself in a fairytale mansion with two of the quirkiest little old ladies imaginable.